DAUGHTER OF DARKNESS

JULIANA HAYGERT

COPYRIGHT

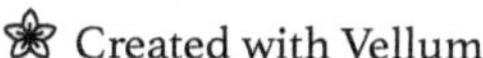 Created with Vellum

AUTHOR'S NOTE

I hope you enjoy reading *Daughter of Darkness*!

Don't forget to sign up for my Newsletter to find out about new releases, cover reveals, giveaways, and more!

If you want to see exclusive teasers, help me decide on covers, read excerpts, talk about books, etc, join my reader group on Facebook: Juliana's Club!

DAUGHTER OF DARKNESS

This is a work of fiction, of fantasy, and it's not intended to be
historically accurate.
Enjoy!

PRESENT

Devon

I HAD FOUGHT AGAINST DEMONS AND GHOSTS AND ALL SORTS OF evil beings, but humans took the trophy for the most horrible of them all.

From my spot under the dark awning of the pergola in the town square, I played with the ring hanging from my neck and watched as a group of young men, not older than eighteen years old, sneaked across the street from the square toward the old music store.

A sigh rushed past my throat.

These damn kids. I knew them all. I knew their names. I knew their families, what school they attended, and which classes they flunked. I also knew they were as drunk as skunks and had just made a bet to see who could steal the most vinyl records from the store before the alarm rang and they had to flee—they had done it before.

Fucking bastards.

The owner of the store was an old man whose only passion for life since his wife of forty years died not even a year ago was his fucking vinyl. And still, they thought this was a joke.

I tried staying out of this shitty town's drama, but certain things, like teenagers messing with an old man and his livelihood, I couldn't let slide.

Exhaling through my nose, I tucked the ring back inside my shirt and stepped out from the shadows—

A figure appeared in front of me.

"Ryder." I checked the time on my phone. "You're early."

The warrior, dressed in his black armor and with his sheathed sword strapped to his back, shrugged. "I finished my previous mission faster than expected."

He was bragging. I hated him. Not for bragging, but because he was assigned multiple missions, while I was stuck with a riddle to solve.

"Let's get on with this," he said. "Report, Devon."

"Yeah." I glanced over his shoulder to the teenagers getting ready to break the window. "Be right back."

I sidestepped the warrior and ran, faster than any human could, and reached the four teenagers as one of them—Paul—lifted his hand, ready to throw a stone at the glass window.

"I don't think so." I caught his arm and twisted it behind his back.

Paul yelped, dropping the stone.

"Let him go, man!"

"What the fuck do you think you're doing?"

"Dude, chill!"

I bent Paul's arm more and he cried out.

"If you want your arm to remain attached to your body, I suggest you forget this stupid idea."

"We were just having some fun," Paul barked, his voice trembling with the pain.

Fury traveled through my veins, and it was everything I could do not to break his arm right there. Fun? He called destroying a store and giving an old man a heart attack fun?

I bent his wrist and he cried in pain.

"Let him go, man," John cried. He brought his fists up. "Let him go or I'll kick your ass."

I couldn't help it. Laughter, hollow and dark, bubbled past my lips. "In your dreams."

John advanced on me. I seriously didn't get it. The little bastard was drunk, and he could barely throw a punch. Why make a fool of himself?

Swift as the wind, I moved, dropping Paul on the sidewalk, his stomach hitting the pavement hard, and blocked John's weak punch with my wrist. I twisted my hand, grabbing his wrist in turn, and pulled him forward. He tripped and fell beside Paul.

I stared at the other two boys. "Who's next?"

The two boys trembled, their gaze shifting to something over my shoulder. What the fuck?

I followed their line of sight.

Ryder, in his full warrior's armor and weapons, stood right behind me, his arms crossed over his chest. Although we were the same height, Ryder's shoulders were wider, and with his face set into a scowl, he was easily one scary motherfucker.

I fought the urge to roll my eyes at him and faced the boys again. The two kids helped John and Paul up and ran off.

"That ought to keep them on their toes," Ryder said.

"Humans aren't used to seeing warriors in full garb, Ryder. They don't even know we exist."

"I know, but it worked, didn't it? They ran."

"I would have made them run with or without you." I picked up the rock the kids had grabbed and put it back in the flowerbed on the edge of the sidewalk. "I just hope they don't tell their parents about the weirdo with the swords wandering around town."

Ryder shrugged. "I wouldn't mind."

"Of course you wouldn't." The warriors revealed themselves to humans only if necessary, but in truth, we were supposed to pretend to be human—just like I did. "But I mind. Paul's father is the bank manager. I deal with him for my account and investments. And John's mother works at the library. She knows who I am."

"Does she now?"

I groaned. Ryder had been a good friend for most of my life, but sometimes he liked to annoy me. "You know what I mean. They think they know me."

I had been relocated to this fucking town about two years ago, and I didn't think any of the twenty-three hundred residents really knew much about me. But I knew all about them. I knew all of their names, ages, occupations, affiliations. If they hadn't been born here, I knew why they had come to this sleepy town. I also knew their medical and criminal history. Some really fucked up people lived here.

And I was the worst of them all.

To the townsfolk, I was a twenty-one-year-old rich orphan with a penchant for solitude. In reality, their quiet neighbor had been alive for more than five hundred years—if I could count the three hundred and some years I spent in hell.

Time didn't exist in hell. No day, no light. Only pain. Suffering. Misery.

All because of a failed mission I didn't remember.

"I know, I know," Ryder said.

I let out a sigh. "All right, you're here for your fucking report, aren't you?"

"Yeah, but—"

"There's nothing new to report," I snapped. "Nothing has changed. I haven't seen anything, felt anything, found out anything. This shitty little town is boring and not even on a map or GPS. Not even lesser demons come here. To be honest, being here feels like another punishment from the gods."

"You know it's not like that. If they wanted you to suffer, they would have let you rot in hell."

I winced. We both knew warriors didn't rot, which meant I could have spent eternity suffering in hell if the gods wanted me to. "But pulling me out of the underworld nineteen years ago and abandoning me in this place without as much as an instruction of what I should be doing is much better."

"At least you're not being tortur—" Ryder's words died when I shot him a glare. "Besides, they did give you instructions. Fix what went wrong and don't fail this time."

The problem was: What had gone wrong? How had I failed? What mission was it? The not-so-merciful gods erased all my memories related to that failed mission when they pulled me out of hell. I didn't remember a single moment, a single action. I barely knew when it had been and where.

Not that it helped knowing when and where. It wasn't as if a warrior's mission history was available in a book or on a computer.

But the warrior standing in front of me knew. He knew all about that fucking mission, but he couldn't tell me. The gods forbade the other warriors from helping me.

"That's my report," I said, my tone harsh. "Come back in five years. I'm sure nothing will have changed by then."

I spun around and marched away.

"Devon, don't be like that."

I had every intention of ignoring Ryder, but when a chill brushed against my skin, sending a disturbance through the air, I halted and glanced over my shoulder. "Did you feel that?"

Ryder drew out his sword. "I did."

The chill spread, bringing heavy, oily tendrils of darkness.

"Demons," I whispered.

In the blink of an eye, my normal human clothes—dark jeans and polo shirt—were gone, replaced by the warrior's thick dark leather armor, and my sword strapped to my back.

With cautious steps, Ryder and I stalked back to the main square. The darkness was thick and coming toward us.

Ryder twirled his sword in his hand. "Be ready."

I unsheathed my sword.

Half a second later, the little fuckers jumped from the shadows, right at us. Dozens of lesser demons in the form of black shadow snakes. Some were as small as my forearm; some were as long six feet.

I swung my sword in a wide arc, hitting most of them in a single blow. The snakes exploded in puffs of dark smoke that dissolved in the night sky. A few more slithered from the shadows, coming at us from the ground. They hissed their forked tongues, as if teasing us.

All I wanted to do was stomp on them and be done with

it. Killing them with swords while they slithered along the ground wasn't the most practical fight. "I hate these things."

"Me too," Ryder said, and he drove his sword to the ground, piercing through the head of a snake. "But at least they are the lowest of the low."

True. Of all the demons that existed, the snakes were the weakest.

One of the snakes lunged at me, mouth open wide and sharp teeth ready. I waltzed to the side, then stepped over its slimy body and cut off its head. It burst into smoke at my feet.

I looked up, ready to slash through some more, but all I felt was the darkness retreating.

I fixed a narrow gaze on Ryder. "What the fuck was that?"

"I don't know." Ryder's eyes scanned the area, as if expecting another surprise attack. "It wasn't normal."

I nodded. I had been in this town for almost two years now and I had never encountered any demons. Not even shadow snakes. They were weak and drawn to evil and dark places, like the alley of a bad neighborhood in a big city. They stuck to the shadows until the humans came near them and became their victims. "Snake-type demons don't attack like that."

Ryder sheathed his sword. "No, they don't."

The pressure and chill of the darkness dissipated, but a stifling feeling hung in the air. I didn't like it. "Something is definitely wrong."

Makenna

It didn't matter how far we ran or how fast we ran, he always found us. He would always find us. I knew that as strongly as my heart beat painfully against my chest.

I spied past the thick dark green curtain into the parking lot below. I had argued against staying at roadside motels, and Cecilia never listened to me.

"Stop obsessing, Makenna," Cecilia said, her tone too light for the occasion. "We need a good night's sleep. Just ... stop, and come rest."

I glanced over my shoulder and saw her fluffing the pillows on one of the queen beds.

Was this the life she intended for us when we ran away? That I intended for us? We had been running and hiding nonstop for almost two years, and each time we settled for more than half a day, he found us.

I couldn't deny it was better than suffering at his hands, doing his bidding without a choice, but I was so freaking tired of running. My only options were to suffer or to run. Sometimes, only sometimes, I wondered if I wasn't better off dead.

Last time we stopped for more than twelve hours, he had found us. We had to fight our way out. We had to kill.

My stomach turned as I remember the blood, the gore, the darkness. A dark trail was left behind me wherever I went.

"How can you rest when you know we'll be attacked soon?" I asked, venom lacing my words.

I half expected Cecilia to lash out at me, but she was too sweet for that, too calm. I could count on my fingers how many times she had lost her composure, and those had been during the most horrible moments of our lives.

Instead, Cecilia let out a long breath and crossed the room to stand in front of me. She rested her hands on my shoulders and looked at me. "Please, have a little faith." Faith. That was such an odd concept coming from her. How could she believe in faith? Her warm brown eyes twinkled. "We've been on the road for a long time. We haven't slept in almost forty-eight hours. We need to sleep."

Again. She forgot to say again. When we first ran away, we had wrecked the second car we stole. Now, we knew two things: One, we had to take breaks, even if it was for power naps of one or two hours under a shady tree, and two, we couldn't keep a stolen car more than half a day.

Since we didn't have any documents, and barely any cash, we couldn't buy a car. So we stole them—borrowed them, as Cecilia liked to say. We grabbed cars, used them for a few hours, then left them where they would be found by the police and returned to their owners.

"Fine," I snapped, though we both knew I wouldn't relax, not until exhaustion won and I passed out in the bed.

"Good." She patted my cheek, and for some reason, the gesture reminded me of a mother. Sometimes, I thought of her as a mother. She wasn't just my friend. Cecilia was, in some ways, the mother I didn't remember. "I'm going to take a quick shower."

I only grumbled as she walked away and grabbed the duffel bag with the only things we owned: a few changes of clothes and toiletries.

Once more, I thought about the kind of life we were living, about the kind of life we would have in the future. Would we ever escape him? I hoped we would, but I didn't have faith that we would.

I glanced back. Cecilia stood in front of the mirror in the bathroom, the door half opened, and from where I was, I could see as she took off her shirt. I flinched upon seeing the scars covering her back and shoulders. Several long marks etched forever in her skin. She had been abducted years before I had, but I had watched him inflict most of those scars. I had cried as she bled in her bed later, her ragged breath making me fear she would die.

But despite her kind heart and her calm demeanor, Cecilia was a fighter. If it hadn't been for her meticulous planning and waiting, we would have never escaped. At least, not alive.

Even if my freedom was another kind of prison, I owed it all to her.

I lowered my gaze.

And that was when I felt it.

The tendrils of darkness reaching out like claws, grasping the earth, and advancing and desecrating everything in their path.

I froze. Closing my eyes, I opened my senses and felt for the darkness—thick and slow. It wasn't the darkness from demons, unfortunately.

It was *his* darkness.

Slater hadn't come personally. I was sure of it, but the darkness now surrounding the motel had been sent by him along with his men.

It spurred me into action. "Cecilia!" I cried as I picked up my jacket, my wallet, and my phone from the bed.

Holding her shirt over her chest, Cecilia stuck her head out the bathroom door, her long brown hair falling like a curtain around her shoulders. "What?"

"They're here."

Her face paled. "Shit." She put her shirt back on, zipped up her pants, and shoved her feet in her boots. "How many minutes do we have?"

The darkness was closing in faster now. "Two, three at the most."

Her hands trembled as she tied her hair in a ponytail. "No time to run."

I wasn't much better than Cecilia, but I pretended better. Somehow, I was able to conceal the tremors running through my body.

I grabbed the duffel bag and slung it over my shoulders. "We can run, after we stun a few of them."

"We." She snorted. "As if I can do much against them."

I knew she hated when we confronted Slater's men or demons, because she couldn't do more than a few self-defense moves she had learned a long time ago.

I pushed those thoughts away and focused. "Ready?"

Eyes shining with determination, Cecilia nodded. "Ready."

The power hummed in my veins, as if awoken by the darkness encircling us. I extended my hands to my sides and pushed my power to the lights of the motel room. The lights flickered and extinguished. I held on to the darkness, creating a shroud over us. Cecilia and I pressed our backs to the wall right beside the door and waited.

The door burst open and a handful of men—all dressed in black, with a silver pendant with a coiled snake hanging from their necks—exploded into the room. I sent the darkness, thick and palpable, to them. Like fog, the black surrounded them, keeping them lost in a cloud of confusion.

Cecilia and I ran.

Two men waited outside the room. One lunged at Cecilia. She grabbed his wrist, twisted, and bent it outward. The man yelped and leaned forward to take the pressure off his wrist.

Cecilia slammed her knee into his face and let go. The man dropped to the ground.

The other man came at me but didn't touch me. He knew what I was capable of.

As if that would stop me.

I commanded the darkness from the corner of the wall, from the space under the stairs, from the night sky to surround him. The darkness spun until it created a tornado that twisted around the man.

"Run!" I cried, releasing my hold on my power.

The tornado spun the man face-first into the wall, and he dropped to the ground, unconscious.

Cecilia and I descended the outer staircase three steps at a time.

We paused in the parking lot. We had ditched our previous car a few blocks away, and had plans of securing another one as soon as we were ready to leave.

As usual, our stop didn't go according to plan and now we were car-less.

Unless ...

I glanced at the SUV Slater's lackey had driven here. "Get in!"

"B-but that's his car."

"I know, but we can't be picky right now." I slid into the driver's seat. "Come on!"

Groaning, Cecilia ran around the SUV and hopped inside. "I don't like this idea."

"It's the only one we have! We'll ditch the car later; we just need to get out of here first."

I slammed the SUV into reverse as the group of men emerged from our room on the second floor.

"Wait!" one of them yelled.

Oh, yeah, like I would freaking wait.

I stepped on the gas, the tires peeling on the pavement, and we raced down the road. We drove for about ten miles on the dark road outside of town before we allowed ourselves to breathe normally again.

"That was unexpected," Cecilia said, leaning against the passenger seat and relaxing for a bit.

My knuckles turned white as I gripped the steering wheel. "You know it wasn't. I was expecting it."

"I know," she whispered.

My eyes darted to the rearview mirror for the hundredth time, sure I would soon see a car or SUV gunning after us. Instead, the only thing behind us was the moonlight reflecting off the road markers.

I took a deep breath, releasing my death grip on the steering wheel, and immediately felt the shoulders of my muscles uncord.

For now, we were safe.

At least until he found us again.

PAST

Devon

THE WARRIOR STOOD AT THE EDGE OF THE ROOF, LOOKING down at the empty streets. At this time of the evening, the village was mostly asleep, except for the usual customers at the tavern. Despite the curfew being enforced since the attacks had started, a couple of men still sneaked out to drink.

One of those would be the next victim, the warrior was sure.

He didn't have to wait long for two men to stumble out of the tavern, tripping over their own feet. Their laughter rang through the night. The town's guard was sure to hear them, but not before something happened to them.

Like a shadow, the warrior jumped off the roof and followed the two men. One of them came upon his house not two minutes later. The lucky bastard tripped on his doorstep as he pushed open the door, falling on the floor of his home. He crawled into the dimly lit room and kicked the door shut behind him.

The second staggered several houses down, then he turned into an alley.

Not five seconds later, the warrior felt it. The change in the air, the thickness and the chill enveloping the area, the evil closing in.

A demon with a long gray body, black eyes, and sharp fangs materialized in the middle of the alley a few feet in front of the man.

The drunk's eyes went wide, and a startled scream caught in his throat. He stepped back to retreat and fell on his butt, gaping at the demon.

The warrior reached behind his back and unsheathed his sword, the black hilt resting comfortably in his palm.

The demon advanced on the drunk.

The warrior rushed from the shadows and slashed his blade across the demon's torso, slicing into its chest. The demon let out a howl of pain and rage. It hadn't died, but it did what the warrior wanted—it shifted its attention to him, leaving the drunk man alone.

"Run," the warrior commanded.

It took a moment, but the drunk man scrambled to his feet and fled, half-crawling and falling over himself as he tried to escape.

The warrior always wondered what the humans who encountered demons and survived told the others. That they had seen evil in the flesh? That they had escaped a demon? Would others believe them?

Not that the warrior really cared about it. Whether humans knew about demons or not, his job didn't change.

He still had to hunt down demons and kill them.

Just as he would do to this one.

The demon let out a snarl, showing off its long claws, and lunged for the warrior.

The warrior sidestepped the demon, dodging the attack. He whirled, facing the demon's back, and swept his sword wide, cutting off the demon's head.

The head fell to the dirt ground with a wet thump.

Now it was dead.

The warrior cleaned the blade on his pants, then sheathed his sword on the scabbard across his back and a small white baton appeared in his hand. The warrior knelt beside the demon's body and pierced the chest with the tip of the baton. The demon's body dissolved into black smoke that faded into the night air.

He repeated the process with the head.

Then, the baton disappeared too.

Having finished his mission, the warrior stood up, ready to leave, when another figure appeared in front of him.

"Ryder," the warrior said, calling the man by name. Like him, Ryder was a warrior. He too sported the same black leather armor and carried the same magical blade on his back.

"Devon," Ryder said. "I'm here to deliver a message."

The warrior straightened his back. "What message?"

"The gods are calling you," Ryder said. "They have a mission for you."

DEVON LINGERED IN THE SHADOWS OF THE TREES, WATCHING AS the young woman knelt by the edge of the lake, pulling her skirt above her ankles so as not to get the hem wet, and washed her hands. She glanced at the water, the rays of the sunset igniting her fair face, and she smiled as if greeting a friend.

Something in the warrior's chest tightened.

She couldn't be older than eighteen. And she was the one the gods had told him about? She was supposed to be evil? With her brilliant smile? Her pretty face? Her delicate hands?

A little squeal and the sound of rapid footsteps came from his right, and the warrior reached for the sword strapped to his back. Two kids burst past the tree line, stumbling toward the girl—her siblings.

Still smiling, the young woman stood. "Selina, Calvin. What are you two up to?"

"He pulled my hair!" the girl spat. She was a miniature version of the woman with brilliant golden hair and bright blue eyes.

The boy, probably younger than both, shook his head, loosening his ponytail. "No, I didn't."

The woman laughed. "Of course you didn't. And what did she do to earn her fate?"

"She kicked me in the shin!"

The warrior frowned. Had the boy confessed he had pulled the girl's hair?

The woman put her hands on her hips and stared at the girl. "Why did you kick him?"

"Because he was being a pest," the little girl said simply.

The young woman rolled her eyes. "And here I thought you two were playing."

"We were," the little boy said.

"Until he started bothering me," the girl said.

The young woman shook her head. The long, heavy

golden braid falling down to her waist barely moved. "You two should try to get along for more than five minutes."

She retreated to a lone cherry tree a few feet away from the lake and sat down on the wooden bench underneath it. With a sigh, she leaned back against the tree trunk. The soft pink of the tree's flowers and the rays of the setting sun gave a soft rose-gold hue to her cheeks.

The girl took a seat on the bench. "I try! He's the one who always bothers me."

The little boy trotted to them. "Am not!"

The young woman laughed, the sound echoing through the air like little bells.

In the distance, movement caught Devon's attention. An older woman appeared from the open door of the stone manor atop a small hill. "Kianna, Selina, Calvin! Supper is ready!" she shouted.

"We're coming," the young woman answered as the kids took off toward the house. Another smile adorned her pink lips as she stood and watched her siblings running up the hill.

With a sigh, she bent at the waist and picked up the heavy basket filled with clothes. She propped it on her hip and took a step toward the house. Then, she stopped as if she had remembered something. With a crease between her brows, the Kianna rose on her tiptoes and snatched a flower from the cherry tree. She slid it behind her ear, as if it was a common gesture, then she glanced out to the lake once more as if sharing a secret or wishing for a miracle.

Despite fighting his growing curiosity, Devon wondered what she saw when she watched the lake.

A moment later, Kianna turned and trotted up the hill as if she didn't care about the lake at all.

PRESENT

Kenna

"Here we are," Lia announced as she brought the car into the driveway.

It was dark out and the few lamps along the street didn't illuminate much, but I could see the shape of the narrow two-story house in front of us.

"This is ours?" I asked, skeptical.

Lia shrugged. "Well, we're renting as of this afternoon, so yeah, it's ours." She reached for her purse on the backseat. "Home, sweet home. Come on."

With a skip to her step, Lia exited the car and rushed to the front porch.

I didn't move a muscle.

By the time we got settled in the house, we would have to move again. For the last two years, Cecilia—*Lia*—had insisted we stay at roadside motels and crappy apartments.

"It's time we stop and make a life for ourselves, Makenna," she had said before the last move.

I thought Lia had been joking. Dreaming out loud, as she usually did. We both did. Who didn't want to stop moving and settle down and live in peace?

But there was no peace for us. There never would be. Not while Slater lived.

Despite my protests, Lia had arranged—behind my back—everything. Since the last time they found us at the motel three months ago, we had zigzagged across the country, only stopping when necessary.

And we hadn't been caught once.

That gave Lia the confidence to move forward with the second part of her plan: securing fake documents and settling down in a nice, quiet town in the middle of nowhere.

With a grunt, I grabbed my backpack at my feet and followed the older woman into the house. Lia had turned on the lights and was now walking from room to room.

She peeked her head from what looked like a kitchen in the back and smiled at me. "I know it's small, but it looks great." She disappeared again.

I glanced around. What was so great about scratched floors, peeling paint, spiderwebs, and dust? I took two steps into the foyer and placed my hand on the wooden rail of the stairs leading to the second floor. Loose, as I thought. To the right was a living room with a small fireplace. Red bricks, chipped and worn with age, climbed the wall. To the left, a glass chandelier hung precariously from the ceiling. I sighed. The house looked old. It was falling apart.

Just like us.

"How long are we staying here?" I asked, raising my voice so I could be heard from anywhere in the house.

Lia appeared from the other door in the dining room. "I signed the lease for two years, but hopefully more."

I frowned, sure I hadn't heard her right. "Wait. What?"

"Why so surprised? We've been talking about finding a place for us for a long time."

For more than seven years, but who was counting? "We can't stay here. Not for more than a week, maybe a month, and that might be too long."

Lia reached for my hands. "It's been months, Kenna." Since we started moving aimlessly, we had changed our names. I wasn't Makenna anymore. For the last three months, I had been only Kenna. "He won't find us here."

I pulled my hands from hers and took a step back. "He'll never stop looking. Even if it takes him ten years, twenty! He'll find us."

She shook her head. "We can't run forever. You're young. Hell, I'm young too. We deserve to live our lives."

What lives? I barely remembered my childhood, and the only images etched in my memory were bad ones. Bloody ones. As for Cecilia ... she had been taken when she was twenty. That was eighteen years ago. Did she really know another way of life?

I looked down at the dull wooden floor, ashamed of myself. Cecilia had suffered for so long. We both had. Of course she would want a better life. She really did deserve it. But here ... living in this house, in this small town on the other side of the country, was still not far enough. Perhaps if I convinced her to move to a remote island, or some other faraway corner of the world, then we might have a chance.

At this point, I really doubted we would make it.

And yet, I couldn't stop myself from falling for Cecilia's dream.

Tomorrow. I would talk to her about this silly dream tomorrow. We could use a good night sleep first.

"Okay," I whispered.

Her brown eyes lit up. "Really?"

How could I say no to her? "Really."

Smiling, she advanced to me and squeezed me in a tight hug. "Everything will be okay. You'll see." She kissed my cheek, then continued her perusal of the house. She went back to the kitchen and opened the back door. The outside lights came on, illuminating what looked like a small porch. "Oh my word, come see this!"

What? Did the house come with a pool? For Lia to be renting it, it had to be super cheap, and I doubted a cheap house came with a pool.

Knowing she would bother me until I let her show me the backyard, I dragged my feet out to the porch.

A big cherry tree sat on the right side of the yard, leaning over the short wooden fence and spilling over to the neighbor's backyard. Its soft pink flowers were in full bloom and emanating a sweet scent.

"Wow," I whispered.

"I know," she said. "It's so pretty."

It really was. It was mesmerizing, actually. If the tree was this pretty at night, I wondered how gorgeous it would be during the day, when the sun was high in the sky and shining down on its petals.

"I don't think I have ever seen a cherry tree this close," I muttered.

"My parents used to have a few in the orchard on our family ranch." Her voice gained a sad lilt, as it usually did whenever she talked about her family. She hadn't seen them in eighteen years. She didn't even know if they were still alive, but because we were and always would be in danger, she didn't dare look for them. "All right. We have a lot of work to do." She went back inside the house, only to cross the kitchen and the hallway and exit through the front door.

She had probably gone to get the few bags we had in the car. Not that we had much, but Lia had planned even that. She had sold the last gold piece she had stolen from Slater, and with the money, she had bought a crappy Corolla that had seen better days. We also used some to buy clothes and food, and purchase fake documents. We saved a little because Lia insisted we would need money to buy furniture for the house.

Of course, she didn't tell me about this plan until a week ago, when she finally bought the car and picked up our documents. At first, I refused to go along with her foolhardy plan. She had been lying to me. She knew, better than me, how dangerous it was to stay in one place for long. I indulged her, because I thought that little streak of hope was enough to keep her going. I didn't actually think she would do it.

I shook my head and a sad laugh bubbled out of my throat as I remembered how eager and excited Lia had been. She always tried to find the bright side. She had helped me survived many dark nights. That was one of the reasons why I loved her so much.

I walked back into the house and glanced at it again. The stained foyer wall, the broken board on the stairs, the cracked footboards. Maybe if we handled it with love, this house could become a home.

But for how long?

I shook my head. No, I wouldn't think of that right now. For a moment, even if only for a night, I would dive into Cecilia's dream, and I would pretend everything was all right.

Devon

MY FOOTFALLS AND INCREASED BREATHING THRUMMED IN MY ears as I ran across the town's main street. This late at night, it was rare to see anything open, much fewer people out. After ten, even the only gas station and the connected convenience store closed, which was why I chose this time to go out and exercise—so I wouldn't be bothered by anyone.

Rarely, I bumped into Paul, John, and their delinquent friends. But unless they were doing something bad—like fucking breaking into to the record store—I gave them a wide berth and kept running.

Thankfully, I hadn't seen anyone out and I also didn't have to report to Ryder. As much as I liked seeing my old friend, it also pained me more than I dared to admit. Unlike me, he and the other warriors kept going on missions— quests assigned by the gods where the warriors searched for and apprehended or killed demons, keeping the world at balance—because they hadn't fucked up like I had. And what pissed me off the most was that I had no idea what I had done wrong, how I could fix it, or how I could escape this meaningless human life.

I turned onto my street and slowed, upset with myself for letting my thoughts wander back to my punishment. My fucking curse.

How could I not think of it, though? Eighteen years, ten months, and six days ago, the gods pulled me out of hell and offered me a second chance.

"Don't fail this time," they said.

I had spent three hundred years in misery, and they wouldn't even give me a clue about what came next? "If I don't know what happened the first time, if I don't know what I did wrong, how can I fix it?"

"When the time comes, you'll know," they said. They handed me a ring and said, "Our gift to you. It'll bring light even in the darkest of times."

Then, they sent me to Earth.

I had been roaming the world for almost nineteen years, searching for whatever I was supposed to find, but how did I even start if I had no idea what I was looking for?

Finally, I settled in Misty Hill. But not because I had wanted to. The gods had sent me here for some reason, one I hadn't found out yet. But even if they told me to move again, I wouldn't. Until the gods came to me and told me more about my mission, I wouldn't move. I would stay here and live a lonely, aimless life, my only interest taking the next breath.

I came to a halt, my running shoes skidding on rough concrete and my hands resting on my hips as I sucked in cool air.

I had new neighbors.

Two women had parked their beat-up Corolla in the driveway of the house next door. Slowly, I walked to my house, watching as they carried their bags from the car to the house. From my front porch, the darkness was engulfing, but I blinked, adjusting my eyes to the dark, and saw almost as clear as day: one looked like in her mid-thirties, the other was not much older than a teenager.

I frowned. Who were these women and what kind of neighbors would they be? If they disrupted my peace ...

I closed my hands into fists and forced the air out of my lungs.

Relax, I told myself.

If they bothered me, I could arrange for them to be kicked out of the house. That simple. For now, I'd watch them in case they spelled trouble.

PAST

Kianna

ONCE A YEAR, KIANNA TOOK ALL HER BOOKS FROM THE SHELVES in the manor, cleaned the surfaces, and then reorganized them. It was her way of connecting with her books and sometimes finding a hidden gem she had forgotten about—and reread it.

"Have you really read all of these?" Catherine asked as she put a few books back on the shelf in the living room, the way Kianna had told her to.

"Yes," Kianna replied from across the room. She sat on the floor, several books spread around her, as she piled them by author.

"And they are all romances?"

Kianna looked up. Cat held a book up with only two fingers, as if it was disgusting to touch. A smile spread over

Kianna's lips at her best friend's silly action. Cat had always been silly and fun to be around. If Kianna had to guess why the two of them became friends as children, she would say it was because Cat could make her laugh like no one else could.

"Yes, most of them are love stories," Kianna admitted.

Cat wrinkled her nose and shook her hair, her mop of dark curls bouncing. "So, I assume you know all about romance. And yet, you're not betrothed. Are you waiting for your prince?" The smile on Kianna's lips faded. "I didn't mean it like that. I didn't ... sorry."

Kianna didn't understand why she got so upset when talking about love and marriage and the future. Love and marriage had been out of the question for a few years now.

At eighteen, she didn't even think she was suitable for marriage anymore. Not with the calluses in her hands and the constant pain in her back. Maybe when her father had been alive, and their farm had been prosperous, when they had more helpers and she didn't need to work, she would have had suitors. Now, she barely stepped a foot off the farm, much less in town. Even if there were potential suitors, they didn't know of her existence.

Upset with the turn her thoughts had taken, Kianna grabbed a book and squeezed it hard as if it was her enemy. Why was she thinking about marriage anyway? She didn't need a man to make her happy. She was plenty happy with her mother and her siblings. Between the manor, the farm, and her family, she didn't have time to think about anything else.

"It's okay." Kianna stood up. "Love and marriage is all in the past. All that matters now is the farm and my family." She picked up a pile of books from the floor and took them to the empty shelf next to her. "Never mind me. Tell me about you and that young man you mentioned last week." Kianna glanced at her friend. "John? Joseph?"

"Jonah," Cat said, her cheeks reddening. "I went to the village with my mother yesterday."

"Did you see him?"

Cat nodded. "I lied to my mother about having to stop at the bakery, just so we would walk past the blacksmith."

A smile spread over Kianna's lips. "Did you see him?"

"Yes." The red in her cheeks darkened. "He actually stopped his work and came outside to greet us."

"Really?" Kianna felt glad for her friend. If she had to live vicariously through Cat, she would. "And?"

"My mother was surprised, but after we left, she told me he was handsome."

Kianna clapped her hands. "That's great!"

Cat came from a modest family. She didn't have many prospects for marriage, like Kianna once had. Truth be told, if Cat married the son of a blacksmith, she would raise her family's social standing.

"She wants me to invite him for supper," Cat said, sounding nervous. "But—"

"Catherine!"

Cat's face paled and she hid behind the sofa.

Kianna placed her hands on her waist. "Why are you hiding?"

"Because I'm not supposed to be here," Cat whispered.

"What happened?"

"She was receiving a punishment," Giles said, walking into the living room. The old man smiled at Kianna, showing off the wrinkles around his eyes, and lowered dipped his chin —a sign of respect for the daughter of his boss.

Kianna's grandparents had hired Giles when her father

was a little boy. Later, when her grandparents died, Giles had remained to aid her father.

And when her father died and all the other workers left, Giles stayed with her family, promising to work for them until the day he died. But Giles had his own family to take care of, and having Catherine for a daughter could be quite exhausting.

Cat spied from behind the sofa. "Can't you pretend you didn't see me?"

"If your mother finds out you're gone and I knew about it, she'll skin us both," Giles said. "Come. The sun is about to set. Time to go."

Cat looked at Kianna as if she could save her from such a cruel fate. Kianna chuckled. What was the worst that could happen? Cat's mother would punish her again, and they wouldn't see each other for the next two days.

They could survive that.

"Go, Cat." Kianna waved her off. "Go before your next punishment is to spend an entire week locked in your bedroom."

Cat's eyes went wide.

Giles nodded, serious. "That could happen."

"Fine!" Cat stood up, pouting. "I'm going, I'm going."

Giles turned to Kianna and sniffed the air. "I can smell cinnamon."

Kianna offered him a small smile. "There might be something in the oven."

"I bet it'll taste delicious." The old man nodded at Kianna again. "Good night, miss." He walked toward the door.

Cat dragged her feet, flinging her arms side to side, as if trying to grab a rope that tied her to Kianna. "Don't make me go," she whispered.

"I heard that!" Giles said, from somewhere in the manor.

"Damn it." Cat stopped playing and waved at Kianna. "See you tomorrow. Hopefully."

Then, she ran after her father.

Kianna's smile lingered while she finished organizing the books and putting them back onto the shelves. She stepped back and admired her work. Half of them were done. Tomorrow, she would tackle the other half.

Following the scent, Kianna sauntered to the kitchen. Kianna leaned in front of the wood stove and carefully opened the little metal door. She spied the rising cake. Just a little longer.

By the time the cake was done, her family should be back.

Kianna stared out the window and checked the sun's position. It was almost fully set. Her mother and her siblings had gone to the market to sell produce and buy a few necessities. They should have already returned.

If they weren't home in fifteen minutes, she would follow the road to town to meet them.

To distract herself, Kianna grabbed the broom and swept the ceramic kitchen floor. Then, she set up the table in the adjacent dining room. Four plates, four cups, and four—

"You really didn't have to."

Kianna straightened. That was her mother's voice, but it was too sweet to be talking to her siblings unless they had been angels in town, which she doubted.

"It's nothing," a new voice said.

Kianna's brows knitted together. Curious, she crossed the hallway, opened the front door, and came face-to-face with her mother.

"Kianna, dear," her mother said with a smile. Her hands were full of what looked like books. Books? Her mother stepped to the side, giving Kianna a full view of the owner of the strange voice. "This is Devon," she said. "He saw me on the road and offered to help."

The crease in Kianna's forehead deepened. Why would a stranger offer help? Besides, even though her sister and brother were little, they could have carried something, lessening their mother's burden. But as it was, the kids ran around behind them on the porch, already teasing each other —which often led to a fight.

Devon bowed his head at Kianna. "Hello."

Kianna stood her ground. "Hi." She gestured to the wooden bench to her right. "You can leave everything there. Thank you."

"Kianna!" Her mother lost the smile. "I would like to at least offer a glass of water to this young gentleman before he leaves." She took a step, but when Kianna didn't move, she tsked. "Kianna, please."

Kianna stared at the stranger. The first thing she noticed was his face. He had a serious face with sharp angles and thick eyebrows. His nose was straight, and his lips a light rose color. His dark eyes stared at her, and she felt as if she were diving into endless ebony pools. His dark hair was tied back into a messy ponytail, a few strands loose, framing his face. His clothes were black cloth and fit him well, even though he was tall, taller than her father had been, and wider too. He was slim, but his shoulders were broad.

Kianna shook her head, ashamed for having noticed more of him than she should have. She forced her thoughts to the matter at hand: a fine young man didn't simply wander around at the country offering to help women in need.

She wanted him gone.

"I'll bring some water," she barked.

Her mother sighed. "Don't be silly." She pushed past Kianna, stunning her daughter with her mother brazenness; Kianna stumbled back.

The stranger reached forward and grabbed her wrist before she fell on her butt. "Careful." His dark eyes fixed on hers.

Heat crept through her cheeks and she jerked her arm free.

"Come," her mother called. Without ceremony, the stranger walked into their home. "Please, put those here." She gestured to a side table in the foyer.

The stranger deposited the bags on the table, then he turned and sniffed the air. "I smell cinnamon."

The heat in her face increased. "I'm baking something." She rushed to the kitchen in the back of the house. She pulled out the cake from the stove. She baked it for her mother and siblings, not some stranger, but it couldn't stay longer in the oven or it would burn.

Kianna returned to the dining room and set the cake in the center of the dining table.

Her mother's eyes widened. "You made this?"

"Yes," Kianna said.

Her mother smiled. "It looks amazing." She looked at the stranger. "Devon, I'm about to make supper. Why don't you stay and eat with us? You can have a slice of cake as well."

The stranger glanced at Kianna. She was sure he could see her flaming cheeks, her incredulous eyes, but he didn't seem to care. He smiled at her mother. "Thank you for the offer, Ophelia. I'll stay, but only if I can help in the meantime."

Kianna stared at them shocked. Ophelia? He was already on a first-name basis with her mother?

"Well, now that you mention it ..."

Her mother asked the stranger to take some equipment to the barn behind the house, where the smaller farming tools were stored. She mentioned something about a broken wagon and he told her he would look into it.

He offered a bow from his waist, and marched out of the house through the back door. From the window, Kianna watched the kids, who raced around the yard at the back of the house. The stranger made them laugh before heading to the barn. When she was sure he was out of earshot, she whirled on her mother.

"What were you thinking?" Kianna demanded. "Bringing a stranger into our house?"

Her mother picked up a pot and filled it with water. "Why are you being so mean? He seems like a gentleman."

"But why? Nobody just helps for no reason."

Her mother frowned at her. "Is that your view of the world? Oh, my dear, you need to believe there's good out there."

"What if he's a criminal?"

"Kianna!" Her mother raised her voice and Kianna flinched. Her mother rarely yelled. "Stop this nonsense right now. Please, help me with dinner and be polite to Devon." She handed a knife to Kianna. "Now, cut the carrots, please."

Kianna took the knife, but as she sliced the carrots, her mind didn't stop. A young man alone on the road ... where was he going? Why would he offer to help and discard his plans to help her mother? She peeked out the window. Why was he now fixing the wagon? She saw nothing out of the ordinary about him.

He knelt on the ground beside the barn, tools spread around him, working on a broken wagon.

It didn't feel like a coincidence.

But then ... who was this man, and what did he want with her family?

Kenna

I STOOD IN THE FOYER AND GLANCED TO THE LIVING ROOM. I had started peeling the old, stained paint from the walls this morning, but I was so freaking sick of working on the house for the last three days. We woke up early and went until late in the night, only stopping for meals or to discuss our plans for the future.

One of the main topics Lia and I discussed was her finding a job. We couldn't live off the little cash we still had, and besides trying to get a job as a waitress somewhere, there wasn't much I could do, not without a high school diploma. But Lia had finished high school and even started college before her life was stolen from her. She had now applied for every job position available in town—which weren't many.

I had started looking at waitressing jobs, but Lia had

threatened to take my recently acquired smartphone from me if I didn't focus on studying.

Right now, I wanted to focus on the house, because there was no way I could live in a house falling apart.

If we stayed here for long.

Which I honestly doubted.

My mood soured in two seconds flat. Deciding I needed a break, I threw the scraper on the plastic covering the floor and marched to the kitchen to grab a snack. I opened the fridge and the cabinets, and per usual, nothing really appealed to me. I craved something sweet and soft ... I could always bake a cake.

I had never cooked, but I was sure I could follow some videos on YouTube and bake a cake. It couldn't be that hard. When Lia got back home from buying more supplies for our home remodel, she would be impressed.

I clicked on the YouTube app on my phone and—

The doorbell rang.

My insides froze, and the phone slipped from my hand, landing hard on the wooden floor.

"No, no, no," I muttered, both as a request not to have broken my brand-new phone, and for me to be mistaken about the doorbell. It had been my imagination.

The doorbell rang again.

Thousands of thoughts raced through my mind. It was Slater and his goons. They had found us, and now our brief peace and quiet would only serve as a torment our own memories inflicted upon us and—

A knock echoed through the door.

I frowned.

If it was Slater and his goons, they wouldn't ring the bell or knock on the door. They would break down the door, without warning, even if it was the middle of the day and the neighbors could see us.

Still, as I walked to the door, I channeled my power. The lights in the foyer flickered, and I inhaled deeply, calming myself. The flickering stopped.

Holding my breath, I opened the door.

A girl with short brown curls and bright hazel eyes smiled at me. "Oh, hi." She dropped her hand, which had been about to rap on the door again. "I knew you were here."

I narrowed my eyes at her. She was probably my age, and she had a t-shirt from Misty Hill High School football team. A student and probably a cheerleader.

"Hm, can I help you?" I asked.

She extended her hand to me. "I'm Caroline, your neighbor." I stared at her hand, but didn't take it. Never losing the three thousand-watt smile, she dropped the hand and pointed to the house to my right. "I live there with my parents." She bounced on the balls of her feet. "I noticed someone had moved to this house a couple of days ago, but it was only this morning that I saw you and your mother, I'm assuming."

"Yes," I muttered.

"I was leaving for school, so I couldn't come say hi. But now I'm back and I wanted to say hi." She raised her hand and waved at me. "Hi."

"Hi."

"So ... what's your name?"

"Kenna."

"And your mother?"

"Lia."

"Where did you guys move from?" When I didn't answer right away, she continued, "Are you transferring to school here? There's only one high school, quite small actually, so I bet we'll be in most of the same classes. Why did you guys move here? Your mother got a new job?"

Her words were like bullets coming from an automatic rifle, fast and hitting hard. With each question she shot, I got dizzier and dizzier. "Hm, Caroline," I interrupted. "You said you just came back from school, right? Don't you have homework?"

"I did it all on the bus," she said, sounding proud of herself.

"What about your parents. Are they home?"

She shook her head. "They are doctors at the emergency room here. They work crazy hours. It's rare when we're home together."

For some reason, that made me feel a little bad for her. I didn't remember much before being taken by Slater when I was eleven. I didn't even remember my parents, or if I had any siblings, but I knew how much I had longed for them, for faceless figures to find me and rescue me and take me home and care for me.

Knowing this eighteen-year-old girl spent most of her days alone made me a little less irritated with her, but not enough to invite her in. I opened the door slightly more and gestured to the mess everywhere. "As you can see, it's a little chaotic in here, and I have a lot to do, so ..."

The girl's smile faltered. "Hm, of course. You just moved, and I know this house needs some serious love and care." She took a step back. "Well, when you're done or need a break, you can come spend some time with me." She gestured to her house again. "Now you know where I live." She let out a nervous chuckle.

"Sounds good," I said, attempting to smile too, but I was sure it had come out more like a grimace.

Head low, she turned and raced down the porch steps and across the yard to her house. I closed the front door, suddenly feeling heavy. Dirty. If only I could tell her that I wasn't trying to be rude, not really, but this was my way of protecting her. Lia and I couldn't make friends. We couldn't. If we did, they would be at risk too. They could be killed.

And there had been already too much death around us as it was.

Devon

MY NEW NEIGHBORS HAD BEEN HERE FOR THREE FUCKING DAYS, and I had learned nothing about them. That had never happened before.

By now, I should have known their names, date of birth, where they were born, and why they were here. But so far, I had only learned from the old man across the street that their names were Lia and Kenna. No last names. I couldn't even search them online like that.

Not knowing who they were and why they were here bothered me. I had woken up twice last night after dreaming they were demons disguised as humans trying to kill me in my sleep.

So, when I saw Lia arriving home with her trunk full, I thought it was the perfect opportunity to approach them. Lia bent over the trunk, trying to pull a box from inside when I halted beside her.

"Hello."

She dropped the box and jumped, her eyes wide and her face pale, as if she had seen a ghost. No, as if she had something to hide.

"Oh my word." She pressed a hand over her heart. "You startled me."

"I'm sorry," I said, trying to sound friendly. I usually didn't come off as such. "I didn't mean to. I just thought it was the perfect opportunity to introduce myself." I extended my hand to her. "I'm Devon Knight. Your next-door neighbor." I gestured to my house, almost an exact copy of hers. Just better cared for.

She took my hand. "I'm Lia Jones. Nice to meet you." She pulled her hand away.

"Let me help with that." I reached for the box in the trunk.

"Oh, no, there's no need," Lia said, her voice tight.

I picked up the box, realizing there were plenty of bags from the hardware store. Cans of paint, brushes ... they were fixing the house. "It's okay. I can do it."

I didn't give her a chance to tell me no again as I hurried to the front door. Carrying bags, Lia rushed after me and opened the door for me. "The house is a mess ..."

"It's okay," I said again, but I confess I was a bit surprised when I stepped into the foyer.

The handrail was gone. A few boards from the hardwood floor were missing. There were more cans of paint and brushes in the hallway leading to the kitchen. To the right of the door, a plastic sheet covered most of the floor, and to the left, a chandelier rested on the floor.

"The house is great, but it was in a bad shape, so we're fixing it." Lia dropped her bags on the first step of the stairs. "You can leave it here." She pointed to a corner of the foyer.

"We?" I asked, pretending I hadn't seen the younger girl with her.

Averting her eyes, she wiped her hands on her jeans. "Yes, my daughter lives here with me."

It might be just me, or my warrior training, but I was convinced these two women were hiding something.

As I deposited the box in the appointed corner, a bang resounded from the back of the house. My body stiffened, on alert.

"Shit!" a voice said.

I sniffed the air. "Something is burning."

"Oh no," Lia muttered. She pivoted and raced to the kitchen.

I followed her, ready to protect the human. I skidded to a stop in the kitchen doorway. Smoke billowed from the open oven. The other girl, Kenna, retrieved a pan from inside wearing cooking mittens. She kicked the oven closed with her foot, cutting off the smoke, and dropped the cake on the kitchen's island. She coughed and fanned the smoke away from her face.

Unlike the rest of the house, the kitchen was mostly intact. The walls and cupboards were intact, and apparently the appliances worked—when Kenna wasn't setting the oven on fire.

"Shit," Kenna muttered again.

"What in ...?" Lia stared at the oven, then the burnt cake. "Were you trying to cook again?"

"I was bored, and I was craving something sweet." Kenna threw the mittens at the cake. It landed on the burnt mound and fell to the side, right on top of an open notebook. I frowned. Books and notebooks and pens littered the island. "Shit."

"Watch your language!" Lia rasped.

Kenna, blinking away the stink of smoke from her eyes, looked our way. Her eyes widened as she saw me.

My breath caught.

Her eyes ... blue as the ocean under the bright sun. Although I didn't care for her the orange dye streaking her brown hair, the color mixed with her fair skin emphasized how bright her eyes were.

"Who are you?" She turned a glare to her mother. "Who is he?"

"Oh, his name is Devon and he's our next-door neighbor," Lia said. She looked at me. "This is Kenna, my daughter."

I extended my hand to her. "Nice to meet you."

She stared at my outstretched hand, then turned to her mother again. "What is he doing here?" The bite in her tone added to my suspicions.

"He was—"

"I saw your mother struggling with the boxes. Thought I would help." I almost barfed in my mouth over my lie. "Besides, I thought it would be a good opportunity to introduce myself."

"Okay, you've met us," Kenna said. "Thank you for your help. You can go now."

"Kenna!" Lia admonished. "Don't be a jerk." Lia offered me a shy smile. "Sorry. It's just ... we're not used to having company." Her brows draw together. "What about your parents? Are they home?"

Behind Lia, Kenna shook her head. If I thought Lia had

been wary of me, I was certain Kenna was. She wanted me gone five minutes ago, which only piqued my curiosity.

"They passed away long ago," I told her my automatic lie.

Lia's brown eyes shone with sympathy. "I'm sorry."

Muttering curses, Kenna picked up the pan and threw it in the sink.

"It's okay," I assured her. "Like I said, it was a long time ago. I've been on my own for a while now."

"It must have been lonely," Lia said, her voice low. I could see her entire demeanor changing. From wariness to sympathy. "You know what? I'm about to make dinner." Kenna stared at Lia with her mouth open in shock. Lia pretended she didn't see it. "Why don't you stay? It would be nice to share a meal with a friendly neighbor."

I looked at Kenna. She was glaring at me, seething from every pore.

For some reason, I took pleasure in irritating her. "Of course. I would love to."

Lia spun around in the kitchen. "Okay, let me see." She let out a nervous chuckle. "Sorry about the mess. We're still organizing everything, and with the repairs, it'll be a mess for a while." She opened a cabinet full of condiments. "Kenna, please, set the island for us."

Nostrils flaring as she let out a long, angry breath, Kenna picked up her books, piled them up, and took them away. While she was gone, Lia grabbed a pot and filled it with water from the tap. Next, she pulled pasta from one of the cabinets and frozen meatballs from the freezer.

My brows curled down. What the fuck was I doing? I had never had so much interest in my neighbors before. Once I researched all their sordid details and found out they weren't hiding anything mythical or a magical side, I was done with them. But these two ... I blamed the fact that there was nothing online about them. That was the only reason I was curious and even accepted Lia's invitation to stay for fucking dinner.

Had I shared a dinner with a human since becoming a warrior five hundred years ago? Well ... there was a short period of time, before my punishment, that I didn't remember, but I honestly doubted I had shared a meal with a human family then either.

It just wasn't me.

Stomping her feet, Kenna came back to the kitchen and grabbed dinner plates from inside the cabinet near the sink.

"I can help," I said, reaching for the plates.

My hands cupped hers.

Blurred images exploded in my skull.

A girl in a beige and soft yellow dress stumbling back and falling; me reaching for her, grabbing her wrist, and keeping her steady.

"Devon?" I blinked, and the images went away. Kenna raised an eyebrow at me. "Are you okay?"

I took the plates from her. "Yeah, I am." I turned around and placed the plates in front of three of the four stools around the kitchen's island, aware of Kenna's eyes watching my back.

When she moved and went to grab glasses, I let out a slow breath.

What the fuck was that? It had been my imagination, I was sure. A vision? A memory? But why? Of what? And why had it happened when I had touched Kenna?

Kenna stepped to my side and placed the glasses beside the plates. Then, she opened a drawer where the utensils were. Trying to be useful so I wouldn't get kicked out, I looked around and found the napkins. I brought them to the island.

Kenna shook her head at me, then whirled to the counter and messed with her phone.

I didn't want to get kicked out. Not yet. Because if I had been curious about my new neighbors before, it was nothing compared to how curious I was now.

PAST

Kianna

AFTER AN ENTIRE DAY WORKING ON THE FARM, KIANNA WAS tired. When the sun began to set, signaling the end of the work day, she couldn't be more relieved. Until she saw the tools still in the field. Some of them couldn't be left out in the weather, and some had to be cleaned before being put away; otherwise they would rust and break. And they couldn't afford new tools right now.

Kianna looked around. Giles had already left. Catherine had come to call him for supper. Kianna couldn't blame him for leaving with only a muttered goodbye. Besides his age, his house was a good walk from her family's farm, and he liked to be home before the sun went down.

She smiled. Tomorrow, she would make sure to stop earlier and ask for his help before he left.

With a long sigh, Kianna knelt down and picked up a few

of the smaller tools, bunching them up in her apron. Movement to her right caught her attention and she looked up.

Devon.

He was still plowing the second half of the field, where they would soon plant new seeds.

She stared at him, not because he was shirtless and his muscles flexed with each of his movements, or because his long, black hair, tied in a low ponytail, stuck to his sweaty back—her cheeks heated at that thought—but because he was a mystery to her. The quiet man, who wasn't much older than she was, had been here for almost five days, and since then, he had been working relentlessly. He woke up early, ate the breakfast her mother handed to him, then went out to work. He took a break for a quick lunch, then worked past sunset. Most nights, he joined the family for dinner after a quick wash, but he remained mostly quiet, observing the family.

Sometimes, Kianna wondered if he had lost his memory, but didn't want to ask. He had suffered some kind of accident, lost his memory, found himself alone and wandering down the road, and when her mother showed him kindness, he couldn't resist.

But if that was true, why wasn't he trying to find his family instead of persistently working for hers? It didn't make sense.

Shaking her head and pushing away those thoughts, Kianna carried the tools to the wooden bench beside the barn. She dropped the tools on the ground, then lifted the handle of the pump, working it up and down until water spit out into the basin. She washed her hands, grabbed a clean rag, and wiped down the tools.

Her arms and shoulders hurt as she brushed the dirt

away from the tools. She tried not to, but she kept stealing glances at the young man still working in the field. The last traces of light lingered like a ghost on the horizon, and he was still working, as if he wasn't tired at all.

With that stamina and energy and strength, he couldn't be human. She laughed. Right, because what else could he be?

The sun had almost disappeared behind the trees on the horizon, when Kianna heard giggles, followed by annoyed screams. She couldn't help but smile as she glanced in their direction. Her mother and her siblings were finally back from the village. They had gone to check on the new school that had been built. Her mother had hopes that the kids would be able to attend it, even though they didn't know the logistics yet. Who would take them to the village? Then bring them back? But until they were accepted, they wouldn't worry about details.

Calvin pulled on Selina's long braid and took off, running into the house.

"You ... pest!" Selina ran after their brother.

Shaking her head, her mother walked around to the back and approached her. "Those two," she said with a sigh. "When will they stop bothering one another?"

"When they grow up and marry and leave the house," Kianna said. But as the words sank in, her stomach turned. Not even she seemed like she would secure a marriage to help her family. By the looks of it, she would forever work in the field and grow old alone and wrinkled. God, she hoped her siblings had a better life than that. "So, how was it?"

Her mother's face fell. "I'm not sure. There were a lot of wealthy families there."

"Being rich or poor can't be a qualification to be accepted into the school."

"It isn't a written one, but you and I know they will favor the children from wealthy families."

Kianna gripped the large scissors, her knuckles turning white. Once upon a time, they had been well-off too. If it had been a few years ago, she would have been accepted into the school without a second thought. Now that they had lost almost everything, they were gossiped about and met with pity. "This is absurd."

"Even Jocelyn was there, babbling about tradition and culture and manners." Her mother sighed, and Kianna bristled. Jocelyn used to be a good friend of her mother's, but she hadn't spoken to them since they had been forced to economize. "It's fine, though. If they can't get in, we'll manage some other way. I need to think about finding them a tutor."

"I can continue tutoring them," Kianna said. "I don't mind."

"I know, sweetheart, but it's either a new tutor or another farmhand, and unfortunately, I can't split you in two."

Kianna glanced at the young man working the field. Sweat covered his shoulders, making his skin glisten under the setting sun. Kianna averted her eyes. "Devon is the new farmhand."

"Finding Devon was a blessing," her mother said, practically swooning. "A few days ago, I would say you're right, but if we want to profit this season, even if only a little, we need to expand the field, plant more, and for that, we need another worker." Her mother glanced at the darkening sky. "All right, enough talk. It's getting late, and I still have plenty to do. I should check that the children didn't injury each other while washing, and then I'll prepare supper." She patted Kianna's arm. "I'll call you when it's ready."

Kianna watched as her mother dragged her feet into the house through the backdoor, her shoulders hunched, her head low. All that had happened since her father's death, all the weight that had fallen on her mother, was dragging her down. Besides trying to take some of that load off, Kianna couldn't do much.

Unless she married a rich nobleman, who would take care of her family? The idea of marrying for convenience was repulsive, but she didn't dwell on it. No rich nobleman would look at her in the state she was currently in.

After a long sigh, Kianna went back to work. She had to finish cleaning the tools before dark; otherwise, she would need to light a candle or gas lamp, and if she could avoid it—gas was now expensive for them—she would.

But her thoughts kept rolling. About her father, her mother, her siblings, their financial situation. If things kept going the wrong way, they would have to get rid of the only things they still had: the farm and the big stone manor behind her.

Lost in thought, Kianna rubbed the rag over the scissors' blades. They slipped from her hands, opening as they fell, the blades running over her palm.

A yelp rose from her throat as the cut stung, the pain spreading through her entire hand and up her arm.

In a flash, Devon stood in front of her, his dark eyes wide, worried. "What happened?"

Cradling her hand, Kianna stepped back from the bench, feeling stupid. "Nothing. I'm fine."

Devon stared at her hand, his brows curling down. "It's not nothing." He reached for her hand, but Kianna retreated another step. "There's blood on your dress. Let me see it. Please."

Blood? Kianna glanced down at her hand and dress. Blood pooled on her palm and dripped down the bodice of her dress. Oh no. Blood stained like nothing else. She had just lost a dress, and she couldn't afford to lose any.

Frustration and pain mixed together, and Kianna felt like crying. "I'm fine," she snapped.

"Kianna, your face is pale, which means you're not fine. And you should clean up that cut."

Kianna took another step back. "I'm fi—" The world revolved, her vision blurred.

"Kianna!" Devon rushed to her, slipping his arms under her before she hit the ground. He pulled her up against his hard, sweaty bare chest, holding her firmly. "Hang on."

Devon

WHEN KIANNA SCREAMED, DEVON PANICKED, BUT THE FEELING gripping his chest when she almost fainted was even worse. It hurt as if he was the one who had been cut.

Clutching her to his chest, Devon hurried into the house and deposited Kianna on a chair in the kitchen.

"I'll be right back," he said, after making sure that, if she fainted, she would fall forward to the table, and not back on the ceramic floor. Then, he dashed to the cabinet in the kitchen with the ointments and medicinal herbs. He grabbed a few and turned back to her. He deposited the box on the table and sat beside Kianna. "Let me see."

Kianna resisted, as she usually did whenever he was involved, but only for a few seconds. Groaning, she extended her hand to him.

Devon sucked in a sharp breath. There was a lot of blood, but the cut didn't look deep. Maybe it had hit a small vein and that was why it was bleeding so much.

With gentle movements, Devon cleaned the blood away, confirming that the cut hadn't been bad, and applied a healing ointment over it.

Kianna hissed. "It stings."

"Then it's working." He grabbed a bandage and started wrapping her hand.

He dared look at her face. Her beauty struck him. Her long blond braid was loose down her back, her skin was fairer than most, but only because of the blood loss, and her eyes—Devon had never seen bright blue eyes like hers. If he had been human, he was sure he would have already fallen for her, even though she treated him with coldness and wariness most of the time. But it was all a facade; he knew that. To protect herself, to protect her family, to protect her heart.

In truth, Kianna was one of the most gentle and caring people he had ever met in his life. She worked hard on the farm, and she didn't complain, at least not out loud, about their condition. She tutored her siblings in her free time, and she took care of them whenever needed. She cooked, she cleaned the house, she washed the clothes, all with a smile on her face. She treated Giles with respect and care, and she almost looked like a regular young woman whenever Catherine, her best friend, visited.

Devon knew nobody was perfect, but he couldn't think of one single flaw Kianna had.

He frowned. He still didn't understand why the gods had told him she was evil and sent him here to watch her. It was as clear that Kianna didn't have one streak of evil inside of her.

"What are you staring at?" Kianna brought her free hand to her cheek. "Do I have something on my face?"

Devon cleared his throat. "You're still pale."

She averted her eyes. "I think ... I didn't faint because of blood loss. I mean, it wasn't a lot of blood, but I haven't eaten in a while."

Devon's gut tightened. "Since when?"

"This morning," she whispered.

Something like anger lashed through his body. "Why?"

"Because I was busy. Honestly, I didn't even notice. Until now." She pressed her free hand over her stomach. "Now I'm starving."

Devon tucked in the edge of the gauze, closing the bandage. "I'll get you something."

He started rising, but her hand shot forward, grabbing his wrist. He frowned at her grip, a little shocked that she was touching to him like that. A faint pink tint spread through her cheeks. "It's fine. Mother said she'll be down soon to make us supper." She stared at the bandage around her hand. "I wonder if I can start it for her."

"Stay seated." Devon stood. "I'll start it."

Kianna glanced at him, her brows high. "Can you cook?"

"A little," he said.

It wasn't a total lie. He hadn't cooked in many, many years, but he knew he could at least start the fire, heat the water, prepare the rice. When Ophelia came down, she could take over.

Devon grabbed a glass, filled it with water from the pitcher, and handed it to Kianna.

"Thank you," she whispered as she took the glass from him.

Devon stared at her for another second. He shouldn't feel like this. He shouldn't care about her or her family. He had been here less than a week and he felt like he had already fallen down an endless hole.

The more time Devon spent with Kianna and her family, the more confused he was. He didn't remember his human life, no warrior did, but he probably had a family, he was sure of that. He didn't remember being loved and taken care of, and sitting down together for meals. And, even though Kianna was wary of him and quiet whenever he was around, he was experiencing it all again. Ophelia treated him like a son, Selina and Calvin loved to play with him, and even Kianna's coldness felt comforting.

It all confused him. New feelings—no, forgotten ones—stirred inside his chest.

And the strongest feeling was toward the girl seating in front of him.

"What is it this time?" Kianna asked, patting her cheeks again. "Am I still too pale?"

Devon hadn't meant to stare at her for so long, but when it came to her, he didn't have much choice, or control. "No, you look pretty, as always." Red quickly spread through her cheeks and she stared at the glass of water in her hands. Damn it, he shouldn't have said that. "I'm going ... to start supper now."

Devon turned to the wood stove and filled a pot with water.

But he couldn't resist. He watched her from over his shoulder. Quietly, Kianna stood from her seat and tiptoed to the corner of the dining room, where there was a tall shelf full of books. He had seen her reading before, especially under the cherry tree at the edge of the lake. As she fingered the spine of the books now, choosing her next read, Devon made a mental note. Next time he went to the village, he would stop by the book shop and buy a new book, or several, for her.

For some reason, the idea of giving her a present filled him with anticipation.

PRESENT

Kenna

WE HAD BEEN IN THIS TOWN FOR A WEEK NOW, AND NOTHING had happened. With every passing hour, I expected Slater and his men to break through the front door and take us away again, but it had been quiet. I sometimes doubted this peace was real. Even the darkness that usually followed me, bringing demons, had been absent.

My will to remain impassive about this move slipped away to hope. Hope that this was it. We had finally escaped Slater's clutches. We were free.

But, since we had stopped running, I was getting easily bored.

Lia had gone out on a job interview around mid-morning, and I sat on the back porch to read. But around noon, my stomach growled, and I headed to the kitchen. The fridge had a few leftovers, but as usual, nothing called to me, so I decided to cook.

After my cake fiasco, I was determined to succeed. A lot of people cooked, why couldn't I?

I prepped everything: thawed the shrimp, cooked the pasta, but when it was time to work on the sauce, things went downhill. Because of our limited cash, Lia and I had visited a couple of yard sales and acquired a lot of old things, especially kitchen stuff like a toaster, bowls, and a set of blue pots. Among those things was a food processor. I cut an onion into big slices and put it in the food processor. The moment I pressed the "on" button, a weird hissing sound came from the freaking thing, followed by smoke.

"Oh, shit," I muttered as I pressed the off button. But the thing didn't stop. More smoke came from the food processor until sparks shot out from under the blades. I yelped and reached for the power cord, but as I pulled it from the outlet, another spark flashed from the thing, prickling my hand. I screamed as I cradled my hand against my chest. "Shit, shit, shit."

The back door burst open, and for a moment, my heart stopped.

This was it. Slater was here, and he would take me.

Devon looked a little disheveled with his dark hair messed up by the wind. "What happened?" His eyes scanned the place, as if searching for an enemy. Then, his gaze found the smoking food processor, and my hand pressed against my chest. "What happened?" he asked again, his tone less urgent.

I frowned at him. "W-why are you here?"

Straightening to his full height—the guy had to be at least six-two—he ran a hand through his hair, pushing the longer strands back. "I was in my backyard. I heard your scream."

"And you just burst inside someone else's home when you hear a scream?"

His thick brows curled down. "Yes."

With my good hand, I gestured toward the food processor. "As you can see, I had a little technical problem."

"What about your hand?"

I glanced at my hand. My fingertips were a little red and raw, and they stung as if I had touched a hot pan. "I ... I'm fine."

In three long strides, Devon was right in front of me. He grabbed my hand. Taking in a lungful of air, he closed his eyes for a brief moment, then shook his head and stared at my hand.

What the hell was that?

"You should apply some burn cream to your fingers." He looked around. "Where's your first aid kit?"

I stared at him. What was his deal? I had seen him around his house a couple of times during the past week. He had even come over once when Lia asked for his help with the new dresser she had bought for my bedroom, and of course, she insisted he stay for dinner after.

The more I looked at him, the more I didn't understand him. As far as I knew, he was twenty-one and lived alone. He had mentioned his parents had died, though he never had said how. But besides his shady past, there was probably something wrong with him, because how could he be alone? I wasn't blind and I had to admit to myself he was too gorgeous for his own good. A magazine cover-worthy face with sharp angles that could cut with a glance; red, full lips, which I bet were good at kissing; enigmatic, dark eyes that bored holes into my soul. His silky hair was cut short, save for a few longer strands on top, which stubbornly fell over his forehead every few minutes. And as if his perfect face wasn't enough, he was tall, with wide shoulders. His polo shirt fit his hard chest nicely, and his arms were corded with lean muscles. Handsome, hot, single, and discreet. How wasn't that the perfect recipe to have at least a girlfriend?

Perhaps he had one, and he just hadn't mentioned her yet.

I took a step back, bumping my waist on the kitchen counter, and he dropped my hand. "I'm fine. I can take care of this."

"Kenna." He reached for me again.

What the hell? Why was he being like this? Didn't he know I wanted him gone? Our first night here, I had made a promise to myself. I would stay here without complaint for Lia's sake, but I wouldn't let anyone get close to us. If Slater found us, he would use them to hurt us. He would hurt them.

My distress and frustration got out of hand, making me lose control of my powers for a second. The kitchen lights flickered.

Devon looked up. "What was that?"

I took a deep breath, calming down. "I don't know." For good measure, I walked to the other side of the kitchen. I didn't have plans to treat my burns, but so I had something to do, I grabbed the first aid kit from the cabinet.

When I spied over my shoulder, I saw as Devon grabbed the book I had been reading from the kitchen counter. "I think this is ruined." He held the book up to me.

The book's top corner was black. "Oh no."

I rushed to his side; I grabbed the book with my good hand. I had left the book right beside the food processor, because my intention was to read a few more paragraphs while the sauce was cooking. A spark must have shot out toward it, burning the corner of several pages. I flipped through the pages. A good chunk of text was burned. I couldn't read it like this now.

"Shit," I said.

Devon's lips tugged up, and I tried not noticing how even more handsome he was with that half smile.

"What's funny?"

"You're more worried about the book than your hand."

Shrugging, I placed the ruined book on the kitchen island, beside the GED forms and study books. I hadn't been to school in seven years, but Lia had taught me a lot of what she remembered, especially in the last two years. Every stop we made, she bought me a new textbook—chemistry, biology, math. I had learned a lot on my own, but she was insisting I dive into our new life. I should study, take the GED exam, and apply for college. There were a couple of small community colleges nearby.

Devon stared at the GED forms.

A sense of embarrassment cut through me. What did he think of an eighteen-year-old—nineteen in less than two months—who hadn't gone to school? He was probably now trying to think of an excuse to leave.

It was okay. I could give him one. "I can take it from here." I picked up the burn cream from the first aid kit. "Thank you, though, for coming to check on me."

Devon's dark eyes locked on mine, and I felt he was trying to see past me, to find the reason I was shooing him from the house through my eyes. However, as he stared at me, I realized a girl really could get lost in those ebony pools of his.

"You're welcome," he finally said, his voice tight.

Devon spun around and left, closing the back door behind him.

The moment he was gone. I let out a long breath, as if I hadn't been able to breathe right the entire time he had been here.

I didn't like it.

I didn't like how my body reacted when he got close or how kind he was. I especially didn't like the possibility of him getting too close and getting hurt.

Tonight, I was going to have a talk with Lia. No matter what, she had to stop asking Devon for help and inviting him to dinner. She would understand where I was coming from. After all, I had suffered at the hands of Slater for five years, but she had suffered for sixteen.

If someone understood why we needed to keep our distance for people, it was her.

We had chosen to escape and live, but we both knew we would never be able to live a normal life. The only way of doing that was embracing the solitude that came with our freedom.

Alone, but alive.

PAST

Kianna

THE COLD WATER IN THE KITCHEN'S WASH BASIN WAS A BALM TO her hands on this very humid and hot day. Spring was well underway, but there were days when Kianna wondered if summer had decided to show up early. She wished she could ditch her duties, even if only for a few minutes, to go for a refreshing dip at the lake below the hill. She bet the water was nice and cool.

She closed her eyes and imagined herself swimming through the clear water.

"Here's more." Cat's voice cut through Kianna's dream.

She opened her eyes as Cat deposited a basketful of produce beside the wash basin.

"That's a lot." Kianna reached for a lettuce head. "She said we'll be using all of these?"

Cat shook her head. "Your mother just said you need to wash them all."

Groaning, Kianna washed the lettuce, making sure she got all the bits of dirt from it, then set it aside and grabbed another one. She guessed standing in the kitchen and washing vegetables was better than being under the hot sun and working the field like Giles and Devon were doing.

Despite herself, Kianna glanced out the window. There, in the middle of the field, Devon working like a mad man, his muscles flexing and shifting with each repetitive movement.

Cat stood closer to her and followed her gaze. "Hm. I know you're still wary of him, but you have to admit, he has been a blessing for the farm."

A long sigh traveled past Kianna's lips. "I know."

It was true. Giles was getting old and he didn't have the stamina to work all day in the field, especially when it was too hot or too cold. Her mother was thirty-eight, not too old. But after years working in the field and running the house and managing the kids, her back hurt more days than not, her hands were covered in calluses, and her face was becoming covered in wrinkles. Kianna thought her mother was still beautiful, but it was easy to see all the hard work taking its toll.

"And he's not bad to look at either." Cat winked at Kianna, who groaned. "What? It's true!" She gestured to the window. "Look at him. He's handsome and strong, and he has been helping your family like no one ever did." Again, Cat was right. "If I were you, I would forget all about an arranged marriage and marry him."

Kianna gasped. "Cat!"

The girl shrugged. "What?"

"That's ... not even an idea." Kianna lowered her gaze, focusing on the produce in the wash basin.

If it wasn't an idea to consider, then why had her stomach tightened at the thought? It was silly, really. Just because he was handsome, and helped care for her family and treated her with respect? She didn't know where he came from, his family. What if he was already married? Or had a debt bigger than her family's?

Marrying him, or even thinking about it, was impossible.

"Your mother told me he's staying."

Kianna nodded. She had had her first big argument with her mother when she told her the news last night. "My mother said he doesn't remember anything from his past and he has nowhere to go. So, she offered to let him stay here. He'll work the farm for housing and food and little compensation." She gestured one wet hand at the view outside. "He accepted the offer."

Though, she didn't consider sleeping on a cot in the barn alongside the tools as housing, but he didn't seem to mind. Not that she wanted him sleeping inside the house. If her mother even tried to move him into the spare room, Kianna would put her foot down.

"Who wouldn't?" Cat asked.

Kianna stared at her. "What?"

"I mean, it's just like he said. He doesn't remember anything and has nowhere to go. He's all alone, but he found your family, who has been kind and welcoming to him." Kianna narrowed her eyes and Cat chuckled. "All right, most of you have welcomed him with open arms. Why would he want to leave?"

Kianna's gaze returned to the young man in the field. When Cat put it that way, when Kianna allowed her prejudice and fear of the stranger and his intentions fade, then she could understand it too. If it were her, lost and alone, she would cling to any offered help with all she had.

And that was exactly what Devon was doing.

Then why, even after knowing this, did Kianna feel like she had to guard her family and herself from him?

Devon straightened, lowering the plow he had in his hands, and glanced to the bottom of the hill. Two seconds later, Kianna's mother walked past the window, going to the front of the house. Selina and Calvin ran after her.

"What's going on?" Kianna dropped the vegetables and dried her hands on the apron tied around her waist.

Cat furrowed. "I don't know."

The two rushed through the house. Kianna paused at the heavy, double wooden doors in the foyer as a strident, loud voice carried.

"Oh no," she muttered.

She flung the doors open and immediately regretted it.

A large carriage with a red velvet top and golden embroidery rested in front of the stone steps leading to the manor, and a plump woman, with bright red lips and wheat-colored hair pulled into an updo atop her big head, waved from the open window over the door. "Ophelia! It's been ages!"

A coachman hopped down from the front of the carriage and opened the door. The woman took his hand and climbed down the steps, until she was standing a couple of feet from Kianna's mother, her fancy dark blue gown spilling around her.

"Hello, Jocelyn," her mother said, her voice edged with concealed anger. "What brings you here?"

Kianna's stomach tightened as she stared at the woman's fake smile. "Oh, I was just on my way to the village and remembered I used to stop for tea every now and then." Her eyes scanned the manor looming over her. Kianna wished she could put a veil over the woman's face, or cover her eyes with her hands. The manor hadn't been properly cared for the last several years, and it was starting to show. Certainly, that would be the newest topic added to her gossip list. Her dull gaze returned to Ophelia. "I just wanted to make sure everything was all right."

Her mother's hands balled into fists, and Kianna could see how she was fighting to control herself in front of their neighbor, fighting not to straighten her plain, dirty dress, or pat her messy hair or fix her brown waves, or hide her wrinkling, makeup-less face.

Anger coursed through Kianna, and it was all she could do not send the woman on her away.

"We're fine," her mother said, her voice tight.

"Oh, I'm sure you are, dear." Her fake smile boiled Kianna's blood. "Didn't I see you a couple of days ago at the new school assembly? I did, didn't I? Oh, my kids have been accepted into the school. They start next week. I bet yours were too, weren't they?"

Kianna would bet the few gold coins she had saved with much effort that the woman knew they hadn't been accepted, not yet, and was asking to rub it in their faces.

Finally, the woman's gaze landed on Kianna. "Oh, my dear, you're looking as lovely as ever." Another lie. Kianna knew that with her ragged dress, dirty apron, scuffed shoes, and her loose, wild blond hair falling in terrible tangles down her back, she did not look lovely. "Have you called on your friends lately? Hattie and Olive? Oh, I heard their engagements are moving well along. Soon, we'll be receiving wedding invitations."

Kianna's stomach dropped. Hattie and Olive were engaged? They were getting married? She knew it would eventually happen, but thinking about it was one thing. Knowing about it was another.

What did she care? It wasn't like Hattie and Olive had ever been her real friends. Once her father died and their situation had changed, Hattie and Olive never spoke to Kianna again. There was that time, not long ago, when Kianna went to the village to visit the apothecary. She saw Hattie and Olive, but when she went to greet them, the girls pretended they hadn't seen her and left.

"That will be *lovely*," Kianna said, forcing a smile at the woman.

"Yes, I was just saying that—"

Devon traipsed down the hill and stopped right in front of Jocelyn, his back to her.

They all stared at him in shock, Jocelyn most of anyone.

"Excuse, ma'am," Devon said, addressing her mother. He sounded out of breath and disconcerted, and even after working all day long under the baking sun, Kianna had never seen Devon out of breath. "But I need to show you something." He gestured up the hill, to where the field stretched over the property. "There."

Her mother's face contorted, from guarded to worried. "What happened?"

Taking a deep breath, Devon swayed and took two steps back.

Dirtying the hem of Jocelyn's dress with his muddy boots.

The woman let out an exasperated gasp, her face turning red. "Why, you!"

Devon spun to her. "Oh, my apologies. I didn't see you there." Was he serious? He hadn't seen the big carriage and the larger woman in the dress? He reached to her, brushing the skirt of her gown with his dirty hands—where it hadn't been dirty before. He lowered his head. "My apologies."

With a hiss, Jocelyn stripped herself away from his reach. "Mr. Flynn, let's go." She narrowed her eyes at Devon, then at Kianna's mother, before gliding into her carriage. She didn't wave goodbye as the carriage rode away.

With a half smile, Devon turned back to them. "Sorry if that was over the top, but I couldn't stand the way she was treating you."

Kianna swallowed a gasp, Cat let out a yelp, her mother smiled, and her siblings shrieked in delight.

"That was ... it was well deserved," her mother said, approaching Devon and patting his arm. "You did well. Thank you." Her mother let out a long breath and waved her arms to the side. "I say we take the next couple of hours off and enjoy a long, lazy lunch. I think we deserved it."

She ushered the kids inside the manor to wash up before laying their paws all over the furniture.

Devon glanced at Kianna. "I'm ... tell your mother I'm going to finish one thing I was doing, then I'll wash up and meet you all for lunch." He lowered his gaze and started marching up the hill.

Something tugged in Kianna's chest, a feeling she didn't want to acknowledge, but she couldn't ignore either.

"Devon," she called before she lost her courage. He whipped his back head and stared at her. Kianna felt the corner of her lips sliding up in a small smile. After all, what Devon had done for them had been pretty great. "Thank you."

The half grin was back, illuminating his entire demeanor. "My pleasure."

PRESENT

Kenna

"Are you almost done?" I asked Carol.

Seated on the foyer floor, with her books in her lap, Carol glanced up at me. "Just have ..." She counted the math problems on her homework sheet. "Four more. Then I'm done."

I grumbled under my breath and resumed painting the living room wall. Carol was persistent. Even though I had practically shooed her away a few days ago, she still came to my house as soon as she arrived home from school, and talked nonstop about things until I closed the door in her face.

It was for her safety, I told myself. Lia and I were playing house right now, but when we had to run again, she would only get hurt in the process.

However, two days ago, Lia had opened the door and invited Carol in. She made us a snack and set us up on the back porch with cookies and coffee. I had no other choice than to talk to the girl, and I was frustrated when after thirty minutes by her side I realized she wasn't half as bad as I first thought.

Later that night, I had an argument with Lia about the risks of letting other people get close to us.

"We can't live halfway, Makenna," she had said, calling me by my real name for the first time in weeks. "We can't join society, but hide from it. We can be careful, but still live. Do you know what I mean?"

I did know what she meant, but it didn't feel any easier. I had lived in darkness and terror for five years, then been on the run every second of the next two years. She couldn't blame me if I was suspicious and wary.

Wary. That was the best word to describe myself right now.

"All done." Carol's voice dragged me out of the dark emotional hole. I glanced over my shoulder. She pushed her books away, then grabbed another roller and stood by my side. "Didn't we do this wall yesterday?"

"No, we did that one." I jerked my chin to the wall on our left.

Well, since she wanted to spend time with me, she could help me with the house remodeling while we talked.

Lia and I had come up with a backstory for us, so when people asked where we came from and why we moved here, we had something ready: my father, Lia's husband, had died in an accident a couple of years ago. After that, money was short and Lia thought it was better to move to a smaller town. Why Misty Hill? Because she liked the town as we were driving through.

That was it.

And that was exactly what I had told Carol during her thousand-question interview. When she asked me again if I wanted to go to school—Carol had just turned eighteen and she was a junior, so she still had a full year of high school ahead of her—I said no. It was already April and school ended the first week of June. To make it worthwhile, I would have to join her junior class, but I was almost nineteen. I didn't want to be the oldest at her school. So, it was easier to take the GED and be done with it.

"... and you know what she said?" Carol asked. The girl never stopped talking. At first, it annoyed the hell out of me, but in the end, it filled the awkward silence. It was easy to talk to her when all I had to do was goad her so she would keep going with her story.

"What?"

"That she was going to tell my parents I had pulled her hair and called her names. Can you believe that? Such a bitch."

I chuckled. I couldn't help it. Carol talked about the bitchy girls at her school as if I knew who she was talking about—and I had to pretend I did.

"Such a bitch," I repeated.

"Right? Ugh, I wanted to slap her."

I lowered the roller and looked at her. "Why didn't you?"

Carol's eyes widened. "I mean ... that's not right, right? Even if she's mean to me, to everyone, I can't be mean to her too."

I frowned. If it were me, I would have called my powers, enveloped her in darkness, and brought forth her worst nightmares. She would cry for a week. But that was usually how I dealt with Slater's goons and demons. I probably shouldn't do that to normal people. "I guess you're right," I said, making a mental note to not do that to innocent humans.

I sighed. I had so much to learn about living like a normal person, it wasn't even funny.

"So ... there's a party this Saturday," Carol started.

I froze.

All right, I had allowed Lia to force a friend on me, and I was trying to be nice to the girl, but going to a party? With other teenagers? I wasn't ready for that yet.

"Oh-kay," I mumbled.

"It's at—" Her phone dinged. Lowering the roller, Carol fished the phone out of her pocket and checked the message. "Shit. It's my mother. She's coming home for dinner. That's a miracle." Her mouth made a small O. "Oh, shit, the kitchen is a huge mess. I better go clean up before she comes home."

"What?" I gestured to the wall. "I thought you were helping me here!"

She dropped the roller into the tray. "I'm sorry." She retreated to the foyer. "I'm so sorry." She picked up her backpack from the floor. "I'll come back later if I can."

I chuckled. "It's fine. Just go." I waved her off.

"Bye." She slung her backpack over her shoulder and rushed out the door. I heard it slam closed, followed by her stomping on the steps and front stone path.

I was still smiling a couple of minutes later, thinking of how crazy and agitated and rather contagious Carol was. Maybe Lia was right. All I needed right now was a friend my age, and the chance to be a teenager and to live a little.

I had to admit, relaxing a little and forgetting about all the bad things from the past was addicting.

I lowered the roller to the tray and noticed the paint was almost gone. I looked around the living room. Several of the cans had been used already, but there were two that were still closed. I made a quick calculation: the amount of paint cans we had already used and how much of the walls we had already covered. Shit, we would need more cans of paint.

This remodeling thing never ended.

I grabbed the empty cans in my arms and dragged my bare feet to the kitchen, where I found a big trash bag and threw them out. Then, I stopped by the sink and washed my hands. I glanced out the window. My hands stilled under the running water when I saw Devon on his porch, seated in a lounge chair, with a thick book in his hands. He looked so cozy and manly with his feet propped up and his gaze fixed on the book's pages.

I glanced down at my hands, remembering the day I had burned them and he had come to my rescue. That had been a few days ago, and since then, he had come by once to help Lia with something. I had lectured her yet again about getting too close to the townspeople, a point that became moot after she convinced me to allow Carol to become my friend.

But what about Devon?

To be honest, I sometimes wondered if he was alone and reclusive not because of a flaw, but because of some horrible secret, like he was a serial killer. How horrible would that be? A handsome man like him—a serial killer?

I shook my head and stomped back to the living room.

I leaned forward to grab the roller back when the doorbell rang.

It was probably Carol, but Carol had left a few minutes ago. She knew the door was unlocked. She never stood on ceremony when she came over. If it was her, she wouldn't ring the bell; she would simply walk in and scare me.

So who was it?

I couldn't help the rapid beating of my heart as I edged closer to the door. This anxiety, this fear, was a reflex. I couldn't control it. Every time the doorbell rang, I tensed, afraid it was Slater.

Holding my breath, I opened the door.

"Hello, dear." A tall woman with a round middle smiled at me with her bright pink lips. "I'm Roselyn, your neighbor." She pointed to a house twice the size of mine across the street. "I've been meaning to come meet you and your mother, but I've been busy." She shoved a beautifully decorated cake in my arms. "Welcome to the neighborhood."

I held the cake as if it were a bomb. "Thank you."

She glanced over my shoulder, to the stairs without a railing, to the cans of paint spread out across the living room floor, to the chandelier still on the dining room's floor. "Oh, I see a little remodeling going on. That's good." Her eyes shifted to the outside of the house, her nose wrinkling. "Do you and your mother plan on fixing the exterior too?" She leaned closer. "Between you and me, your house could at least use a fresh coat of paint. It would make the entire neighborhood look better."

I stared at the woman incredulously. What the hell had she just said?

"That's on the to-do list," I mumbled.

"Good." She clapped her big hands together. "Now tell me, where's your mother?"

I frowned. "At work." Lia had taken one of the jobs she had interviewed for and started immediately.

"Oh, really, where does she work?" The lady pinched her lips. "It can't be anything too glamorous, not in this town. So, I'm guessing she's a waitress? Maybe a maid? Who is she working for?" I blinked at the woman. Was she serious? "Is she any good? I had to let my maid go, and I could definitely use someone right about now." She narrowed her eyes at me and took me in from head to toe. I was barefoot, in a pair of loose, stained jeans, and an old t-shirt with holes and paint stains. My long hair had been pulled into a loose bun atop of my head. I knew I didn't look that great, but the way she looked at me made my stomach curdle. "Do you work as a maid too? I can pay you nicely for the rush service." She opened her bag and fished her wallet from inside. "After, we can come up with a rate, depending on how I like your job." She smiled at me. "What do you say?"

A bout of anger whiplashed through me. My powers awoke, and I felt my fingers tingling as my magic begged to be released. The lights in the living room flickered, and I took a deep breath, trying to rein in my power.

Devon

MRS. THOMPSON'S STRIDENT VOICE REACHED MY EARS. Frowning, I got up from my chair and looked around, trying to locate her. I couldn't see her, but when she spoke again, I knew where it was coming from.

"Between you and me, your house could at least use a fresh coat of paint. It would make the entire neighborhood look better."

What the fuck?

I swallowed the anger rising inside me.

It was not my problem. It was not my problem. It was not my problem.

"Maybe a maid? Who is she working for? Is she any good? I had to let my maid go, and I could definitely use someone right about now."

All right, that was it. I couldn't stay out of it.

Faster than any human, I ran to Lia's and Kenna's house, jumping over the low fence without any effort, and entered their house through the backdoor. I glanced around and grabbed the first thing I saw—painter's tape.

"What do you say?"

I made my way through the hallway to the foyer. On my way, the few lights that were on flickered, and I frowned as a tendril of darkness brushed through me.

Kenna stood in front of the door, one of her hands curled into a tight fist, her knuckles white. In front of her, Mrs. Thompson looked like a predator ready to bite off someone's head. Kenna's.

"Here," I said, rushing to Kenna's side.

Mrs. Thompson's eyes widened. Kenna stared at me. Slowly, she let out a long breath and flexed her fingers, as if they were stiff after being squeezed like that.

"What—?"

"I found it in the kitchen," I cut her off before she gave away my ruse. I handed her the tape, then turned my best nonchalant grin to the devil standing on the porch. "Hello, Mrs. Thompson. How have you been?"

"Devon," she said, as if my name tasted sour. Fine by me. "I'm ... fine." She offered a tight smile to Kenna. "I'll be back to meet your mother later." Without waiting for a response, the woman climbed down the stairs and rushed back to her house as if she was running from a demon.

If only she knew …

"W-what was that?" Kenna asked. I looked down at her. She had old clothes on, paint stains everywhere, even on her arms and her bare feet, and her brown hair was bunched atop her head. Like this, she looked so small, so fragile, with her forehead barely coming to my chin, and for some reason, a sudden urge to protect her hit me hard. Hadn't I just done that? "Why are you here?"

I took a step back and ran a hand through my hair, trying to tug at the long strands that hadn't been there in almost nineteen years. "I'm sorry. It's just … I could hear her from the back of my house and I don't like her. To be honest, that woman makes me sick. And the things she was saying to you —" I shook my head once.

"So you just came over, and she fled?"

One corner of my lips tugged up. "Yeah, she doesn't like me either. I don't make it easy, seeing as she doesn't deserve my respect."

"I see. So every time she comes over, I should just call you? That will make her leave?"

"It should work," I said, feeling a grin forming on my mouth. Kenna hitched the cake higher in her arms. "Here." I reached over and grabbed the cake from her. My fingers brushed against hers.

A foreign image filled my mind.

A young woman in a dress and a long blond braid smiling at me.

"Thank you," Kenna said.

I squinted, trying to see the girl's face in my mind, but everything was blurred. Pride filled my chest.

"Devon?"

I blinked.

What the fuck was that? That was the third time it happened. Every time I touched Kenna images flashed in my mind. Visions? They felt like memories.

"I'm okay." Averting my gaze, I started toward the kitchen.

"By the way," Kenna said, her feet barely making a sound as she followed me, "thank you."

The sense of pride was back, but this time it was real. In the present, and despite all my reservations and the loud bells ringing in my mind, I smiled. "You're welcome."

PAST

Devon

IF IT WAS POSSIBLE, DEVON WOULD STAY WITHIN A MILE OF Kianna at all times. But it wasn't possible. He had to send word to the gods, to report to the other warriors. So when Ophelia announced she needed to go to the village, Devon volunteered to accompany her.

Devon had never been to this particular village, but on this side of the country, they all looked the same: a poor quarter with dusty roads flanked by ramshackle houses and shops, and a wealthier district, surrounded by stone walls, where the nobles and lords of the village resided in their opulent mansions.

As they rode into the town in the small wagon, pulled by a horse who was in desperate need of more food, Ophelia's gaze lingered on the stone walls in the distance, longingly. Before her husband had died, she would have spent much time on the other side of those stones, dining with the wealthy elite of the town.

They parked the wagon to the side of the road, the horse tied to a low rail. People milled about enjoying the spring day or going to the shops or to work. The scent of rice cake and chicken soup carried through the air.

"Here." Ophelia handed him a jarful of cherries. "Give this to Laina at the apothecary. She'll know what to do."

Devon frowned at the jar but didn't question it. "Anything else?"

She shook her head. "I can do the rest. Just meet me here in about an hour so we can be home before lunchtime."

"Yes, ma'am." He bowed his head to her and she waved him off.

With a faint smile, Devon walked away. Ophelia always reprimanded him when he called her ma'am, but most of the time, he felt weird calling her by her given name.

Despite all his lies, he had come to respect Ophelia and care for her family.

Care for Kianna.

No, it wasn't right. He did not care for her. He couldn't. He was an immortal warrior. He couldn't care for a human like that.

The apothecary was located on the other side of the village—maybe that was why Ophelia had given him only one task—but Devon arrived at the small shop in no time. He took in the shelves full of vials with liquids and powders and herbs, all covered in a thin layer of dust. A small wooden table stood at the back.

A woman walked out from a door behind the table and smiled at him. "How can I help you?"

"I'm here to give this to Laina." He showed her the cherries.

"Oh, yes, I'm Laina." She reached for the jar. He reluctantly gave it to her. Carefully, she deposited on the table. "One second." Then, she walked to one of the cabinets flanking the table. She opened one of the cabinet doors and retrieved a small vial full of red liquid. "Here it is."

Devon narrowed his eyes. It looked like watered down blood. "What is that?"

"Kianna's perfume." His eyes widened and the woman chuckled. "She sends me the cherries and I make the perfume for her."

Devon took the vial from the woman. "How much do I owe you?"

The woman shook her head. "Nothing."

"Are you sure?"

"Of course. I owe much to Kianna's family. This is the least I can do."

A human feeling took hold in Devon's chest—curiosity. "May I ask you what happened? Why you owe the family?"

"My parents died when I was barely a teenager. Ophelia took me in, and she offered me a home in exchange for work. At first, I stayed out of the way, learning from the other maids at their manor. But time passed and Kianna was becoming a lady. Ophelia assigned me as Kianna's maid." A soft smile adorned her lips. "I grew fond of the girl, and considered her as a daughter." Her smile faded. "But then the master died, and the debt collectors came. Most of the help was fired, including me. But Ophelia helped me secure this job."

"And that's why you make Kianna's perfume for free."

She nodded. "I wish I could do more."

Me too, Devon thought.

But he was doing a lot; he knew that. They hadn't had proper help on the farm for years now, and he had taken on the lion's share of the work.

And what frightened him the most was that he didn't mind. He wanted to help.

Devon thanked the woman and left to meet with the warriors before his time was up. He was lost in thought, scared of his feelings, when he turned into the alley to meet them.

Ryder, Lucien, and Warren stood side by side at the end of the alley, sporting their leather armor and swords.

"You don't look good," Ryder teased. "What happened?"

Devon tucked in the vial with the perfume in his pocket and faced the warriors. "Nothing."

Lucien narrowed his eyes. "You're lying."

A protective feeling surged inside him. "Does it matter? I'm here to report. I've been following Kianna for almost two weeks, and nothing has happened. There's no darkness around her, and she definitely doesn't have any powers." He paused, sure of the backlash his next words would bring. "She isn't evil. The gods are wrong about her."

Warren crossed his arms. "The girl may not be evil, but her powers are."

"That's the thing; there's no power," Devon insisted. "We can sense the darkness, and I sense nothing from her." The only things Kianna stirred were human emotions that should have been dormant.

Ryder pointed to Devon's hands. "What is that?"

Devon glanced at them. "What?"

"The calluses," Lucien said. "The redness. Your hands are scratched and raw."

"Have you been working for them?" Warren asked, his tone disapproving.

Devon stiffened. "Isn't maintaining a cover part of the mission? Kianna's family is struggling. I had to make myself useful to stay close."

Ryder shook his head. "You are on dangerous ground."

"It doesn't matter," I said. "It's working."

"Did the gods tell you how long you have to protect Kianna?" Lucien asked.

"Only that I have to protect her until the danger passes," Devon said. The only danger right now was an entire field of produce rotting, snobby neighbors, and debt collectors. Devon could easily deal with those.

"Be on the lookout," Warren said. "The gods wouldn't have sent you to her for nothing."

"I know." In the one hundred years he had served the gods, he had gone on countless missions, and the gods had never been wrong. And that scared him. "If we're done here, I should go back."

Ryder pressed his lips into a thin line, clearly not voicing what else was on his mind, and Warren shifted his weight, done with this meeting too.

Lucien nodded. "Go. Do your job. Meet us back here in one week."

"Will do." Devon walked away.

"Devon," Ryder called. Devon paused and glanced at the warrior over his shoulder. "Be careful."

Devon dipped his head once, then strolled out of the alley. He patted the perfume vial in his pocket, as if assuring himself it was still there, as if he was still connected to Kianna somehow, even though he wasn't supposed to get attached to her or her family.

But how could he not? If only he could have stayed back and watched over Kianna from the shadows, he wouldn't have gotten so involved. But the gods specifically ordered him to get close to her and her family, to become a human, to become a friend.

What was he supposed to do while her kind, caring family struggled? They desperately needed help, and he could offer them that. It was better than sitting back and waiting for something to happen.

That was done. He had stepped into their lives, like the gods wanted, and got involved with the family. There was nothing he could do to change that now.

Truth be told, he didn't want to.

Forcing out a long breath out, Devon searched the road, taking in the sort of shops displayed.

A bookstore on a street corner caught his attention. He remembered his mental note: get more books for Kianna. He had no idea what he would tell them about how he had gotten money to pay for the books, but right now, he didn't care.

All that mattered was to see her smile at him again.

PRESENT

Devon

So far, my reports had been delivered at night, because the warriors could easily hide in the shadows, but this time, I was summoned during the day.

I drove my Maserati past the Misty Hill Inn and stopped at the edge of the parking lot behind it. Ryder, in his full warrior garb, stepped out from behind a row of tall trees and marched to my car. The sword strapped to his back disappeared, and he slipped into the car.

"Drive around the town so it doesn't look suspicious," Ryder said as soon as he closed the door.

"If people see a stranger in my car, they will think that is suspicious." I crossed my arms. "We stay here."

"Killjoy," Ryder mumbled. I shook my head, amused. Ryder's missions were technical, and he never got too close to humans. It wasn't as if he wanted to get mixed up with them, but I knew he was curious. "Anyway, report."

I glanced out of the car, staring at the tall trees around the parking lot, and the green shrubs. The high spring sun filtered through the leaves, like divine golden rays.

A play of the gods.

That was how my life felt right now.

"Still nothing," I said. "Besides those lesser demons a couple of months ago, nothing else has happened." I could tell Ryder I had new neighbors, but that was my human side meddling and not related to my mission. I sighed. "I don't know what the gods want from me. I've been at this for nineteen years! I need clues or nothing will change."

"It hasn't been nineteen years yet."

"I know!" I groaned. "Ryder, I know you're not supposed to tell me what happened and what I'm supposed to do here, but point me in the right direction. Tell me one single word that will make sense." Living like a fucking human was getting to me. "Please."

"Devon ..." Ryder shook his head. "I can't. If I utter half a word, the gods will send me to the underworld for the next three hundred years. You've been my friend for centuries, and I would do anything for you. Almost." He paused, watching me with knowing eyes. "Besides, I believe in you. You can figure it out and make it right this time."

"But—"

"No, Devon, don't ask more." Ryder opened the door and slipped out of the car. "I'll contact you in a few days. Good luck." He pushed the door closed and marched into the forest.

I stared at the spot between the trees where he had disappeared, my mind reeling, my chest heavy. I hadn't felt this agitated in a long time. Probably since my first few days back from the underworld, when I believed I would be able to solve this mystery fast and be done with it. The anxiety only grew as the days passed, and I found no clues, no directions, nothing. But after two years of worrying and barely sleeping, I gave up. I was fucking tired, exhausted, and angry with the gods and the warriors who came to check on me.

For a few years, I had felt like a fucking ghost, drifting through the human world.

But even that became tiring eventually.

Then ... I didn't know. I just tried to live quietly and pay attention to everything around me. I didn't go searching for clues like I did when I first came back, but hoped to simply stumble on something, anything.

Like a fucking fairytale.

I was sick and tired of this.

I drove back into town, only half of my mind on the traffic of Misty Hill. At this time of the day, kids were in school and most adults were busy at work. The streets were mostly deserted.

I stopped my car in front of the library.

One thing I had carried over from my human life—at least I thought so since I didn't remember the details—was the love of reading. I had no idea how it had begun, but I loved getting lost in books, especially fantasy books about good prevailing over evil. Humans thought it was fiction, but I knew better. Before I had been stuck in this boring routine, that had been my life.

Because of my love for books, I had become a patron of the town's public library since the first week I had moved here. And because of the quantity of money I had donated to date, I was almost like a celebrity in town. In the beginning, I was quiet and never asked for anything, but they kept sending me reports and updates of things happening at the library.

My life was so fucking boring, I ended up getting more involved than I had planned.

It was hard to admit, but I enjoyed this small part of my life.

I entered the library and was greeted by Miles, an old man who had been the receptionist here for years. He looked frail, but content. Even though I had suggested he retire already—I would anonymously cover any funds he needed—he had refused. His wife had died years ago, and his kids were grown up and living away with their families. He had nothing left but the library.

I couldn't take that away from him, too.

"Mr. Knight!" Miles grinned at me. "So good to see you." He clasped my hand with both of his. "Although, I must confess, I wasn't expecting to see you. What can I do for you today?"

With my free hand, I patted his shoulder. "I'm fine, old man. Just thought I would stop by and pick up some new reading material."

"We received some boxes this morning with new books. I opened most of the boxes to organize them, but I didn't have time to enter them in the system and put them out yet." Miles gestured to the back of the library. "If you would like, sir, feel free to browse through them."

"That sounds like a go—"

"Miles," a voice called out. A moment later, Lia emerged from between two tall shelves, a heavy leather ledger in her arms. "I'm confused about this." She lifted her eyes from the book and halted, in shock.

"Oh, yes," Miles said. "Hm, Mr. Knight, this is—"

"Lia Jones." I nodded at her. "What brings you to the library?" My gaze found the little rectangular tag pinned to her shirt. "You're working here?"

She smiled. "Yes. I started here a few days ago."

"This is the good side of a small town," Miles said, mildly amused. "Everyone knows everyone, even the new faces."

"Lia and her daughter are my new neighbors," I told him. "Lia often invites me for dinner at their house." I leaned closer to the old man and pretended to whisper, "She's a great cook."

"Oh, don't lie." Red tinted Lia's cheeks. "By the way, I was planning on making a homemade lasagna this evening. You're invited to stop by."

"Can I come too?" Miles joked.

"I wouldn't be opposed to that," Lia said, though her smile faltered a little.

"I have an appointment later in the afternoon," I said. "I'll try to make it, but if I don't show up, thank you for the invite."

"Well, I'll save a slice for you, even if it's in a Tupperware so you can take it home."

I had smiled more in the last two weeks than during my entire warrior life. The muscles in my face screamed. "Thank you." I nodded at them once more. "Now, if you'll excuse, I'll take a look at those books."

Lia and Miles stepped aside to let me pass, and I disappeared between the shelves. As I marched to the back of the library, I massaged my face. Any more smiling and I would need to apply ice to my cheeks.

I found the boxes and carts with the new books in the storage room. I decided to help a little since I didn't have any place to be. I emptied all the boxes, piled the books on the cart, and then took them all to the computer in the corner of the storage room and entered them one by one in the system. Why didn't they have a barcode reader in the back yet? I thought I had donated enough money to have barcode readers everywhere in the library. As I typed the numbers and titles, I made a mental note to take that to the manager.

It was easy to get lost in the task and forget about the problems crowding my mind. Perhaps I should do more. Find a hobby. Read more books. Exercise more. Anything to keep myself and my mind busy. I bet that would help pass my eternally long days.

I barely thought of anything as I worked, until I grasped one of the books. The cover grabbed me. In the center of the cover was a dark silhouette of a couple with a big cherry tree behind them. Its branches curved down, as if embracing the lovers. Protecting them.

Something about this cover, about this book, called to me.

I frowned and read the blurb. It looked like a romantic fantasy, like the one Kenna burned the other day. Perhaps I should take this to h—

I put the book down and picked up another book, resuming the work.

But as I tried to lose myself in the job, I realized I couldn't. I kept stealing glances at the fucking book and thinking of Kenna, of her reaction when I took the book to her.

Would she like it? Would she throw it at me? Would she thank me?

Like a fucking idiot, I grabbed the book again. I made another mental note: Buy a new copy of the book for the library, because this one was going out as a gift.

PAST

Kianna

AFTER THE INCIDENT WITH JOCELYN, KIANNA SAW DEVON IN A new light. She tried not to, but it was impossible. He was everywhere she looked. Always ready to help, always offering an encouraging smile, always surprising her.

The quiet farmhand had warmed up even to Selina and Calvin, the two pests who never did what they were told. When she least expected it, Kianna would glance out of the window and see the kids playing around Devon. At first, it always looked as if her siblings were bothering him, until Devon dropped his tools and gave chase to the kids, making them squeal and laugh in delight.

The sight warmed her heart.

This time was no different.

Seated on the wooden bench on the back porch, Kianna sewed shut the holes in Calvin's pants and Selina's dresses.

She sighed, convinced that soon she would need to buy new clothes for them. The fabric was threadbare. There was only so much she could do with a needle and thread. Besides, Selina had Kianna's old dresses to use, but Calvin was still growing and needed new clothes often.

More money they couldn't afford to spend.

Upset, Kianna looked up from her work. Her mother was in the field with Giles, while Devon fixed a broken tool right beside the barn. Selina and Calvin were supposed to be cleaning tools, but instead were poking at each other, trying to provoke a game of chase. Finally, Calvin couldn't stand it anymore. He dropped the tools and ran at Selina. She let out a squeal and ran from Calvin.

She squealed even louder when Devon shot to his feet, hooked his arm around her waist, twisted her out of the way, and pushed her to give her a head start. Her laughter echoed through the field as she ran.

Calvin stomped his foot in the grass. "Not fair!" He tried to go around Devon, but Devon stepped to the side, blocking the way. "Get out—"

A sound like a roar came from Devon as he charged Calvin, who stared at the man, too surprised to react. Devon wrapped his hands around her brother's waist and pulled him over his shoulder, as if the boy were a sack of potatoes. Calvin laughed as he jerked to get free.

Playfully, Devon let Calvin slip down his back, holding the boy by his ankles. Calvin shouted and laughed at the same time, begging for Devon to not drop him.

Selina came back. She jumped up and down and clapped her hands in excitement. "Drop him! Drop him!"

As if Calvin didn't weigh more than a flower, Devon

pulled him back up to his shoulders, then knelt down to settle the boy on his feet.

"You!" Calvin snarled before lunging at Devon. Since he barely reached Devon's waist, Calvin couldn't really do much, but Devon pretended to be wounded by the boy's attacks. Devon dropped to his knees and fell backward as Calvin attacked him.

A wrestling match ensued.

As much as Kianna wanted to ignore them, she couldn't. She found herself smiling and laughing with them.

Until Devon turned his back to her, and the sunlight hit his drenched white shirt, showing off every inch of his muscular back, shoulders, and arms.

The laughter died in her throat. Heat coiled low in her stomach. Even her neck and cheeks burned.

"Kianna!" Kianna whipped her head in the direction of the side yard. Waving a piece of paper in her hands, Cat rounded the house and ran into her direction. Cat slowed down when she got close and frowned at Kianna. "What happened to your face?"

Kianna brought her hands up to her face and patted her cheeks. "What? What is on my face?"

Cat took the seat beside Kianna and narrowed her eyes at her friends. "You're ... blushing." Cat looked around, but she didn't have to look long. Devon still played with the kids, his long, hard body on display under the fitted brown pants and semitransparent shirt. "Ah, that's why."

Kianna snorted, dropping her hands. "That's nonsense." It truly was. Devon was an attractive man, but he was nothing more than that. Not to her, at least.

"Whatever you say," Cat drawled, clearly unconvinced.

Eager to change the subject, Kianna glanced to the paper in her friend's hand. "What's that?"

A smile spread over Cat's lips as she straightened the paper and showed it to Kianna. "The lamp festival was announced. It'll be in a couple of weeks."

Gasping in delight, Kianna took the paper from Cat's hands. "Finally! I thought they would skip it this year."

"The festival?" Calvin asked. He had stopped playing and now walked toward Kianna and Cat.

"Is it?" Selina asked, sounding hopeful. She too left Devon behind. "Is it the lamp festival?"

The siblings leaned over Kianna to take a look at the paper. She couldn't help but notice that Devon had approached them too, a slight furrow between his brows.

She cleared her throat and returned her attention to the paper. "Yes, it's the lamp festival."

Calvin and Selina smiled at each other. The siblings loved the lamp festival. Kianna loved it too. Well, everyone in town loved it. It was the most anticipated event of the year.

"What's the festival?" Devon asked.

Cat gasped. "You don't know about the lamp festival?"

"He doesn't have any memories," Kianna whispered. She wondered how that worked. He didn't remember anything? Not even big events? Or his birthday? He still knew the basic things like how to write and read, which were uncommon for the lower class. He knew how to tend crops, to fix broken tools. All of these questions only piqued Kianna's curiosity.

"Oh." Cat glanced at the farmhand. "I'm sorry. I forgot."

Devon shrugged. "It's okay."

"The lamp festival is great," Calvin said, smiling up at Devon. "There's food, and dancing, and art exhibitions, and—"

"And the lamps!" Selina finished. She rocked on the balls of her feet, clearly excited. She turned back to Kianna. "Will there be a dance demonstration this year?"

Kianna pointed to the lower section of the paper. "No, but there will be a dance competition."

Selina's smile fell. "Competition?" She glanced to Calvin. "We're not that good. We can't compete."

Kianna put her hands on her waist. "Says who? I don't see why you can't compete. Treat it like a demonstration. Just go up on the stage and dance your heart out. If you don't win, that's okay. At least you'll have fun."

Selina and Calvin looked at each other as if conferring about the matter in their heads. Devon crossed his arms over his sweaty shirt, and fixed his eyes on Kianna.

Her cheeks warmed under the weight of his gaze, but she didn't avert her eyes. She held his stare.

"We'll do it," Calvin announced.

Immediately, Kianna realized what she had been doing, and embarrassed, turned her attention back to her siblings.

"But we have a condition," Selina said.

"And what's that?" Kianna asked, curious.

"You have to help us practice," Calvin said.

"Of course," Kianna agreed.

"What about me?" Cat asked, sounding offended. "I want to help too!"

Selina shook her head. "You have two left feet."

Cat exaggerated a gasp, her hand pressed against her chest. "Hey!"

The group laughed, and Kianna couldn't help but notice the way Devon's lips curved up as if he too wanted to smile and laugh at Selina's joke. Moments ago he had been playing and laughing with her siblings. Why did he hold back now?

Selina clapped excitedly. "When can we start?"

Kianna glanced at the field. There was still so much to do. She had to finish sewing the clothes, then start on supper, and when she was done, she should help with the crops. "I don't—"

"As soon as she finishes this." Devon pointed to the clothes in her lap.

She stared at him with big eyes, silently asking him how she would do that. "Don't worry," he said, his voice gentle. "I'll take care of the field. You go help them."

Kianna worried her lower lip with her teeth, considering. This was so kind of him. "Are you sure?"

The half smile was back to Devon's lips. "I am."

Despite herself, Kianna smiled back at him.

Devon

THE WARRIOR GLANCED AT THE MANOR ATOP THE HILL. A candle flickered past the windows, indicating someone, probably Kianna, was still awake, despite it being almost midnight.

The young woman never stopped. She woke up early and went to bed late. She prepared breakfast, cleaned up after everyone, worked in the field, schooled her siblings, washed, sewed, and swept ... it was a never-ending routine.

And she never complained. At least not out loud. He knew that she had to be hurting on the inside. Or exhausted.

Despite all she had on her plate, when Selina and Calvin

asked her to help them practice the dance for the lamp festival, she only hesitated because she knew the weight of her duty. Devon couldn't help but take care of that. He could handle the field while she spent a couple of hours with the kids.

The smile on her face had been worth it.

Her beautiful face. Her beautiful spirit.

Devon looked to the dark sky, dotted with millions of stars. The gods had to be mistaken. There was no other explanation for it. He would bet his soul, which belonged to the gods, that she didn't have one evil bone in her body. Not even a sliver in her blood.

She was the most kind and hardworking person he had ever known.

And the most beautiful woman he had ever laid eyes on.

His heart squeezed and he let out a string of curses.

Why did these feelings snake inside his chest uninvited? He wanted to resist her charms, but every time he looked at her, he found himself powerless. Despite his strength, she could disarm him with a single look, with one small smile.

Devon shook his head and turned his back to the manor. He had to stop these thoughts, these feelings. He was a warrior of light, and he had a job to do here. Nothing more.

Devon patrolled the perimeter of the property. He walked by the cherry tree and the bench Kianna liked so much—in the little free time she had to herself, she could be found on the bench, usually with a book in hand.

Devon stopped short. There they went again, his thoughts turning back to her.

What was wrong with him?

A groan started in his chest. Determined to accomplish this damn patrol without any more interference, Devon stomped past the lake. He rounded the estate line in the middle of the forest, then cut back behind the field. He glanced at the growing crops. Ophelia had told him the field didn't use to be so close to the house, but once her husband died and they sank into debts, they had to sell many of their possessions, including their house in town and most of the estate, leaving only the area around the manor. Thus, the field butted up to the back of the family home. If they didn't make a profit this year, even a little, she would have to consider selling the rest of the estate, and moving them to a small house in the town's poorest neighborhood. She didn't know how they would feed themselves then, but at least they wouldn't be spending so much on the manor, in the field, and on employees.

If only he could help. The warriors of light were allowed to have houses in the human world if they wished and money, lots of money. Devon didn't have a house, but he did have money, and every time he saw Kianna and her family struggling, he wished he could give it all to them.

But how would he explain his fortune?

Devon halted in his tracks once more.

Holy ... why was he worrying about them?

He closed his eyes and let out a long breath. He had a job to do, damn it. He wouldn't, couldn't, be this involved with this family. It wasn't right.

Devon opened up his mind and senses.

His eyes shot open and his skin crawled.

He could sense it. The darkness. Thick and powerful. It was far away, but not as far as he would have liked.

With a knot between his brows, Devon glanced at the forest, where in the distance, the darkness awaited.

Perhaps the gods weren't mistaken after all.

PRESENT

Kenna

The sales associate opened the door for me. "Come back
soon."

"I will," I said, with a small smile. "Thanks."

I walked out of the small store and inhaled the fresh spring air—this town could be little and hickish, but the streets were clean and beautiful, with lots of flowerbeds around well-manicured bushes and trees.

And the people were nice. The lady in the store had been a little curious, wanting to know where I had moved from, which school I had gone to, if I was going to college and what my major was—everyone Lia and I met so far had wanted to know the same things—but she had been kind and helpful.

I started home, swinging the bag in my hand. Finally, I had found my favorite perfume. It was a sweet cherry perfume done by a small perfume company. They didn't distribute to bigger grocery and drug stores, thus making it hard to find. But I never gave up looking for it. The cherry scent ... I loved it. It warmed my soul and made me happy.

In an unusually good mood, I skipped back home.

I turned the corner to my street and skipped to a stop when a little girl and a little boy came running my way. They slammed into me, and the girl latched on to the strap of my bag, pulling hard.

I held on harder. "Hey!"

She tugged again. "Let go!"

I reached for her and grabbed her wrist. "I don't think so." The girl couldn't be older than ten, and the boy? He was probably eight. The girl shot daggers at me with her blue eyes, and the boy kicked my shin. I glared at him. "That's not nice!"

"What do you know about nice?" the girl snapped.

What did she mean? I took a good look at them. Their clothes had holes and stains, their hair was messy as if it hadn't seen a brush in months, and they were way too skinny.

Were they homeless?

My heart sank.

"Here." I pried the girl's hand from my purse. "I can give you some money and you can buy yourselves some food. Is that okay?"

The girl and the boy exchanged a meaningful look. Could they read each other's minds? Impossible.

Well, I knew of impossible things that were real ...

They turned back to me and nodded.

I grabbed my wallet and fished out a twenty-dollar bill. Cash was limited right now with our meager funds and Lia's low salary, but something tugged inside my chest. I wanted to help them. Needed. Hopefully, they would be able to buy dinner with that.

"Thanks," the girl said, reaching for the bill.

I pulled the money back. "Just ... don't steal anymore, okay?"

The girl frowned. "I'll try."

I stared, not expecting such honesty. I thought she would downright lie to my face.

I handed her the money.

The two kids took off running.

A second later, the school bus stopped a few yards from me and Carol hopped out.

"Hey." She walked to me as the bus left. "What are you doing out here?"

I gestured to the other side of the street. "I was almost robbed by a girl and a boy."

She halted by my side. "The girl is yay high—" She put a hand beside her shoulder. "—with long blond hair and blue eyes, and the boy is a little shorter, with brown hair and grayish eyes?"

I stared at her. "Yes? Do you know them?"

She nodded. "Everyone in town knows them. Sabrina and Kevin. She's eleven and he's nine. They are siblings, but they live with foster parents a few blocks from here."

"A foster home? They looked homeless."

"I know." Carol sighed. "Their foster parents don't really care. Social workers tried to take all the kids from them, but apparently, it isn't that easy."

"So they go around robbing people?"

"They probably only did it because you're new." Carol hooked her hand around my arm and steered me toward our houses. "They are good kids, but don't really have anyone to take care of them."

My heart tugged again. I didn't even know them, and yet, I found myself wanting to go after them and help. To do more for them.

As we walked the few yards to our houses, Carol told me about her day, citing the names of her friends and classmates as if I knew these people. I guess she assumed I did since she told me so much about them.

I turned into my house's driveway, but Carol didn't follow me. "Aren't you coming in?"

"Not right now. I'm gonna drop my books at home, sort out what homework I have to do, then I'll come over later."

"Okay," I said, surprised by my disappointment. Despite Carol being annoying, talkative and bubbly, I wanted to spend time with her. I was probably going mad. "See you later."

She waved at me as she headed home.

I stayed in the same spot, a little lost. I had been feeling so many emotions I wasn't used to, it was scary.

"Hey."

Lost in thought, I hadn't noticed someone had snuck up to me.

I turned and found Devon standing a few feet from me.

I swallowed hard as warmth spread through my cheeks. Despite my attempts to not stare at him, I couldn't help it. The man was drenched in sweat. Black strands fell over his eyes, and his white shirt clung to his shoulder, chest, and stomach. Holy shit, with all those muscles, he probably spent the entire day at the gym.

A sweat drop rolled down his cheek, past his jaw, down his neck, and I found myself wanting to lick—

I blinked, snapping out of it. "Hi." I fixed my gaze on his eyes. There were only his rich, deep dark eyes. "Out for a run?"

He nodded. "Yes."

I stared at him again. "So ..."

"Right." He ran a hand through his hair. "Hm, I ... I have something for you."

Devon

HER BRIGHT BLUE EYES ROUNDED AND HER PINK LIPS MADE A little O. A breeze blew, brushing her long brown hair back. I wanted to reach out and run my hands through it.

I shook my head. What the fuck was I thinking?

She smoothed the surprised expression from her face. "Something for me?"

"Yeah." Why did I feel so anxious about this? "It's in my house. Do you want to come with me and get it?"

A small knot appeared between her brows. Once more the urge to reach out and touch her, this time to smooth the knot out, hit me.

"S-sure," she said.

I stepped to the side, allowing her to fall into step with me. Side by side, we walked up the driveway to my house. In those few seconds, the silence wasn't awkward. It was exactly the opposite, but I couldn't help wanting to talk to her.

I glanced at her, trying to find something to talk about.

The small bag in her hand caught my attention. "Were you out shopping?"

She lifted the bag a few inches, then dropped it again. "Yeah. I found my favorite perfume in a small drugstore in town."

"I'm assuming that's good?"

"Yeah, it is. It's hard to find."

"You're making me curious." Which was surprising to me. Normally, I couldn't care less about those sort of things.

Her lips tugged up. "It's nothing special." She fished the perfume out of the box. "See, nothing special about it." A small rectangular glass vial and bright, red-purple liquid inside. The brand name was some farm, but the drawing on the side was well done.

"Cherry?" A cherry tree, flower, and fruit illustrated the bottle.

She nodded. "I'm addicted to it."

I frowned, curious to smell the perfume now.

What a fucking ridiculous thought.

Shaking my head, I went up the porch steps. I entered my password on the lock and twisted the knob. "It's right in here." I reached over to the side table in the foyer and grabbed it. I extended it to Kenna.

She stared at the book in my hand, her eyes wide. "How? ... Why?"

"I was at the library the other day. I saw this book and remembered the one you burned the other day."

She lifted her eyes to mine. Her stare, so surprised and unguarded and intense, took my breath away. Did she know how pretty she was? How beautiful?

The lights on the porch twinkled once. Twice. Three times.

"What the hell?" I stepped inside my house and flicked the switch. The lights were off. How could they be flickering?

Kenna grabbed the book from me, her hands briefly grazing mine.

An image filled my mind.

A young woman with long, blond hair wearing a worn beige dress, seated on a wooden bench, holding a piece of paper in her hands. She smiled at the kids in front of her.

My chest tightened as she lifted her chin. Finally, I would see her face clearly.

The image faded before I could get a good look at her.

In front of me, Kenna hugged the book. "That's thoughtful of you." She cleared her throat. "I-I should go now."

Shaken by what just happened—was it the fourth time I touched Kenna and a random image appeared in my mind?—I swallowed hard and took a step back. "Yeah, yeah, of course."

She gestured to the book. "Thank you."

"You're welcome."

Kenna held my gaze for a moment longer, then turned her back to me and dashed to her house. I stared after her, entranced by her and the stupid knowledge that she was wreaking havoc inside my chest. And what was with these fucking images? Once more, I wondered if they were memories of the time I had lost, but what did Kenna have to do with them? That was three hundred years ago.

I closed the front door and went to my kitchen, where I grabbed a bottle of water from the fridge and gulped it down. Running was supposed to not only maintain my human body, but clear my mind, to burn my energy so I could relax.

Yet, here I was, the thoughts in my mind reeling and turning too fast for me to try and make sense of any of it.

I opened the backdoor, leaned on the doorjamb, and inhaled the rich spring scent.

Cherry.

I stared at the cherry tree and its branches, angling over my backyard. The air was heavy with cherries.

A groan ripped through my throat.

God damn it. It seemed that the more time Kenna spent here, the more she filled my thoughts.

Trying to regain my focus and forget her for at least one second, I closed my eyes and took a deep breath. Surrounded by the scent of cherry, I meditated for a moment, searching for my center. I was a fucking warrior of light and I would push this girl from my mind one way or another.

My senses rushed outward.

And bumped into darkness.

I stared at the horizon, where the darkness was hiding, just out of town.

This wasn't good.

Tonight, I was going hunting.

PAST

Kianna

"Here." Kianna turned the book around and showed the text to Selina and Calvin. Though the siblings were different ages and would have been in different levels in school, it was much easier for Kianna if she taught them the same thing. So, she fell right in the middle—she taught them what a ten year old would be learning.

"All of this?" Calvin grimaced. He hated reading, much less writing about what he had read afterward, but it was a requirement if he ever wanted to measure up to the other kids who were able to attend an actual school.

A sliver of annoyance snaked inside Kianna's veins. She had way too much to do. Teach the siblings their daily lessons, prepare the lessons for tomorrow, check the clothes on the clothesline, wash a few more, prepare dinner, check if there was anything she could help out with in the field before the sun went down, make sure the tools were functional and clean enough for tomorrow, have dinner, put the kids to bed, clean the kitchen, wash herself, and only then she could think about going to sleep. It would be past midnight again.

What she wouldn't give for a day off, a day she could do whatever she wanted—she would spend the day sleeping.

"This is too long," Selina said, adding fuel to the fire.

Kianna clenched her hands under the table before she lunged over it and slapped each one of her siblings hard. She had never hit them, but she wouldn't promise she never would.

Cat slapped the table, startling Kianna. "Be quiet and read the stupid thing." She poked a finger to her own book, open in front of her. "I'm trying to study here."

Cat couldn't afford school either. Her mother didn't allow her to come over every day, because she was afraid Cat would goof off and not study at all, but Giles was able to intercede, and Cat ended up studying with Selina and Calvin at least three afternoons in a week. The only difference was that she was in a more advanced level.

Selina and Calvin muttered some complaints, but lowered their gazes and read from the book.

Kianna let out a relieved sigh. She glanced at her best friend seated beside her and mouthed, "Thank you."

Cat winked at her, then she, too, returned her attention to her book.

Having already finished her studies, Kianna watched, waiting until they were done to explain the text. To not waste time, she pulled out paper, ink, and a quill, and began her notes for the next day's lessons.

Not two minutes later, Selina complained. "I'm hungry."

Kianna fought an eye roll. "Lunch wasn't three hours ago, and supper will be in two."

"I'm hungry too," Calvin mumbled. "Can't we have a snack?"

Kianna opened her mouth to tell them to quiet down and read—

"I'm kind of hungry too," Cat whispered.

She glared at her best friend.

Cat pouted and batted her eyes.

This time, Kiana didn't suppress her eye roll. "Fine. Keep studying. I'll see what we have." She got up from the chair and dragged her feet to the kitchen.

Kianna cleaned her hands in the wash basin and glanced out the window. It was only spring and the sun was already too hot to handle. Her poor mother, Giles, and Devon were outside, working in the field and baking under the sun.

Kianna had wanted to trade places with her mother—she was young and healthy. She could endure the heavy work in the field under the scorching sun, while her mother stayed inside, teaching the kids. But her mother insisted Kianna was smarter than her, and the better choice to homeschool the siblings.

But as Kianna watched her mother wiping her sweaty forehead with a dirty rag in the middle of the field, Kianna's heart squeezed. Her mother was too old for this kind of work. If only they could afford to pay one more worker, one more farmhand as energetic and strong as Devon.

No, no one was as energetic and strong as Devon.

And he wasn't even being paid. All he got was a roof over his head, food on his plate, and a short allowance to buy cheap, personal things. Why he endured such hard work for scraps, Kianna would never understand.

Well, she hadn't asked him about that, about why he was working himself to death for people he didn't know.

Kianna grabbed the carrots and the apples from the ice box and washed them on the basin over the counter. Once more, she looked through the window.

It was easy to spot him in the field. It was as if Kianna's brain was tuned to him and her eyes just knew where to look.

As a testament to how hot it was outside, Devon had taken his shirt off and tied it around his long hair to keep the loose strands back. His smooth skin dipped and crested over the muscles of his shoulders and back. He moved with vigor, making his muscles contract and expand. Glistening with sweat and the brightness of the sun, Devon looked more like an angel than a normal man.

Heat crept up her cheeks. Kianna averted her eyes, ashamed of where her thoughts had veered to.

She couldn't think of him like that. She couldn't think of him like that.

Easier said than done.

Kianna set the carrots and apples on a cutting board and began chopping them. She tried focusing on preparing the snack, but her mind and body betrayed her. When she least expected, her eyes looked up and spied on Devon.

However, the next time she looked out the window, she was surprised to see Devon beside the barn, drinking water from the pitcher left in the shade. He raised his chin, swallowing the water, his Adam's apple bobbing up and down.

Kianna's breath caught.

Devon set the glass down and turned to the manor. He looked directly at Kianna. His lips curled up.

Kianna dropped the knife and took a step back from the cutting board, breaking the line of sight with Devon. She had better pay attention to what she was doing or she would lose a finger or two.

Annoyed with herself, Kianna inhaled deeply, trying to reason with herself. Why did she feel like this? Why was she so attracted to this strange, quiet, and mysterious man? Why couldn't she rein in her mind and heart? She had to prove to herself this was just lust. He was an attractive man and he was close. That made it easy to think she was falling for him. Because she was falling for him. That was stupid. It was just lust.

Just lust.

The backdoor opened and Kianna yelped, startled.

She pressed a hand to her chest, trying to calm her racing her.

Devon, still shirtless, walked in. "I'm sorry. I didn't mean to startle you." His dark eyes stared at her with such interest, with such attention. She felt her resolution melting away.

"No, it's okay." She turned back to the cutting board. Better to face the knife than to risk staring at his bare chest.

"I ..." Devon took a step closer. Her back to him, Kianna held her breath. "I have something for you."

Kianna couldn't help it. She spun around and faced him. "Something for me?"

Devon offered her a gift. "I know how you like reading, so ..."

Kianna hesitated for a second, but her curiosity won. She grabbed the wrapped rectangle and ripped the wrapping paper. "A book." And it wasn't any book. It was one that she had been meaning to buy. A fantasy romance about warrior females and angel knights. She hugged the precious gift. "You bought a book for me?"

Devon ran a hand through his hair, pushing the shirt-turned-bandana back a little. "I was running an errand in the village and spotted it in the bookstore." He paused and she waited, her heartbeat hurting from the anticipation. He gestured toward the book. "Well, I thought of you and got the book."

Kianna glanced down to the book as if it was a precious treasure. But how? How could he afford a book like that? Books were expensive. Had he spent his meager money on her? Why?

She wanted to ask him all those questions, but she couldn't find the courage.

"Thank you," she whispered, choking up. It had been a while since someone had done something nice for her. And Devon wasn't just someone. "I haven't had the time to read lately—" Or the money to buy new books. "—but I really appreciate the gesture."

A small smile adorned Devon's lips. "You're welcome."

PRESENT

Devon

I BARELY REMEMBERED MY HUMAN LIFE BEFORE BECOMING A warrior of light, and I had lived as an immortal for a long time, so long that many feelings and things humans did or said sounded foreign to me.

But there was one taste I had acquired since being rescued from the underworld and thrown back onto Earth: cars. When my days were too boring or too stifling, I either went out for a long run or for a long drive. I liked my Maserati the most about having to live as a human. There was nothing like lowering the windows, putting on a rock ballad and driving aimlessly.

But I couldn't drive forever, and so I ended up back at my house in the shitty Misty Hill town.

It was late afternoon when I came back from a six-hour

drive, and as I was bringing my car up my driveway, I saw Kevin sneaking around Kianna and Lia's house.

Like everyone else in this town, I knew about Kevin and Sabrina's past. Abandoned at the age of three and one, placed in the foster care system. I was sure the ones they lived with now were probably the worst of the bunch, and yet, they didn't have much say in it.

Worried Kevin might be sneaking into my neighbor's house to steal something, I cut off the engine of my car and followed him. I rounded the corner of the house when he opened the backdoor and slipped inside.

The little fucker.

I raced up the porch steps and caught the door before he closed it.

"Gotcha!" I said, reaching for him.

But I froze as I took in the scene.

Around the kitchen island, Kenna stared at me, a knife covered in butter in one hand, a slice of bread in the other. Carol was right beside her, a milk carton in her hand. Sabrina sat on one of the stools, her books open in front of her. The spot beside her was empty, but there were more books there—Kevin's.

My shoulders sagged.

"W-what happened?" Kevin asked, his eyes huge and his face pale, as if he was afraid I would hit him. Fuck. His foster parents probably beat the crap out of him for no reason.

"I ..." I straightened.

Kenna lowered the knife and the bread to a plate. "What are you doing here?"

"I ..." I tried again. Why not be honest? The siblings wouldn't be offended, I was sure. "I saw Kevin sneaking around the house. I thought he was gonna ..." My words faded as something I rarely experienced filled my chest. Shame. Shame for having assumed the worst of the little boy.

"You thought he was coming in to steal," Sabrina finished. "I don't blame you. I would probably have assumed the same."

I narrowed my eyes at her. Had an eleven year old just said that?

Carol nodded. "Yup, I would have thought the same."

Finally relaxing, Kevin took his place beside his sister. "I wasn't stealing, though."

I glanced around the odd group. The siblings and Carol were studying, and Kenna was making them a snack. "I can see that." I gestured toward them. "If you don't mind me asking, how did this start?"

Kenna grabbed spinach and tomatoes from the fridge and set them beside the bread and butter. "Well, Carol is always here, despite my many hints that she should leave."

Carol chuckled. "She thinks she can scare me away."

"As for Sabrina and Kevin," Kenna continued, "they tried to steal my purse the other day. At first I was mad, but then Carol explained their situation." She shook her head. The siblings looked down at their books. "I just couldn't do nothing, you know? So ... they have been coming here after school for the past three days."

"She makes us snacks," Kevin said.

"And helps us with our homework," Sabrina said.

"Don't forget about your clothes," Carol added.

"Oh, yeah." Sabrina gestured to her shirt and pants. I hadn't realized until now, but for the first time ever, their clothes looked clean and well cared for. "She washed our clothes, mended them, and even got us some new things."

I stared at Kenna. What the fuck was she doing? Was she

trying to adopt them or something? She was eighteen, for fuck's sake. She didn't have the maturity or means to take care of two kids.

Despite it all, I was shocked. Touched, actually—another human feeling that only came around once every century. Instead of reprimanding the siblings and reporting them, she took them in. She was helping them.

"We stay here until we can't anymore," Kevin confessed, his voice low.

My chest constricted. Of course. Staying in their foster house meant being one more kid "bothering" their foster parents, and eventually, it all led to a punishment or a beating. Staying hidden for as long as they could at Kenna's house meant they would be safer for longer.

My eyes returned to Kenna, who passed the plates with sandwiches to her guests. Her long brown hair had green streaks now, and her nails were painted turquoise. She looked relaxed and nonchalant in jeans, a tank top, and barefoot, but she couldn't fool me.

Under all that guarded attitude was someone who cared deeply.

It was like Kenna had entered an unknowing challenge: impress Devon at every turn.

She was definitely winning.

The sound of a door opening came from the front of the house. "Kenna?" Lia called. "I have groceries. Can you help?"

I had no idea what made me move, but without hesitation, I stepped into the hallway. "I can help."

Her arms full of paper bags, Lia smiled at me. "Oh, you're here."

"We are too," Sabrina said, coming right behind me. Kevin stood with her.

"Great." Lia jerked her chin to the car. "Help me with the groceries, then I'll cook supper for us while you guys finish your homework." Sabrina and Kevin rushed past her, toward the car. Lia looked at me. "Devon, you're staying too, right?"

I opened my mouth.

"He's staying!" Carol shouted from the kitchen. I heard a shush from Kenna and some covert mumbling from Carol.

I frowned. What the fuck was I doing? I had no idea, but I couldn't stop now. "Yes, I'm staying."

"Great." She walked past me and dropped the bags on the kitchen island. She grinned at Kenna and Carol. "I love a full house."

The corner of my lips tugged up as I turned to help with the groceries.

Then, I wiped the smile off my face. I was here because of my mission, nothing else. Every time I touched Kenna, I saw a vision. I would find a way of casually touching her again tonight to see if I had another one, because I was now convinced these visions were connected to my mission.

That was the only reason I endured Kenna, her mother, and her friends.

Or so I told myself.

PAST

Devon

DEVON WIPED THE SWEAT FROM HIS FOREHEAD WITH THE SHIRT he had slung over his shoulders. In this heat, he didn't even know why he bothered putting on a shirt when he got out of bed in the morning.

His eyes scanned the field. Giles worked as hard as he did, and Ophelia was farther away, doing lighter labor. Until about an hour ago, Kianna had been in the field with them.

He straightened and stared past the field, down the hill, to the cherry tree and the lake behind it. He couldn't help the tug in his chest as he took in the blonde girl seated at the bench, holding a fiddle, watching as her younger siblings rehearsed their dance for the competition.

At first, Kianna had resisted rehearsing more than once a day, but knowing this dance was important to Selina and

Calvin, she soon gave in. Now they spent half the time allotted for schooling, rehearsing instead.

Often, Devon spied out from the field to watch the dance. Though he was intrigued that Kianna could play the fiddle, he still thought the best parts were when Kianna got up from the bench and showed the siblings a step or two, corrected them, or added the next move to the dance.

As if the gods granted his wishes, Kianna rose to her feet and stood between her siblings. She lifted her arms, moving them side to side, her hands undulating with the movement. A breeze blew past, ruffling the skirt of her dress and blowing her long tresses back. The lake's surface shone behind her, becoming a halo around her.

An angel.

She couldn't be evil, because Devon was sure she was an angel.

His feet moved before he could register what he was doing. When he finally came to, he was halfway down the hill, his eyes glued to the young woman dancing beside the cheery tree.

Devon hesitated for a moment, but he had earned a break. He would just watch Kianna, Selina, and Calvin for a few minutes, then he would drink some water, and go back to the field.

Calvin was the first one to see him. "Do you want to dance with us?"

Kianna and Selina stopped the move they were practicing and turned to Devon. His cheeks heated.

"Oh no, I can't dance," he said quickly. "I was just taking a break and saw you dancing."

"Want to see what we have so far?" Selina asked with a smile. She seemed excited about having an audience.

Devon nodded. "Sure."

Selina grabbed Kianna's wrist in one hand, and Devon's in the other, and pushed them back to the bench. "Then sit there and enjoy."

Devon stumbled onto the rough wooden bench, right beside Kianna. Instantly, he scooted to the edge of the bench.

"Sorry," he mumbled.

She narrowed her bright blue eyes at him. "For?"

He gestured to himself. "I'm sweating and smell bad." Her eyes followed his hand, and he could swear he felt her gaze brushing over his skin. She was looking at him, staring at his chest and stomach.

Red tinted her cheeks and she averted her eyes. "It's okay." She cleared her throat, grabbed her fiddle, and waved at the kids. "Are you ready?"

"Yes!" Selina and Calvin shouted in unison.

Kianna began playing—though she didn't seem like an expert, she could play well enough for a simple song—and the kids danced.

After five seconds, Devon's head turned to the side, and his eyes fell on the young woman seated beside him. She had a faint smile on her lips, her chin bobbed with the beat of the song, and her hands moved skillfully over the strings through the chords. For a moment, he wished she would be the one entering the competition. He would have loved to see her dancing.

Her nails caught on the strings and she missed a beat. "Sorry. Keep going." She caught up and the kids found the rhythm again.

"Ta-da!" Selina said.

Devon blinked and glanced to the kids. They had stopped dancing, and Kianna stopped playing.

And he hadn't seen much of the dance.

"That's it for now," Calvin said. "Kianna still has to teach us a few more moves."

"So." Selina bounced up to him. "What do you think?"

Devon stared at her. "I think ... that with enough practice, you two will do great."

"Really?" the little girl squealed. "It's all because of Kianna. She's the expert."

Kianna shook her head. "No, no. You two are the ones dancing."

"But they wouldn't be that good if they didn't have a good teacher." The words flew out of Devon's mouth before he thought them through. Kianna stared at him, her eyes narrowed. Damn it. If he could, he would take those words back.

"Can we take a quick break?" Calvin said, pulling Devon's attention. The little boy patted his throat. "I need some water."

"Me too," Selina said.

"Sure." Kianna held her fiddle tight. "Five minutes."

The kids dashed up the hill, toward the house.

Kianna stayed seated beside Devon under the cherry tree, clutching the fiddle.

The damn curiosity was back and Devon couldn't help it. He said, "It's obvious you used to dance, and you're good at the fiddle too."

The young woman laid the instrument in her lap and stared at it as if it was a forgotten lover. "I used to take lessons. Dancing, singing, music, painting. I wasn't good at them all, except for dancing. I loved it so much. I think that's the reason I was a decent dancer."

Decent? From the way her hands moved, her neck elongated, her chin jutted out, and her back arched, she had been a lot more than just a decent dancer.

"But you're good at the fiddle too."

She shook her head, her blond hair falling over her shoulders. "I could follow a rhythm and play simple songs, but I was never really good at it. But when the kids have to follow a rhythm, it's enough."

"What about the festival? Will you play for them, then?"

"No, goodness, I would never." She chuckled as if that was funny. "There will be a band playing for the contestants. I'm sure they will play the full song and sound much better than me."

But Devon doubted any of them would be as gracious and beautiful as Kianna.

Devon frowned.

Mission. He had to focus on his mission. Nothing else.

"If you say so," he said, his voice suddenly cold. He rose to his feet. "I should get back to work."

Kianna looked at him, her delicate brows curled down. Was that disappointment in her gaze? No, it couldn't be. "Sure. You should."

After a slight bow of his head, Devon stomped up the hill. Cursing himself for the stupid feelings stirring inside his chest, he stopped in front of the barn and served himself a full cup of chilled water. But instead of drinking it, he threw it over his head, hoping his senses came back to normal.

But as he brushed a hand over his face, he knew it had been a waste of good water.

His senses had been askew since he had first seen Kianna, and until the gods liberated him from this mission, he was convinced he would be more and more enthralled by her charm.

His chest squeezed.

One day, this mission would come to an end, and he would have to leave Kianna and her family behind.

Devon didn't want to think about that.

PRESENT

Kenna

STUDYING FOR THE GED ALWAYS GAVE ME A HEADACHE. THERE was so much I missed, so much I still had to learn ... I wondered if I would ever catch up. It was normal to graduate from high school at eighteen or nineteen. If I continued like this, I might get my GED when I was twenty-two. And then I would go to college too? How old would I be when I graduated? Thirty?

Of course, I was exaggerating, but it felt like that for the most part. Carol would graduate from high school next year, while I felt like I could be in the same class as Sabrina.

I took a Tylenol for the coming headache, picked up the book from the kitchen island, and headed outside. It was early afternoon and the heat was picking up, despite being spring, but I sat on the grass at the cherry tree's roots and cowered under its shade.

For some reason, I really liked this spot. I inhaled deeply. It was probably because of the tree's scent, which reminded me of my cherry perfume.

I cracked the book open and began reading. The headache faded—it wasn't studying. Reading was fun and relaxing—and I fell into the story world.

In the back of my mind, I couldn't forget that Devon had given the book to me. Why had he done that? Because he had seen me burn the other one? That wasn't a good enough answer. I had almost died of surprise when he gifted it to me, which in turn had fueled my powers. The lights of his porch flickered, and he had thought there was something wrong with them. At that time, all I wanted was to thank him properly, but I was afraid I wouldn't be able to control my powers, so I fled.

The other day, when he had come to check why Kevin was sneaking into my house and ended up staying for dinner, because Lia insisted, I opened my mouth several times to let him know I was enjoying the book, but couldn't do it.

What was wrong with me?

I shook my head and went back to the book.

I read and read, not really paying attention to the time, until Sabrina and Kevin walked into the backyard, back from school.

"Still reading that book?" Sabrina asked.

Smiling, I shot to my feet. "Yes, I'm trying to take it slow." Although, I had only read fifty pages. I would have to slow down or I would be done with it in no time. "Hungry?"

"Always," Kevin answered. He dragged his backpack across the yard and kicked up the porch steps.

"Something wrong?" I asked as we entered the kitchen.

Sabrina threw her backpack on the floor and sat on one of the island stools. "He almost got into another fight."

Sabrina had told me about the fights. Kevin was a small boy for his age. Instead of nine, I had guessed he was eight, but most people thought he was seven. Apparently, there were some big kids in his class, and one boy who was already eleven—he was repeating the grade—liked to pick on Kevin, since he was half his size.

"Want to talk about it?" I asked, trying to remain calm. I didn't care if his foster parents didn't give a damn. I did. And if this continued, I wouldn't stay quiet. I would go to the damn school and teach that boy a lesson.

Kevin shook his head. "No. I just want to eat."

I smiled. "Well, I've got a surprise." I grabbed the beautiful chocolate cake from the range and placed it in the middle of the island. "Ta-da!"

Kevin's eyes rounded, and Sabrina's jaw fell open.

"You made this? For us?" Sabrina asked, sounding a little touched.

I snorted. "I wish. If I tried, I would probably burn the house down. No, I bought it from the store, but for you nonetheless."

I couldn't explain, not with words, why I felt so drawn to these two kids, why I wanted to help them, why I wanted to buy them cakes and new clothes with the little money I had. Every time I looked at them and saw a ripped notebook, or a new bruise on their faces, or their dirty clothes, or their skinny arms and stomach, my heart hurt. Thankfully, Lia felt the exact same way. She was happy I had not only Carol as a friend now, but Sabrina and Kevin too.

And Devon.

Lia wasn't into younger guys, or I would have thought Lia

was in love with Devon. There was no other explanation as to why she kept inviting him to dinner, or was so glad to hear when I bumped into him outside.

The siblings devoured three thick slices of cake before settling down to do their homework. I wanted to go back to my book, but I pulled out my GED book and studied beside the kids.

Not long after, Carol arrived from school. She had stopped by her house, as usual, to drop her book bag off and sort through her homework, then she came to my house. She had brought one notebook and one book with her, but this time she had something else too.

"Look what I have here." She waved something in her hand.

Sabrina looked up from her books. "What's that?"

Kevin's eyes shone. "Tickets? Are those tickets?"

Sabrina gasped. "For the light festival?"

Carol's smile was brighter than a lighthouse. "Yes!"

Sabrina reached for the tickets. "How did you get them?"

"I think my parents got them," she said casually. "They always receive a bunch at work. I saved one for me, and there's five there."

"One for each of us," Kevin said. "And the fifth?"

"For Lia," Carol explained. "If she wants, of course."

The confusion went on for too long. "Wait." I raised a finger, as if asking for a time out. "What's going on? What festival?"

Sabrina stared at me with a furrowed brow. "The light festival."

"Oh my God, you've never heard of the festival?" Carol asked incredulously.

"Hm, I've been here for a month." I shrugged. "Of course I never heard about the festival."

"The light festival," Kevin said. "It's a big festival in Willow Grove."

That name wasn't strange. Wasn't that town forty minutes from here?

"It's the biggest festival in the region," Sabrina said. Her smile died. "We only went to it once, a couple of years ago, but I remember it was the best thing ever."

I looked at the remaining two tickets in Carol's hand. "What's this festival about?"

"Oh, there's food and games," Carol said.

"And dance!" Sabrina almost jumped from her stool. "They have dance demonstrations. It's always so cool. One day, I want to participate in one." Her face fell. "I love dancing."

Something tugged in my chest. What I wouldn't give to go back in time and dance again. I barely remembered my life before Slater, but I did remember dancing. I had studied classical ballet, jazz, and tap, and I remembered loving it all. It had been many, many years since I last danced.

"But the best part is the lights," Kevin said, bringing me back to the present.

"Right." Carol clapped her hands. Was she excited too? "After it's dark, they have a light parade. People in beautiful costumes, wagons, cars, all with hundreds of tiny, colorful lights on them, walk and dance by a long street."

"Then there's the fireworks," Sabrina added. "After the parade, they set off lots of fireworks while people cheer and dance some more."

Kevin let out a long sigh. "It's awesome."

It sounded great, but too crowded. Maybe one day this

would be my kind of thing, but I lived in hiding, even if lately it didn't feel exactly like that. I had to avoid places with too many people.

But with Kevin's big eyes, and Sabrina's excited smile, how could I not go?

I grabbed the tickets from Carol's hand. "I'm not sure Lia will come, but I'll take you two to the festival."

The screams that came from those two little kids almost made me deaf. They shot up from their spots and crashed into me, embracing me tight. I was the cheese in their sandwich, and I could count on my fingers how many times I had felt this happy.

I hugged them back.

Carol laughed. "You know I'm coming with you, right?"

I rolled my eyes. "As if you'd let me forget."

PAST

Kianna

THE SCENTS WASHED OVER THE VILLAGE, REACHING KIANNA'S nose even before she was close to the main street. Warm sugar, cinnamon, vanilla, and other spices. People milled the streets from every side, all of them following the same direction. This was the one evening that the entire village stopped —poor, rich, old, and young. They all celebrated together at the lamp festival as friends.

Finally, the smaller street opened to the main street and Kianna's heart warmed. In bright contrast with the night sky, colorful lamps and ribbons lined the streets. Stands with food and jewelry and games were spread out along the street, and musicians gathered at every corner, playing songs that ranged from sorrowful to happy ballads. People strolled up and down the street, stopping to buy food, to look at the necklaces and hairpins, to play the games, or simply to talk to each other.

Selina and Calvin skipped ahead of Kianna and her mother, while Devon stood a few steps behind them, taking it all in. It was odd watching him as he looked around.

Every year since her father's death, her mother set up a stand of rice balls, filled with vegetables from their farm, with Giles and his wife. Kianna and Cat helped, but Kianna was always able to sneak out for a few minutes since she had to take her siblings to the dance demonstration—or competition.

The stand was set up right in the center part of the street, where everyone walked by, which meant that hopefully, they would sell lots of rice balls this evening. Especially since it was a beautiful spring day, which would attract more people than usual.

Cat saw Kianna coming from a mile away. Her lips stretched into a big smile and she rushed forward. "Give me those," she said, taking the pans from Kianna's arms.

"How is it going?" Kianna asked, her eyes on the group of people parked in front of the stand, trying all the food.

"Come see."

Kianna followed Cat behind the stand. Giles and his wife were hard at work, luring the customers with their animated talk and enchanting them with the food. Underneath the stand, two pans sat empty.

"Oh my word," her mother whispered from beside her. "If it keeps selling like that, we'll run out of rice balls."

"That's a good thing, right?" Cat dropped the pans over the table on the back of the stand.

"It sure is," her mother replied. She and Devon followed suit with the pans they had been holding.

Kianna glanced at the many customers flocking around the stand. "Do you want me to stay?"

Her mother shook her head. "It's fine. I think the four of us can manage. You and Devon take the kids to the dance competition. If I can, I'll come watch them later."

"All right." Kianna kissed her mother's cheek, waved at Cat, then fled with Devon. She stopped in the middle of the street and glanced around. "Where are those two pests?"

"There." Devon pointed to a stand of ring toss.

Sure enough, Selina and Calvin watched the game, practically drooling with excitement. Kianna's heart tugged. If only she had some change left to buy them some rounds ...

Kianna and Devon gathered the kids and strolled to the end of the street, where it opened to the main square. Like the rest of the festival, the square was decorated with colorful lamps and ribbons, but here there were fewer stands, because most of the space was taken by an improvised wooden platform, which would serve as the stage for the dance competition. The dancers, mostly dressed in beautiful gowns and suits and costumes, already stood around the stage, waiting for the competition to start.

Kianna glanced at her siblings. They were the most beautiful kids in the world, but unfortunately their clothes weren't the best. Kianna had washed one of her old dresses for Selina —it was pretty, but already old and out of style. For Calvin, she had found one of her father's old button-up white shirts, which she cut up and sewed again in the right size.

If Kianna narrowed her eyes, they looked perfect.

"Are you two ready?" she asked.

Selina looked at her with her big blue eyes. "I don't think so."

Kianna nudged her with her elbow. "Sure you are."

"You two rehearsed a lot," Devon said. "I'm sure you'll do great."

"Just remember to have fun," Kianna said. "This is not a competition. It's a demonstration. Just have fun."

Calvin puffed his chest. "I'm ready!" He took Selina's hand in his. "Let's do this."

Selina dipped her chin. "You're right. We can do this. Let's go."

Kianna pressed a hand to her chest as she watched her siblings marching to the side of the stage. Looking every bit like grown-ups, Selina and Calvin talked to the lady holding a thin ledger—probably the organizer. They checked in, then waited.

Nervous for them, Kianna wrung her hands in her dress.

Devon reached for her and clasped her hands in his. "Don't ruin your pretty dress."

Kianna froze as several thoughts and feelings rushed through her.

Her dress wasn't pretty. It was a simple dark blue thing she had tried embellishing with silver embroidery. Compared to the other women's dresses, she felt terribly underdressed.

Devon's hands weren't as full of calluses as she thought they would be.

In fact, his skin was warm, cozy.

It felt nice to have her hand in his big one.

Shocked, Kianna pulled her hand from his. "I-I'm just nervous for them."

He stared at her, a small smile in his lips. "I know."

Kianna cleared her throat, embarrassed by her thoughts, and averted her eyes. She focused her attention on the empty stage. It had been a challenge to ignore the man beside her, but after a few minutes, the musicians took their places on the right side of the stage, and the competition started. She got lost in the dances.

There were some inexperienced acts, but most of the dancers to hit the stage were good.

Kianna saw the line beside the stage moving. She glanced around, but her mother was nowhere to be seen. She would miss the kids' dance, which was a good thing if that meant she was selling her rice balls like hot cakes on a winter night.

"Hey." Cat stepped to her side.

Kianna stared past her. "Where's my mother?"

"She couldn't come," Cat said. "The stand is too busy and the costumers seemed to like to chat with her more than me, so she sent me here instead."

"It's okay," Kianna said, her voice low. She was a little disappointed, but she understood.

Finally, it was Selina's and Calvin's turn. They walked onto the stage and halted in the center. From where she was, Kianna could see Selina's hands shaking slightly. When the little girl looked at her, Kianna took in a deep breath and let it out slowly. Selina followed her cue and did the same.

The band started playing, and the kids danced to the song.

Their first movements were unsure and a little stiff, but as the beat increased, they let it go and danced their heart outs.

A smile spread through Kianna's lips.

The song ended, the kids froze in their final pose, and the public clapped. Kianna clapped the loudest of them all. She even let out a cheer. Devon chuckled at her side.

The kids hopped off the stage and ran to her. She embraced them both and kissed the top of their sweaty heads. "I'm so very proud of you."

"That was great," Cat said, patting them on the back.

"You two did well," Devon said.

"Thanks," Calvin said.

"I was so nervous," Selina admitted.

"I know, but you overcame it," Kianna said.

Cat grimaced. "I should get back. I'll let your mother know you two were great." She waved at them, then dashed away.

Kianna, Devon, Selina, and Calvin stayed near the stage and watched the rest of the performances. There was a ten-minute break after that, so the judges could vote out and decide on the winners, then the lady from before came onto the stage and announced the winners.

As Kianna expected, Selina and Calvin didn't win. There had been better pieces and more experienced dancers in the competition.

"Remember what I said?" Kianna asked. "Don't think of it as a competition. It was a fun demonstration, right?"

Calvin nodded his head. "Right."

Selina, on the other hand, didn't seem happy about it. She was passionate about dancing, even more than Kianna had ever been.

A pang cut through Kianna's chest. If only they had more money. If they hadn't lost it all, Selina could have taken dance classes like Kianna had.

"Here." Devon extended his closed hand to Calvin. The little boy stared at his fist. Devon grabbed Calvin's arm and dropped a bunch of coins in Calvin's hands. "Go play some games." Calvin's face brightened. "Share with Selina."

Selina's lips pulled up into a big smile. "Thank you!"

The siblings ran to the nearest game stand.

Her brows curling down, Kianna turned to Devon. "Why—?"

"Come on." Devon turned and walked away.

Kianna stared after him for a moment. What was he doing? Why was he being so nice and attentive and gentle? Why was he making her heart flutter so much?

God, more than that, how could she look at him and not feel attracted to him? He had washed his long hair, pulled it back into a loose ponytail, and put on a nice, clean black shirt and pants.

Since the first time she had seen him, she had found him good-looking, but now she thought he was handsome.

Devon disappeared into the crowd and Kianna rushed to catch up with him. Side by side, they meandered from stand to stand, looking at trinkets, tasting samples, and talking about the festival and what they liked so far.

To her surprise, spending time with Devon was easy. Simple. Comfortable.

She liked it.

The next stand they stopped at was a jewelry one. Kianna's hand hovered over the necklaces and bracelets and earrings. She didn't consider herself vain, but she missed having jewels. Now, she had only the small pearl earrings she was currently wearing, one thin necklace her father had given her for her birthday right before his death, and one hairpin that had been her grandma's.

Her eyes scanned through the rings and one called to her. A silver band and a bright blue stone. It looked like the stone had been shaped and cut around the metal, and then sunken. Small claws clutched the stone.

It was delicate and beautiful.

"It looks like your eyes," Devon said. Kianna frowned. "The bright blue of the stone matches your eyes."

It didn't matter if it matched or not, she didn't have money to pay for the kids' games, and she certainly didn't have money to waste on a superfluous ring.

A heavy sigh escaped her throat. Needing to get away from such things, Kianna turned her back to the stand and walked on.

Her mind lagged as a horse appeared right in front of her. She ordered her legs to move, but they were too slow—

An arm hooked around her waist and pulled her back.

"Sorry!" the rider yelled as he maneuvered his animal through the crowd. Why was he riding a horse in the middle of a crowded street?

But his words were lost as Kianna looked up at her savior. Devon had grabbed her and pulled her back. Her arms were against his chest, his arms tight around her waist, her eyes fixed on his, and his mouth only a inches away.

"Are you okay?" he asked, his voice low. His dark eyes gleamed with concern.

Her breath escaped her, not only because from her near-miss with the horse, but Devon's arms encapsulated her body. Kianna nodded. "I-I think so."

She wanted to move, to regain a respectful distance from him, but she couldn't. She was completely frozen in place.

Like a fly in a spiderweb.

She had been caught while fluttering by and would soon be dead.

Devon

A STRONG, MAGICAL, IMMORTAL WARRIOR RENDERED POWERLESS by a beautiful maiden. It sounded like the storyline of an impractical romance novel, but no matter how much he fought against it, Kianna's beautiful blue eyes had ensnared him.

Gods, was this torture? Or punishment? Had he done something terribly wrong that they now were sentencing him to the woes of a human life, one he could never be truly a part of?

Why send him to this stunning, kind, generous young woman with the excuse of protecting the world from her? Only to see him fail? To have a good laugh at his expense?

He had been a warrior of light for a long time, and he knew the gods could be cruel and heartless, but he had never seen it, never believed it.

Until now.

He couldn't hold in the desire inside him anymore. Without loosening his grip, Devon moved his hand up Kianna's back. He wanted to touch her skin, to cup her cheek ... His fingers grazed the nape of her neck, just above her dress line. Her body tensed, and she sucked in a sharp breath. His eyes flickered to her pink lips.

"It's time!" someone yelled right beside them.

Kianna jumped back two feet and looked everywhere but at him.

Around them, the crowd became agitated. Many people shouted, "it's time," and rushed away.

Devon frowned. "Time for what?"

Kianna looked up at him, but turned her gaze down again. "To light the lamps and make wishes."

The street filled with people holding the fabric lanterns.

He was still confused. "You don't have one?"

Kianna shook her head. "I don't have money to buy one."

Devon pressed his lips tight. He had already spent too much on her and her family. The book, the entry fee for the dance competition, which Kianna didn't know about, the money for the games ... it didn't make a dent in his savings, but how could he explain all these expenses if he was supposed to have nothing?

Yet, as he stared at Kianna and saw the longing in her pretty eyes, he knew he couldn't resist.

By now, he was sure that when it came to her, he couldn't resist anything.

"Wait here," he said, then ran to the nearest stand selling the lanterns. He bought eight lanterns. Holding them in one hand, he ran back to Kianna. "Come on." He grabbed her hand and pulled her toward the stand where her mother and Giles and his family were selling rice balls.

"There you are," Selina said. "I thought you two had gotten lost."

"Or disappeared," Cat said while coughing, which made her words hard to understand.

Devon frowned.

He was glad everyone was at the stand and he didn't have to hunt them down.

"Here." He passed a lantern to each person.

The kids yelled in excitement, Cat bowed her head, and her parents thanked him.

Ophelia took one in her hands and stared at him with big eyes. "Devon, you shouldn't have."

The sincerity in her voice, the eagerness of the kids, and the shock on Kianna's face as she took the second to last lantern from him. It all brought a smile to his lips. "I wanted to," he answered Ophelia, but his gaze was glued to Kianna.

The angel.

His angel.

Kianna's delicate brows turned down. "This is too much. You've been spending too much on us."

So, she had noticed. He had known she would.

Devon shrugged. "I get food and shelter from your family. I don't have any use for my money." He looked to the grinning faces of the group as they lit their lamps. "I think this is a good use, though." He gestured to the lamp in his hands. "What do I do now?"

Visibly holding a smile in, Kianna reached to his lantern and helped him light the wick inside it. The fabric filled with hot air, becoming a white balloon.

"Now, you make a wish and let it go." She closed her eyes, making her wish. A moment later, she opened her eyes again and pushed the lantern up. It floated alongside dozens, hundreds of other lanterns, filling the sky with bright, white dots that rivaled the stars. "Your turn."

He stared at his lantern. What would he wish for?

The thought came to him like lightning.

I wish for all of Kianna's wishes to come true.

With a little push, he let go of his lamp, certain there was no better wish he could make. He stared up at the sky, watching amazed as his lamp flew away and got lost amid all the other wishes.

"What did you wish for?" Calvin asked, his voice carrying a happy lilt.

Devon looked at the little boy. He opened his mouth to tell him and—

"He can't tell you that," Selina snapped.

Devon was confused. "Why not?"

"If you tell me your wish, it won't come true," Kianna explained.

They made wishes on fabric lamps, let it float into the sky, and if someone told their wishes, it wouldn't come true? What a strange thing. Alas, humans were strange creatures.

Because of the lanterns, the festival seemed to have paused for a moment. Every single person on the street or in the square watched the lamps floating away.

Humans were strange creatures indeed.

When the lamps became tiny little dots against the black canvas, easily confused with the stars, the crowd stirred. They lowered their eyes and resumed the festivities—chatting, laughing, walking, eating, dancing, and playing games.

Costumers approached the stand and the group went back to work. Even Kianna snaked around the table to help. She grabbed a small rice ball with a napkin and handed it to a little girl and her mother with a smile.

A smile that illuminated her entire face. A smile that made her more beautiful each time she offered it. A smile that hid her concerns and struggles. A smile that showed how strong she really was.

Once more struck by a very human feeling, Devon itched to ask Kianna to dance with him.

Mustering up courage, Devon inhaled a long breath.

The darkness slammed into him like a brick wall.

It was here. The darkness was here. So, so close.

He stared at Kianna, who had stepped back to rearrange the empty pans. She stilled and one of her hands flew to her chest.

Devon rushed to her side. "What is it?"

"I-I don't know," she whispered. "Something feels odd. It's like ... I don't know. It's crazy."

Could it be? Was she sensing the darkness too?

The dark wave advanced, pushing against Devon's senses.

Eyes wide, Kianna gasped.

The colorful lamps hung above the stand flickered.

What in the underworld …

"Kianna, listen to me." Devon clasped her shoulders and turned her to him so she was looking at him. "Stay here. No matter what happens, stay with your mother and the others. You understand?"

She inhaled a deep breath. The flames in the lamps flickered again. "What are you talking about?"

"It's nothing," he said. "Just … stay here. Okay?" She hesitated. "Okay?"

She nodded and whispered, "Okay."

Not wanting to waste a second more, Devon turned and ran. He slipped into an alley and sprinted toward the darkness. He had to find it. He had to stop it before it found Kianna, before it hurt her.

Outside the main street, the town was practically dead, but Devon still stuck to the alleys. Using his powers, he changed his human clothes to his reinforced black armor, and his sword appeared, strapped to his back.

He turned the last corner and halted in the middle of the intersection.

He could feel it. The thickness in the air. The pressure changing.

The darkness coming.

They stepped out of the shadows. Azerinthe. Little bastards with bodies resembling chimpanzees, with a short, stalky build and black, short fur, but the heads of eagles, with a bald top, no ears, sharp yellow eyes, and long beaks.

But the main difference was the razor-sharp teeth and the long, forked tongue inside that beak.

The demons advanced, grazing their claws on the ground.

Devon unsheathed his sword and spread his feet apart.

It was play time.

PRESENT

Kenna

I HAD COME BECAUSE I HAD PROMISED TO BRING THE KIDS TO the damn festival, but I couldn't lie; it was way more fun than I expected.

Lia had been so excited about me going out with friends that she left the car with me that morning. My only task was to take her to work.

"I won't be here when you get out," I said as I parked the car in front of the library.

She waved me off. "I'll just walk back," she said, as if walking thirty minutes on a hot spring day was nothing. I protested, but she insisted.

Carol, Sabrina, and Kevin were excited about it. They hopped off the school bus and slipped into the car, eager to go. I only shook my head and drove us to Willow Grove, which was about forty-five minutes away.

When we arrived, the festival had already started and the place was crammed with people of all ages, races. The sun beat down on us. Why did I put a jacket over my tee? I took it off and tied it around my waist.

Carol told me the festival was always held on this empty patch of land right beside an abandoned baseball field. There were carnival rides and games, food stands, and an open area with a small stage on the corner where a band played songs. The main street had been decorated with lanterns, and later the light parade would travel the strip of road.

Strings of white LED lights hung from stand to stand, on the arcade, and on the rides.

It was beautiful, contagious, warming.

The smell of popcorn, cotton candy, corndogs, and hot dogs added to the allure of the place.

I glanced around, amused and shocked at the same time. I had never been to such a place, or at least I didn't remember. I had heard about the circus, movie theaters, and carnivals. I had even watched TV, but until recently, enjoying those things had never been a reality.

Now ... now Lia and I were free. We had been hiding in Misty Hill for a month, and nothing had happened. The thought both thrilled me and filled me with dread.

Finally, we had gotten away. Finally, we had been able to hide.

But until when? In the end, Slater had always found us. No matter where we went, where we hid, he sent his lackeys after us. We only got away because he still underestimated my powers—thanks to Lia. If she hadn't instructed me to hide my full potential from him, he would have made better preparations. He would have made his place more secure. Put more guards around me.

We wouldn't have been able to escape so easily.

I was sure he would figure out I was more powerful than he imagined.

Just as I was sure this perfect little life would be taken from me. It would be ripped away, torn to pieces, destroyed and burned to the ground.

And I would be left hurting, crying, regretting.

"Earth to Kenna." Carol snapped her fingers in front of my face. "Where are you?"

I forced a smile. "Right here. I'm right here."

She arched an eyebrow at me, as if she didn't believe me. Thankfully, she didn't push it. Instead, she hooked her arm with mine. "Let's play that game." She steered me to a dance game booth.

There were four dance platforms, complete with a light-up mat and screen. Sabrina and Kevin occupied two of them —Sabrina seemed to know what she was doing, while Kevin went with the flow.

Carol pushed me toward one of the platforms, then took the other one.

"Ours is ending," Sabrina said, her eyes fixed on the screen in front of her. She followed the movements perfectly. "Wait and we can all dance together."

We didn't have to wait long. We all chose the same hip hop song and started at the same time. At first, I was a little tense dancing like that in the middle of a festival, but soon the song, the movements, and the excitement from my dance buddies filled my veins and I let it all out.

Carol whistled. "Girl, you've got some moves."

I chuckled. I had always loved dancing—classical ballet and contemporary the most—but I hadn't danced in years. I thought I had forgotten how. Apparently, all I need was a little nudge.

Kevin was the first out of the game, right after the second song started. Carol lost the game in the middle of the third song. They both cheered as Sabrina and I went on, dancing our hearts out.

I didn't think I had ever had this much fun before.

Sabrina and I went on for another six songs. She was kicked out of the game fifteen seconds before the tenth song ended. I finished it and won the game.

When I turned back, I was taken aback by the crowd that had gathered, watching us dance.

The man managing the booth walked up to me and brought me a small, white teddy bear. "You broke our record. Congratulations."

"Thanks," I whispered, taking the teddy bear from him. I walked down the platform and people patted my shoulders, congratulating me.

Kevin high-fived me. "That was awesome!"

"Yup." Carol nodded. "You're a pretty good dancer."

"Sabrina is too," I said, smiling at the young girl. She shrugged. "Here. I want you to have it."

Her blue eyes shone. She hesitated for a moment, as if unsure she should take it or not. But I pushed the bear into her chest. She wrapped her arms around it and smiled at me. "Thanks."

I glanced around. "What now?"

I shouldn't have said that. Sabrina, Kevin, and Carol meandered through the booths of the festival. We played dozens of games, ate cotton candy and hot dogs, watched musicians play and several dance groups perform, and walked and walked and walked.

I paused at a jewelry stand. My hands hovered over the simple, handcrafted necklaces and earrings, but there was one ring that called to me. It looked odd, with a silver band and a blue center. That ring seemed familiar, but not quite, and I couldn't explain it.

"The sun is going down," Carol said, tugging me forward. "It's almost time for the parade."

Around us, everyone talked about the parade, and most of them already walked toward main street, trying to get a good spot.

Kevin and Sabrina ran ahead of us, to save us a place, while Carol and I strolled up the street, arms hooked. At first, having Carol this close and always holding on to me had been awkward. But now, I was getting used to it, and to be honest, I kind of liked it.

"Thanks," I whispered.

She narrowed her eyes at me. "For?"

"For the tickets. For making me come."

Her mouth stretched into a knowing grin. "You had fun, didn't you?"

I nodded. "Like never before."

She squeezed my arm. "I'm glad."

It came out of nowhere, but with a force I hadn't felt in a long while. The darkness barreled into me like a crazed bull. Gasping, I skidded to a stop and pressed a hand to my chest.

"What happened?" Carol turned to me. "Are you okay?"

My senses weren't perfect, but I had honed them over the years, and from what I could tell, the darkness was outside of town, but advancing fast.

Coming this way.

Coming for me.

And Carol, Sabrina, and Kevin were with me.

I couldn't let them get hurt. I just couldn't.

I disentangled myself from Carol's hold. "I'm fine. I just … I think I need to go to the restroom." I pushed her toward the main street. "You go ahead with Sabrina and Kevin. I'll meet you guys in a few."

She frowned. "You sound odd. Are you sure you're okay?"

I rested a hand over my stomach and grimaced. "Yeah, I think all the food didn't sit well with me," I lied. "I'll be right there." I waved her off.

Carol hesitated but walked on. I watched as she weaved through the crowd, heading to where Sabrina and Kevin had gone.

A desperate feeling filled my veins. The darkness was here. Because of me. It had found me. If it caught me, my life here would be over. My friends could get hurt because of me.

I had to protect them. I had to save them.

Channeling my power, I spun on my heels and sprinted to the edge of the festival, where it was deserted as everyone was gathering around main street.

I halted in the middle of the parking lot and opened my senses. The darkness was closer, stronger. I could wait for it here, or I could go toward it, keep the danger far from the others.

From my friends.

No doubt in my mind, I raced toward the darkness. Past the parking lot, across another road, into a lot with an abandoned building.

I untied my jacket and put it on to protect my skin. Then, I inhaled deeply and called my powers. It filled my veins, pushed against my skin, asked for release.

A moment later, the demons stepped out of the shadows.

I froze.

These weren't Slater's demons or lackeys. I had never seen these demons before. Half their bodies were lizard-like, the other half catlike, with dark scales. Their eyes were a mix of red and yellow, like a river of lava, and their wide mouths were filled with hundreds of small, but sharp teeth.

A chill ran down my spine.

It didn't matter. They had come because of me. They had sensed me. I was a beacon to them.

And now, I had to kill them all.

Devon

MY MIND HAD BEEN TOO FULL OF NONSENSE LATELY—AND MY body full of human emotions. Because of that, I had been going out for runs more than once a day.

I was getting ready for my third run of the day, when I looked out the window. By now, I didn't even need to check the clock. I knew that every weekday at this time Sabrina and Kevin arrived at Kenna's house. In about half an hour, Carol would join them.

What was odd about this day was that Lia's car was in the driveway. Wasn't Lia at work? As far as I knew, she worked most weekdays from eight to five, and sometimes she worked Saturday mornings too.

Things got even odder when Kenna came out of the house with Sabrina and Kevin. The kids jumped up and down and talked animatedly, their voices loud, though I couldn't make out what they said, while Kenna shook her head, a smile touching her perfect mouth.

They piled in the car and drove away.

I tried ignoring them. I really did. But a tug cut through my chest, like a calling, or even magic, telling me to go after them. To follow and check on them.

In my long years, I had learned many things, and one of them was to never ignore the power of a calling.

Grumbling under my breath, I changed into jeans, a polo shirt, and boots, hopped into my car, and followed the tug. I caught up to Kenna as she stopped at the high school and picked up Carol.

Like magic, the tug died. From here, I would have to follow her on my own.

From the high school, they drove out of town.

To the festival.

Of course, the fucking festival.

I had gone there once, out of curiosity, and vowed to never go back again. Alas, here I was, following Kenna and her friends to that forsaken place.

I followed them a safe distance, so they wouldn't notice me. The volume of cars on the road, going to Willow Grove for the festival, was staggering, which made it easy to blend in. It was like everyone in the neighboring towns had left work early, just to go to the light festival.

I watched as they walked through the place, tasting food, stopping by the stands, chatting, and laughing.

The most surprising moment of the evening came when Kenna joined the others at the dancing game. Kevin and Carol tried their best, but both were out of the game soon. But Sabrina and Kenna persisted. I had to confess, I enjoyed watching them. Sabrina was good, but not as good as Kenna.

If I had to guess, I would have said Kenna had had at least ten years of dance lessons. The way her hands moved, her shoulders rolled, her hips swayed with the beat was impressive—and completely alluring.

I couldn't tear my eyes from her even if I tried.

I had to fight the urge to go to her, to watch her dancing from closer, until Sabrina lost and Kenna won.

The wide grin that spread on her face wasn't like any other smile I had seen from her before. She was happy. I could see it.

I could feel it.

From there, they went on.

It caught my attention when Kenna stopped by a handmade jewelry stand. She seemed entranced by the jewelry for some reason.

Carol called out to her, saying the sun was going down, which meant the light parade would start soon. Instantly, Kenna forgot about whatever attracted her to the jewelry and moved toward the main street with her friend.

Several steps back, I followed them.

Like a rolling wave in the distant ocean, the darkness washed over my senses.

I froze.

A few yards in front of me, Kenna froze too. My attention was divided between the incoming darkness, and the girl who seemed to be ditching her friend right before the festival's main attraction.

Kenna pushed Carol forward. Only after Carol walked on did Kenna turn around and move. She weaved through the crowd and I lost sight of her.

Where the fuck was she going?

Opening my senses, I searched for the darkness and for

Kenna. The darkness was still coming, tiptoeing near the edge of town, but I couldn't find Kenna. It wasn't easy to sense a person, and for some reason, she was harder than most.

I looked around, I walked a few steps to the right, to the left, but in the sea of heads in the dimming light, I couldn't find her.

But I knew where the others had gone.

I pushed through the crowd to the main street, looking for Carol, Sabrina, and Kevin. Since most people were still finding spots and settling for the parade, it was easy to find them.

Kevin saw me approaching. "Hey, Devon. You came? I thought you hated this kind of stuff."

I frowned. How did he know that about me? Did I let on more than I wanted to? Or was this kid just attentive?

I shook my head. I didn't have time to worry about time. "Where's Kenna?"

"She said she was going to the restroom," Carol said. "Why? What's the matter?"

Fuck.

"Stay here," I told them.

Something nagged at me as I dashed toward the restrooms. I was sure Kenna hadn't really gone to one, but where else could I look for her?

I skidded to a stop.

People bumped into me as they made their way to the main street.

She had stilled like I had when I felt the darkness. Moments later, she disappeared. Could she have felt it? Could she have gone toward it?

It couldn't be.

But my feet weren't listening to my brain. Step by step, they moved, toward the edge of the festival.

It couldn't be.

It couldn't.

My heartbeat sped up and my walk became a jog.

I took a step into the parking lot and slowed down. Across the parking lot, a woman walked in the festival's direction. A woman with long, blond hair.

I narrowed my eyes.

What ...

It took me two heartbeats to realize it was Kenna. She was the young woman marching back to the festival.

But her hair was blond and her jacket was ripped with a few red stains.

Blood.

She was bleeding.

I raced to her.

Kenna jumped back and raised her hands, as if she would attack me, or defend herself, but once she saw it was me, she lowered her arms and her face paled more.

"Devon," she whispered, putting her hand over her chest. "You scared me."

"What happened?" I looked her over. Her jacket was torn around her right upper arm and her chest, but only the former seemed to be bleeding. "Are you okay?" Despite her injuries, I couldn't shake the fact that her hair had gone from brown to blond in a matter of minutes. "What happened to your hair?"

She picked up a loose strand and brought it in front of her face. "Shit." She waved a trembling hand, dismissing my question, and walked right past me. "It's ... nothing. Just forget you saw it."

"How can I forget it?" I caught up with her. She really wanted to go back to the festival looking like that? Even if people didn't know about her hair, someone was bound to see her wound. Wait, was that a limp? "You're hurt. What happened?"

Kenna took two more steps—yes, she was limping a little —and turned back to face me. "This is none of your ... concern."

I opened my mouth to argue, but shut my lips as her eyes met mine. So bright blue, so enchanting. Suddenly, I was a dumb fly caught in a spiderweb. "Kenna," I whispered, taking a step closer to her. I wanted her to tell me what had happened, why she was in such state. I wanted her to let me help her.

I reached for her.

"There you are!" Carol's voice was like a bucket of cold water.

Kenna took a large step back. She turned to Carol, a faint smile in her lips. "Were you looking for me?"

Sabrina and Kevin ran after Carol, but the three of them skidded to a stop and stared at Kenna a second later.

"What happened to you?"

"What's up with your hair?"

"Did you just dye it?"

"Is that ... blood?"

The three of them unleashed a series of questions, the ones I wanted to ask, but Kenna dismissed them too.

"No time for that," she said. "I was on my way to find you. We have to go."

Kevin's face fell. "Why? The parade just started and we didn't have a chance to see it yet."

"I know. I'm sorry." Kenna fished out her cell phone from

her pocket. "My mother called. She needs me home, so we need to go. Sorry."

I frowned. She was lying.

I wanted to go after her, to confront her, to make her answer everything, but the way she ushered her friends back toward the parking lot, trying to hide her limp and her shaking hands, made me pause.

I would confront her, just not now.

Puzzled, I watched as they hopped into her car and drove away.

Only then I remembered the darkness and the demons that had been lurking around the town's edge before I bumped into Kenna. I opened my senses, trying to pinpoint their location so I could go after them and kill them all.

But the darkness and the demons were gone.

PAST

Kianna

KIANNA STARED DOWN AT HER SHAKING HANDS. PERHAPS IT HAD been the heat of the moment, the excitement of the night. After all, it wasn't always that she had such a great time—mostly because of Devon—but she was sure she had felt something back at the festival.

Something odd, something different.

A thick feeling like a sea of oil stirring inside her, coming for her, reaching its dark tendrils to her.

A shudder rocked her body. Kianna dropped her hands and stared out at the lake, to the faint reflection of the moon on the water's surface. It was the middle of the night and everyone was sleeping. Everyone but her. After tossing and turning for hours, thinking and agonizing about this wicked feeling, Kianna threw her blankets away, put on a thin overdress over her nightgown, marched down the hill, and took her spot on the bench under the cherry tree.

Now, if only she could make her hands stop shaking and her breathing slow, she could relax and go back to sleep.

A shadow fell to her left. Kianna's heart raced. "Who's there?"

"It's just me," Devon said, as he walked closer to her.

The moonlight gave his face a pale glow, making him look like a dark god. Maybe the god of death? He had the characteristics she had read in novels—stoic, strong, tall, dark hair, face cut with sharp angles, and mysterious. The god of death was always a popular character. In some books, he was the savvy villain; in others, he was the cursed lover. Could Devon be anything like that?

Kianna shook her head, expelling such thoughts from her mind. "You startled me."

"I'm sorry." Devon stopped a few feet from the bench. "What are you doing out here?"

Kianna shrugged. "I couldn't sleep. What about you?"

"Same." He took a step closer. "Is it okay if I sit down?"

Kianna scooted to one side of the bench. "Of course."

Devon sat down beside her. "Thanks." He glanced out to the water. "It's peaceful here at night."

Kianna chuckled. "You mean, it's peaceful here when the kids are sleeping."

Devon laughed.

Kianna couldn't help but noticed his face brightened whenever he smiled. Her stomach tightened. Grasping for another subject, Kianna frowned. "Hm, what happened tonight? I mean, back at the festival? Where did you go?"

He had worried her. He vehemently told her to stay with

her family, then disappeared. She had thought he would come back soon, but he never did. The festival ended, they dismantled the stand, packed away their things, and came home without any sign or note from him.

That was the other reason she hadn't been asleep, but she didn't want to admit that even to herself.

Devon ran a hand over his hair, messing up his ponytail a little. "I ... I thought I saw a band of thieves going around the festival. I went to find the village guards to arrest them."

Kianna narrowed her eyes. "But ... you weren't back all night. Was it hard to find the guards?" She was sure she had seen a few guards strolling up and down the festival.

"Yes, it was," Devon said quickly. "But it was even harder to locate the band of thieves after I first lost them. Since the guards thought I was playing a joke on them, they wouldn't let me leave until we found them."

"So you did find them? And the guard arrested them?"

Devon nodded. "Yes. We found them in an alley, escaping the festival with their pockets full."

She watched him for a moment. She had never thought he would be the kind to go out of his way to aid strangers. Well, he had helped her and her family many, many times, but they weren't really strangers anymore, were they?

"That's good," she whispered.

Despite herself, her gaze landed on her hands, folded in her legs. Kianna wasn't shaking anymore, but the memories of that dark feeling still lingered. Would she ever be able to go back to sleep, or would that feeling scare her to the afterlife?

Devon twisted his body her way. "I can see something is bothering you. What is it?"

Slowly, Kianna lifted her hands again. "I'm not sure," she

said, a little startled that she wanted to tell him. "Back at the festival, right before you left, I felt something." She pressed her hands to her chest. "Right here. Something ..." She shook her head. "I'll sound like a crazy person. Never mind."

Surprising her, Devon reached over and grabbed her hands, pulling them away from her. He cradled her hands in his. "Whatever you say, I can assure you, I won't ever think you're a crazy person." His dark eyes stared into hers, so intense, so raw. Those kind of looks had been few, but right now, she found herself wanting more of them.

"I'm afraid you'll stop looking me like that if I tell you," she whispered.

One of his hands moved up. His fingers slid across her cheek, and he cupped her face. His hand wasn't as callused as she thought it would be, and she found herself leaning into his touch.

"Impossible," he said, his voice low. He leaned into her. "Kianna, I—"

"Kianna!"

Kianna jumped up from the bench, almost knocking Devon away and falling on her wobbly feet. "Y-yes!" She glanced up the hill and found Calvin on the front porch, hugging his blanket. She raced up the hill. "What is it? Why are you up?"

"I had a nightmare," the little boy said.

"You're okay now." Kianna pulled him to her arms. "Want to talk about it?"

She felt Devon's presence a few steps behind her. Of course, he would have followed her. Why wouldn't he? It wasn't as if she had been running from him or whatever almost happened by the cherry tree.

Calvin shook his head against her stomach.

Devon knelt beside them. "Hey, you know what I do when I have a nightmare? I drink a cup of warm milk, then I lay back in bed and think of the good things that happened the previous day. With the festival, I bet you have plenty of good things to think about, don't you?"

Calvin nodded. "It's just ..." He glanced at Kianna. "The monster will get you if I close my eyes."

"W-what?" Kianna asked.

"My nightmare," Calvin said. "Monsters came into the village and searched for you. They wanted to kill you."

She glanced at Devon. There was a deep line between his brows.

"Is it the first time you had a nightmare like that, Calvin?" he asked.

Calvin nodded.

"It's okay," Kianna said quickly. "I'm fine. No monster will get me, okay?" It wasn't the first time Calvin had woken up in the middle of the night because of a nightmare and searched for her, but it was the first time he had ever mentioned monsters. Coming for her? What a wild imagination he had. "Come on." Kianna patted his back. "I'll make you some warm milk, then put you back in bed. Okay?"

Calvin nodded again. She slipped her hand in his and tugged him into the house. Beside her, Devon rose to his feet, the frown still in place.

"Good night, Calvin," Devon said, his voice tight.

Kianna glanced at Devon. "Thank you," she mouthed.

Devon dipped his chin in acknowledgment. "Good night."

His eyes remained locked on hers for a moment longer, then he spun around and marched around the house, probably to the barn where he still slept.

"Come on." Kianna ushered Calvin inside the manor and focused on taking care of her little brother, purposefully pushing all thoughts of Devon away from her mind.

PRESENT

Devon

I STARED AT THE BOARD IN FRONT OF ME.

Newspaper clippings of demons sightings, or strange attacks that only the other warriors and I knew had been demons, and places where I had fought them nearby.

Notes of what I could remember from my nightmares.

A list of ideas of what could have happened in the past and why the gods had punished me.

A picture of the ring I carried on a chain around my neck.

And now: photos of Kenna and Lia, and a list of all the visions I had had when touching Kenna. Also, a scribbled note about her blond hair last night at the festival.

Lines of yarn connected everything relevant—red for demons, blue for humans.

I had started the board years ago, when I was first brought back from the underworld with only the ring for a clue. The board started as a three by four, and I had been determined to fill it fast and figure this fucking curse out.

Time passed and I barely covered a small corner of it.

But since Kenna and Lia had shown up, I had added two more boards side by side, and if things continued evolving this way, I would soon have to buy another.

To be honest, I would rather figure everything out before that, and be done with it.

I glanced out the window. From the guest bedroom, I could see the small window on the side of the kitchen and a corner of the porch and the backyard. Kenna had been active since early this morning, going around the house, though I had no idea what she had been up to. The only time it was easy to tell what she was doing was when she showed up on the back porch with a towel bunched up atop of her head. A few minutes later, she walked by the window—with her hair dark brown again. This time, she had added blue streaks to it.

Once more I wondered why she dyed her hair. What was she trying to hide? Was Lia in on it too?

I couldn't sit still. Not when I knew she was a few yards away, and she could have the answers I needed. She had to have them, right? At least a couple of them. Something, anything to point me in the right direction.

I needed some fucking direction.

I went to her house. Lia had left earlier, probably for work, but for some reason, I wanted to speak with only Kenna for now.

I rang the bell and waited.

Not thirty seconds later, Kenna opened the door.

"Devon, what are you doing here?"

The words flew past my throat but got stuck on my tongue. What? Had I really planned to come here and ask who she was? If she was in on it with the gods? If she was part of my punishment? If she knew anything about demons?

What if this was all a coincidence and I scared her away?

I really didn't want that.

I cleared my throat and pointed to the bandage peeking out from underneath the short sleeves of her shirt. "You were hurt last evening. I wanted to check if you're all right now."

Kenna narrowed her bright blue eyes at me. The newly dyed brown hair brought out the beautiful hue of her eyes more, but from the little I had seen, she was still lovely with blond hair.

What the fuck was I thinking?

"I'm clumsy. You didn't know that?" She averted her eyes. "I fell and scratched my arm. It's okay now."

Was she seriously trying to feed me that bullshit? "What about your chest?"

She took a step back as if preparing to defend herself. Or run. "What about it?"

"There was a scratch on your jacket right across your chest," I said. She opened her mouth, but no words came out. I took that as an opportunity and stepped inside her house. "What about your hair? I'm sure it was brown yesterday afternoon. Then suddenly it was blond during the festival."

She retreated. "How do you know what my hair looked like yesterday? Are you spying on me?"

I closed the door behind me. "We're neighbors. There's a high chance I'll see you whenever I step outside." I stalked after her as she retreated toward the kitchen. "So? What happened to your hair?"

She shook her head and whispered, "You wouldn't understand."

In the kitchen, she rounded the island, putting it in

between us. Was she afraid of me? I had no plans of attacking her, but I wouldn't let her off the hook so easily.

"Try me," I said.

"Why? It's not like it matters to you."

I frowned. What did I know about this girl? She and her mother had moved here out of nowhere—I was never able to find out where they had lived before. Their last name was Jones, but for some reason, I thought they were lying. Kenna would soon be nineteen and hadn't finished high school yet. She didn't even try applying for school and finishing it. She was going for the GED directly. Lia had found a job at the library, but her resume was a big blank. She had no prior working experience. They seemed to be hiding something, but at the same time, they allowed people to get close—like Carol, Sabrina, Kevin, and me.

Then, there were the glimpses I got each time I touched Kenna. Had those really happened or was I imagining things? I had to find a way of touching her again right now.

"What? Your grandmother is a mermaid and every time she gets wet, her hair changes color? And you got that from her?" I was being beyond ridiculous, but in a world that wasn't supposed to exist, mermaids weren't that far from demons and divine warriors.

She stared me, one eyebrow cocked up. "Have you been drinking?"

"I rarely drink."

"Then what? Drugs? Because something must be wrong with your mind. Mermaids? Really?" Shaking her head, she opened the cabinet and grabbed a box of popcorn.

I frowned. "Hungry?"

"Not me." She grabbed three sealed packets from the box. Then, she pointed to the backdoor. "But they are."

I glanced at the door just as it opened.

"Hey," Sabrina said as she walked in. Kevin followed her inside and waved at me. "Are we having a party?"

Kenna ripped the plastic from one of the packets and stuck it in the microwave. "Why do you think we're having a party?"

Sabrina gestured to me. "Because he's here."

"Just ignore him," Kenna muttered.

Kevin grabbed a bottle of juice from the fridge, while Sabrina opened a cabinet and grabbed a big round bowl.

"Are you two here all the time now?" I asked before I could measure my words. It was baffling to see the two siblings acting as if they lived here too.

"Pretty much," Kevin said.

"Better than staying at the damn house," Sabrina muttered.

"Hey!" Kenna pointed a wooden spoon at Sabrina. "What did I tell you? Mind your language."

Sabrina rolled her eyes.

What the fuck was going on here? When she first took the siblings in, I was touched. Nobody had even been caring for them; it was kind of refreshing and heartwarming. But why was Kenna acting like their mother or an older sister? Did she really care about these strangers that much? What had they done to earn her affection?

"Oh, tell her about it." Sabrina nudged Kevin's arm.

Kenna grabbed the first packet of popcorn from the microwave. "Tell me what?"

Sabrina took the packet from her, opened it, and poured the popcorn into the bowl. "He had a nightmare with you in it."

"A nightmare?" Kenna put another packet of popcorn on the microwave. "Want to tell me about it?"

Looking at the popcorn in the bowl in front of him, Kevin shrugged. "Not really."

"He woke up in the middle of the night crying," Sabrina said.

Kenna stilled. "What? Kevin, tell me about it."

He lifted his gray eyes to her. "You were in an alley at night, and monsters with dark, shiny skin, huge claws, and sharp teeth surrounded you." He gulped. "I don't want to talk about the rest."

Monsters with dark, shiny skin, huge claws, and sharp teeth? Surrounding Kenna? Was Kevin dreaming about demons?

Kenna stared at Kevin, her eyes big, her body rigid. Then, she shook her head once and rolled her shoulders. She reached over the island and patted his hand. "Don't worry, Kev. I'm all right, as you can see. No monster will get me."

He rolled his eyes and shoved a handful of popcorn into his mouth.

"Have you ever dreamed about the monsters before?" I asked, curious. I hadn't seen which demons had been in Willow Grove last night, but they could have been the ones Kevin described. But why hadn't they advanced? Why had the darkness disappeared?

I glanced at Kenna.

"No," Kevin said. "Never." He shuddered. "And I hope I never do again."

Kenna fished the other popcorn packet from the microwave. "It's all over now. You're awake. No monster can get to me, okay?"

Kevin nodded, then shoved more popcorn into his mouth.

She waved the wooden spoon to the siblings. "Save some of that for Carol. She'll be here soon." She turned and put the third packet in the microwave. She glanced at me. "We're going to watch a movie. You're welcome to stay, if you want."

I hesitated. I stared at her, my mind spinning with all that was happening.

"Are you staying or not?" Sabrina asked.

I blinked. "Yeah. Yes, I'm staying."

How could I not when all the pieces of the puzzle seemed to be hidden in this kitchen.

Around these people.

Sabrina groaned. "You better make more popcorn."

PAST

Devon

DESPITE ALL THAT HAD HAPPENED, THERE WERE DAYS WHEN Devon really doubted the gods had sent him to the right girl. Days like today, when Kianna had several errands to run in town and he tagged along. When she did selfless things like stopping by the apothecary and handing a freshly baked cherry pie to Laila, her former maid. Taking old clothes from her siblings to an orphanage. Helping an elderly woman with her heavy basket. Giving little cookies to a homeless child.

It was impossible to think she was evil, or that she would turn evil. She was kind and caring. The gods had to be mistaken. Devon prayed the gods had made a mistake.

But if they did, his mission would end and he would never see her again.

Devon couldn't bear thinking about that.

He had to stay here, stay with Kianna.

He was done pretending he didn't know what was going on. He might not be human or have experienced human feelings for centuries, but he knew what feeling was blooming in his chest.

Love.

He was falling for Kianna, and he could do nothing to stop it.

Truth was, he didn't want to stop it.

When she finished her errands, Kianna informed him she was ready to go home.

"Are you done too?" she asked, her bright blue eyes twinkling.

It took him a second to remember he had lied and said he also had errands in the village, so he could come with her. "Yes, I'm done."

They left the village, following the dirt road to the manor.

Thunder rumbled in the distance. Kianna looked up at the darkening sky. "I thought the rain would hold until this evening."

Devon glanced up. The dark clouds were rolling in fast, heavy and ready. Thunder boomed over them, closer this time. "The storm is moving in fast."

"We better run, then," Kianna said, lifting her skirt an inch.

Two seconds later, he felt a fat drop on his hand.

Grumbling under his breath, Devon took off his thin jacket and put it over Kianna's head as the sky fell.

"This way." Devon caught her arm and steered her toward the trees flanking the road. The trees were full of blossoms and leaves, creating a canopy to protect them from the rain. He gestured to a branch bent low over the grass, almost like a bench. "Here."

Taking off his jacket, Kianna sat down. She glanced to the rain slamming the road. "I hope it doesn't last long."

It looked like a summer downpour—hard and brief. It would clear up, at least enough so they could go back to the house without getting soaked. However, they would certainly get their feet muddy.

"It should stop soon," Devon reassured her.

"Here." She extended his jacket back to him. "Thank you."

He took his jacket back but didn't put it on. "You didn't get wet?"

She shook her head, her blond hair beautiful as always. "No, thanks to you." She tilted her head at him. "Are you going to stand there until the rain stops?"

Devon frowned. "I don't know."

She patted the spot on the branch beside her. "It might take a while. You better rest."

Devon hesitated. It was one thing to know he was falling for her, but another not to keep his distance, to respect boundaries. The closer he got to her, the harder it would be to stop himself from touching her.

It wasn't wise.

Yet, when she patted the branch again, he didn't resist.

Devon sat down but kept a good foot away from her. "It would have been a nice day, if it weren't for the rain."

Kianna leaned back, a soft smile on her pink lips. "It was a good day. It still is." She turned her eyes to him. "Since we have some time, why don't you tell me something?"

"Like what?"

"I don't know." Her pretty eyes narrowed. "You don't remember anything? From before?"

From before being a warrior? "No."

"I'm sorry," she whispered. "It must be hard, not knowing. Your family must be worried about you."

"I'm fine right here," he said, his voice low but firm, his eyes trained on her. If only she knew how true that statement was.

Blinking, Kianna looked out at the rain again. "When I was little, I loved rainy days, because my father didn't have to work, so he played in the rain with me all day."

Devon knew losing her father had been hard on them, but he was glad she had those memories to hold on to. Calvin and Selina had been young when he died and barely remembered him.

A gentle breeze blew past them, carrying a few strands of her hair over her shoulder. The scent of sweet, delicious cherry invaded his nostrils and filled his mind.

By the gods ...

He jumped up, putting space between them, before he surrendered to her perfume and did something stupid. His back to her, he inhaled deeply, welcoming the refreshing scent of rain into his lungs.

"Did I say something wrong?"

Devon cleared his throat before glancing at her over his shoulder. "What? No. I just thought the rain was stopping."

Please, gods, make this rain stop. I beg you.

As if they had listened to him for once, the rain softened to a patter before stopping. The road had turned to mud.

Devon looked back at Kianna's boots. They were the nice kind, with a delicate fabric and a low heel. The mud would ruin her shoes, and right now, her family couldn't afford new ones.

Devon crouched in front of her.

"What happened?" Kianna asked, her eyes wide.

"You'll ruin your boots if you walk home now." He reached for her hand and tugged her forward. "I'll give you a piggyback ride."

Kianna frowned. "That's not necessary."

"It's either that, or taking off your boots and walking in the mud barefoot."

She stared at him. "It'll be heavy ..."

He was sure she was as light as a feather. He tugged on her arm once more. "Just come."

Her cheeks reddening, Kianna stood and let Devon wrap her arms around his neck. He tried keeping his mind blank as he reached back and grabbed her legs, his fingers splayed around her thighs.

Even more enticing than that was her chest pressed against his back, her breath on his neck, and her cherry scent enveloping him again.

By the gods ...

Devon counted to twenty before focusing on one step after another and getting them home. "Hold on tight," he said.

And she did. Kianna held on to him as if her life depended on it.

PRESENT

Kenna

WHEN I NEEDED A BREAK FROM STUDYING FOR THE GED exam and repairing the house, I went for a walk. We had been here for six weeks now. I still felt like there was so much to discover, even though the town was the size of a button.

During my walks, I met some of the shop owners, greeted the elderly man who was always seated on the bench in the main square, reading a newspaper, had to flee from a hose shower while a middle-aged lady cleaned the sidewalk in front of her house, and jumped out of my skin when dogs barked from behind fences.

It was a quaint and quiet town.

And that worried me.

The demons had sensed me two towns over. Wouldn't they find me here? Wouldn't they come for me and hurt everyone here? Shouldn't Lia and I leave before that could happen?

I hadn't told Lia about the attack the other night. She would freak out on me and forbid me from leaving the house, but I doubted she would want to leave town.

"We've been at this for six weeks now," I said to her while we had lunch together. It had been noon when I started back home. Not eager to be alone in that house, I made my way to the library and invited Lia to lunch. "You know it won't last forever." Although, I wished it would.

"You have to think positive," she said between bites of her salad. I had brought her to a diner on the corner of the main square to eat burgers, not salad, and yet, she wouldn't quit her diet, the same one she had been on the past two years—and hadn't lost one pound yet. "Everything is going so well. I have a job, and you have friends. You'll pass your GED and apply to college."

I frowned. College. There were no good four-year colleges in the area, just a bunch of community colleges. "I don't even know why I'm studying for the GED. It's not like I'm going to go to college." If I wanted to go to a better, bigger university, I would have to move away, and stay in a particular area for at least four years.

If staying here for six weeks made me nervous, imagine four years.

It wasn't practical, not with our lives.

Sooner or later, we would have to move, and I was hoping we did it sooner, before anyone in this town got hurt.

Lia kept talking about college and what majors would be best, as if I hadn't said anything. I let her ramble. She was too enamored by our lives to remember we had a bad guy and his demons looking for us.

They wouldn't rest until they found us.

Until they found me.

After lunch, I made my way home. The sky had darkened considerably since I had gone into the diner with Lia, and the thick clouds seemed like they would burst open at any moment. I rushed my steps, but the tension in my body only increased.

To distract my mind and nerves, I tried thinking of good things. Like how Sabrina mentioned her school fundraiser and how she would have to work a couple of hours a week at the pet rescue center in town. Play with cuddly dogs for free? I would love to help with that. Once she got to my house after school this afternoon, I would ask her when she would like to go. I bet even Carol would want to join us.

Then, I thought that I should stop by the bakery and buy some cupcakes to give to Sabrina and Kevin. They were always complaining that they had found Lia and me, but the other foster kids at their house had no one. Though I couldn't take care of all of them, I could send them cupcakes. Unfortunately, I was terrible in the kitchen, so I would have to buy them.

I turned the corner, heading for the bakery, when the rain started.

"Shit," I mumbled, racing toward the nearest awning. I hid under the red fabric in front of a self-service laundry place, and looked out as the rain fell in fat, heavy drops.

I stuck my hand out from under the awning. Besides being strong, the rain was too damn cold.

I let out a sigh. I could run home, get soaked, then take a hot shower and put on clean, dry clothes.

But did I want to?

I looked at the dark sky. Who knew when this damn rain would stop? If I stayed here, I could wait until tomorrow.

Damn it.

All right, I was going.

I took a step forward and paused as a sleek black car stopped at the curb.

A fraction of the passenger window came down.

Devon's eyes met mine. "Get in."

Devon

AFTER MY MEETING WITH RYDER, I WENT DRIVING FOR A couple of hours. Nothing like speeding down backroads and hearing the engine roaring to alleviate the tension in my muscles.

During my weekly report, I told Ryder a lot about my investigation—the visions I had when touching Kenna, the demons that had disappeared in Willow Grove, her hair changing colors, and more. I had hoped he would see my progress and would reveal something, a bigger clue that would steer me in the right direction. But the warrior had been as quiet as a mime. He didn't even say yes or no, or show any emotions so I could measure his silence.

Nothing. He had given me nothing.

Was this part of my punishment?

I punched the wheel. What the fuck had I done to deserve so much pain and frustration? Why had I been sent to the fiery pits of the underworld and brought back to this world to live like a fucking human?

It was just past noon when I turned back into town. The heavy rain that had been threatening to come down since mid-morning finally showed up, dumping its rage on the town.

I slowed down and cruised past the main square.

As if my eyes were trained to find her, I glanced ahead and saw Kenna cowering underneath the red awning of the laundry place. Had she been caught in the rain unprepared?

My body tensed again and I sped up.

I wouldn't stop. I wouldn't stop. I wouldn't—

Who was I kidding?

I stopped the car beside her, the wheels touching the curb, so I could get closer to her, and lowered a little of the passenger window. Kenna stared at me, her eyes glinting with suspicion.

"Get in," I told her.

She hesitated but rushed forward. Thankfully, the awning reached to the middle of the sidewalk, providing good coverage for her. To help, I opened the door of my car. She hopped in and closed the door.

I reached back and handed her a hand towel I always had in there. "Here."

She took the towel and patted her arms. "Thanks."

I pulled away from the curb. "Want me to drop you off somewhere, or were you going home?"

"Home," she said, her voice low.

I started that way. Here, in this closed space, I was aware of her. Of how her wet, light blue blouse clung to her arms and chest. Of how her hair, now brown with pink streaks, was a little damp, framing her beautiful face. Of her sweet, delicious cherry scent.

I inhaled through my mouth.

Another thing I couldn't help but notice was how the hair of her arms and neck stood on end.

I extended my arm and turned the hot air up. "This might help."

"Thanks," she muttered.

"No problem."

She didn't say anything else on the way home, but the silence wasn't uncomfortable. It was just charged. Tense. As if we both had too many things on our minds, too many things we wanted to talk about, but couldn't find the right words.

Before I could think of anything to say, we arrived on our street. I pulled the car up to her driveway, the closest I could get to her porch, and put the car in park.

"Here," she said, returning the hand towel.

I took it from her, my fingers brushing hers. A jolt of electricity ran up my arm and a vision clouded my sight.

I was seated beside the blonde girl on a low tree branch. A breeze blew past us, her hair moved with it. She turned her face.

I would see her; I would see her face. I would know who she was.

But before her face could register, the vision broke.

I blinked and stared at Kenna's narrowed eyes. "Are you okay?"

"Yeah," I said. I pulled back a little, but I couldn't strip my eyes from her.

That brown hair. It was fake. She had blond hair and I knew it. Was she the girl from my visions? I only saw them when I touched her. It was the only explanation I had. I was ninety-nine percent sure, but I wouldn't say anything until I had proof.

How the fuck would I find proof?

"Thanks ... for the towel, and for the ride."

"You're welcome."

She opened the door and raced out of the car. The rain had lessened since I picked her up, but it still wet her some as she ran up the porch steps to her house's front door.

For some reason, I wished I had stopped her. I wished I could have told her to stay and talk to me. I wanted to touch her again and hold on to her until I could see the face of the blonde girl clearly. I wanted to ask her who she was running from.

But what if I did all that, and the next day, she and Lia were gone? I couldn't risk it. Not yet.

With a low exhale, I pulled out of her driveway and drove into mine, while thinking what I would have to do to get invited to dinner at their house later this evening.

PAST

Kianna

The storm had stopped, but it had brought an unusually cold night to the farm. Before putting the kids to bed, Ophelia and Kianna lit the fireplaces in their rooms to keep warm.

Kianna lay in her bed, under her thick blankets, and despite being tired from walking back and forth from the village, then helping the kids with their lessons, making dinner, and cleaning up, Kianna couldn't fall asleep.

She couldn't stop thinking about the man sleeping in the barn in this cold. There were no fireplaces there, and he probably didn't have a thick blanket either.

It was okay. He would be okay. He would survive the night, and tomorrow she could hand him a couple more blankets.

Thunder echoed through the house.

Kianna sat up in her bed. Was it going to rain more? The temperature would drop too.

Giving in, she threw her blanket aside. She put on a jacket over her nightgown, grabbed a nice blanket from the linen closet, and headed downstairs.

Kianna walked out of the back door and yelped, almost dropping the blanket.

Devon got up from the bench along the wall. "Are you okay?"

"Y-yes," she said, hugging the blanket tighter. "What are you doing here?"

He sat back down, his eyes on the dark horizon. "I couldn't sleep." He was fully dressed, but his jacket was the same as before—too thin for this crazy weather.

Kianna handed him the blanket. "Here. I thought you might be cold."

He turned his dark eyes to her. "Worried about me?"

Kianna clicked her tongue. "Not likely." Why she was being this hostile so suddenly? He had kept her company while she ran her errands, walked to and from the village, lent her his jacket when it rained, and gave her a piggyback ride home after the rain. Overall, they had spent a good day together. With a huff, she sat down on the bench beside him. "Why couldn't you sleep? Was it because of the cold?"

Devon wrapped the blanket around his shoulders. "I don't think so. I just lay down and my mind wouldn't stop."

Kianna hated how curious she was about him, but she couldn't stop the words from forming. "What were you thinking about?"

He stared at her and despite the darkness around them, she could feel the intensity of his gaze on her. "This and that," he said, as if that was a good enough answer.

"I couldn't sleep either," she revealed, though she wouldn't tell him why she couldn't sleep.

More thunder cut through the sky, bringing in a chilly breeze.

Kianna shivered.

"Here." Devon scooted closer to her and stretched the blanket over both their shoulders. He tightened it until her shoulder was buried in the side of his chest. "That's better."

She glanced up at him. He was so, so close. If she stretched her back a little bit more, her lips would touch his. Frowning, she snapped her head forward and fixed her sight on the horizon.

This wasn't right. She was a lady. She shouldn't be pressed to a man she barely knew. To any man, for that matter, especially if he wasn't her fiancé or husband.

She should move. She should scoot away. She should go back to bed.

Instead, she relaxed beside him and whispered, "Thank you."

PRESENT

Kenna

THE EXPLOSION OF THUNDER SHOOK THE HOUSE.

Cursing, I sat up in my bed. Holy shit, this storm. It hadn't stopped raining since earlier that day. In fact, it had only gotten worse as the night progressed.

I hated when it rained like that. The flash of lightning and the sound of the thunder reminded me of the nights spent locked up at Slater's place. If it wasn't the rain, then the booms I'd heard and the light I'd seen had been the battles Slater raged against his enemies and his subordinates—sometimes, against me.

I tried lying back down. I even put on my earphones and played music loud to drown out the sound. I pulled my blanket over my head, so I wouldn't see the lightning flashes. But there wasn't much I could do when I could feel the damn thing.

Giving up on sleep, I threw my blankets to the side and headed downstairs. Staying up and consciously hearing and seeing the rain wasn't the best idea, but it was much better than being in my bed, trying to ignore it, and only feeling more scared and perturbed in the process.

In the kitchen, I grabbed a glass from the drying rack and filled it up with water. I almost dropped the glass when thunder shook the house again.

"Holy shit," I muttered.

This was ridiculous. I wasn't a kid anymore. I couldn't be afraid of storms, even if it was because of bad memories. This fear was unreasonable.

There was only one way I knew how to win against fear— to face it.

Inhaling deeply, I opened the kitchen door and stepped out onto the back porch. A bright flash of light rolled through the sky, followed by loud thunder. I jumped out of my skin, but stayed there, at the edge of the porch, just out of the rain, forcing myself to face it, to overcome it.

A new sound reached my ears between the lightning and the thunder.

A scream.

No, a roar.

I glanced around, trying to find what animal was doing that.

The roar came again.

My head whipped to Devon's house.

It was coming from inside.

Lightning and thunder flashed once more, but this time, I barely moved as I waited for another sign, another scream.

A moment later, the roar came back, followed by a loud crash.

I didn't think.

I ran into the rain, jumped over the fence, and rushed to his house. Shit, the backdoor was locked. I called my power, a piece of cake because of all the darkness around me. I had never done something like this, but besides breaking down the door, it was the only thing I could do. I sent my darkness inside the lock and molded it around the pins, forcing it to move with my will. A faint click sounded, muffled by the storm, and I turned the knob.

The door opened.

Another roar chilled my spine.

I raced into the house and up the stairs.

I halted beneath the doorframe and watched as Devon thrashed in his bed, groaning and breathing hard. His arms moved to the side, and he hit the nightstand, almost knocking it over.

He screamed again.

Careful with the shards on the floor—what once was a lamp was now fallen beside the wall, a million pieces of glass spread around the room—I rushed to him.

"Devon," I called. He didn't stop moving and grunting. Sitting down beside him, I grabbed his shoulders. "Devon! Wake up!"

He lunged at me. Teeth bared, he pressed my shoulders down on his bed, his body hovering over mine. Fear filled my veins as I realized that, like this, he looked dangerous. A monster. Someone who could hurt me.

Then, he opened his dark eyes and blinked.

"Kenna?" Finally aware of what was going on, Devon retreated to the other side of the bed. "What are you doing here?"

Swallowing the fear lodged in my throat, I sat up. "I heard

screams and a crash." I pointed to the lamp broken on the floor. "I thought something was wrong. I'm sorry. I shouldn't have barged in."

He ran a shaking hand over his distraught face. "I-it's okay."

Then I realized two things: Devon was shirtless, and even in the dim darkness of the room, I could see all the muscles in his chest and shoulders. And my arms and hair were a little wet from running in the rain.

I jumped up, afraid of wetting his sheets. "I'm sorry. For barging in, and for sitting on your bed." I took a step back. "I-I should go."

"Wait," he said, standing from his bed. He grabbed a t-shirt and pulled it over his head, and then he grabbed a towel from a closet and threw it at me. "Do you want some tea?" I frowned at him. It was almost three in the morning, and he was offering me tea? "Since I won't be able to go back to sleep now, I'm going to make some tea."

I should go. I should leave and go home and back to sleep. Instead, I nodded.

A moment later, we were in his kitchen. He placed a kettle on the range and picked up two mugs from the cabinets. His house was much like mine, but well kept, with newer, wooden flooring, and more contemporary furniture. His kitchen had sleek gray cabinets, black marble counters, and fancy stainless-steel appliances.

Seated on one of the high, metal stools around the kitchen island, I tried not to watch him too much. But it was way too hard when he was wearing black pants and a thin white t-shirt that hugged his shoulders. His black hair was messy, but for some reason, I liked it this way, maybe even more than when he combed it into a neat style.

Devon poured the hot water into the mugs and handed one to me. "It's chamomile tea."

"It's fine." I took the mug and wrapped both my hands around it. "I like chamomile tea." Careful not to burn my lips, I sipped from the tea.

Devon leaned against the counter on the other side of the island and watched me. "Sorry if I scared you."

I shrugged. "As long as you're okay."

He glanced down at his steaming mug. "I have nightmares often."

"They must be really terrible." What the hell was I saying? "Sorry, that's none of my business."

His eyes on mine, he nodded. "You're right, they are terrible. Even if I'm exhausted, I feel better awake."

Thunder boomed. I almost jumped out of my skin and dropped my tea. "Holy shit."

Devon's eyes narrowed into slits. "Afraid of thunder?"

"Was that obvious?" I tried joking, but I was still spooked.

One corner of his lips tugged up. "A little." He brought his mug to his lips and drank.

I watched him.

Something about him called to me. Maybe I was drawn to him because I shouldn't be doing this. I shouldn't get close to anyone—not him, not Carol, not Sabrina and Kevin. I shouldn't invite him to dinner, or let him inside my house, or check on him in the middle of the night.

I certainly shouldn't be having tea with him at three in the morning.

But I couldn't help it. I felt like, in some way, he was like Lia and me. Like he had secrets and was as lonely as me.

Maybe, just maybe, we could be lonely together.

PAST

Kianna

The young woman stood from where she had been crouched in the field and looked in the direction of her mother's voice. Standing on the back porch, the older woman beckoned for her to come.

With a groan, Kianna trudged through the field. Her hair was tied into a high ponytail, her skirt was raised with pins, her work boots were brown from dirt, like her nails. She stopped beside the barn, took off her boots, and washed her hands before proceeding to where her mother waited for her.

The kids should be doing their homework, and her mother was supposed to be working in the house. It wasn't even time to stop to make supper yet. What could her mother want with her?

She halted before her mother as Cat emerged from inside

the house. Her best friend had been here since dawn, running away from her chores at her own house.

"Did you call me?" Kianna asked politely.

Her mother waved an envelope of expensive silk paper in front of her. "This just arrived."

Kianna frowned. "What's that?"

With a big smile, her mother cracked the red seal on the envelope and pulled out the letter from inside. "It's an invitation. To a ball!"

Cat spied over Ophelia's shoulder. "Oh my word, you've been invited to a ball."

It didn't make sense. No one in town invited them to balls anymore. "What?"

Her mother pointed to the front of the house, where they could see a carriage driving away. "A servant came. He said a man named Lord Sandler moved into the village and he's hosting a ball to get to know everyone."

"And he's inviting me? Why?" Kianna asked. If this man was new in town, then he didn't even know her family had been rich once. Kianna and her family were poor now.

"It doesn't matter," her mother said, an eager tone in her voice. "Don't you see? This is a fabulous opportunity. What if this lord has a son your age? You can finally get married."

And save the family.

Her mother was right. The only way of saving them right now was through marriage, but no one in town looked their way anymore. But a new lord who had mistakenly invited them to a ball wouldn't know that. She could fall into his favor before he found out she was poor, and maybe secure a wedding.

Despite herself, Kianna looked out at the field.

Devon was at the edge, working hard under the hot sun,

his strong shoulders tense, his lips pursed as if something bothering him.

Could he be upset about this invitation? About a possible marriage?

She shook her head, expelling such absurd thoughts from her mind.

"Mother, I'm not sure—"

Cat snatched the invitation from Ophelia's hands. "If you aren't going, then I will in your place."

Her mother glared at Cat and took the invitation back. "Kianna, please, you're doing this. For you. For us."

Certain that there was nothing she could or say that would change her mother's mind, Kianna nodded.

She should have gone back to the field and continued working, but she suddenly felt like being alone. Dragging her feet, Kianna went to the cherry tree at the edge of the lake. She sat on the bench, wondering why she had such a heavy heart.

Devon

THE WARRIOR HAD TRIED NOT TO EAVESDROP, BUT HE HAD BEEN close, and it wasn't like they had whispered. Anyone would have heard them.

But not everyone would feel as upset and jealous as Devon.

Ophelia wanted to take Kianna to this ball, to meet the new lord in town and secure a marriage.

Marriage.

The rake fell from his grip, and he balled his hands into fists.

Forget marriage. Kianna shouldn't be out when there were demons running around. There hadn't been a sighting since the lantern festival, but that didn't mean Kianna was safe.

He looked down the hill. Kianna sat on the bench under the cherry tree, clearly upset by the idea. Cat walked toward her, probably to try to lighten her mood.

If only Cat didn't agree with Ophelia.

Not sure what else he could do to stop Kianna from going, Devon marched to Ophelia, who still stood on the porch, beaming at the invitation in her hands.

"I don't think that's a good idea," Devon blurted out.

A knot appeared between Ophelia's brows. "What do you mean?"

"There's a lot of work to do at the farm," Devon said, grasping for any excuse. "Kianna shouldn't waste time going to a ball."

"Don't be silly." Ophelia waved him off. "If I can arrange a marriage for Kianna, then we won't need to work in the field anymore." She raised a finger at him. "Oh, wait here."

Even more frustrated than before, Devon stood there while Ophelia ran into the house. A moment later, she came back with a small velvet pouch in hand.

Devon frowned. "What's that?"

"I saved this in case we didn't get a good yield from the crops, but I think this occasion deserves this." She offered the pouch to him. Wary, Devon took it and he felt the heavy weight of the many coins inside. "Take Kianna into town, please, and help her buy the most beautiful dress she finds."

She patted Devon's arm, then turned to the house. She went in with an extra skip in her steps.

Devon stared at the pouch in his hands.

This was all of their savings and they were going to waste it on a dress. At the same time, he wished Kianna and her family were saved somehow; he didn't want this plan to work.

Without much of a choice in the matter, Devon pocketed the pouch and headed down the hill to invite Kianna to go into the village and buy her dress.

With each step he took toward her, the hurt and disappointment only grew inside him. He pushed the pain away and focused on his mission.

He was here to protect Kianna, nothing more.

Kenna

"THIS IS GOOD," SABRINA SAID, MUNCHING ON A MUFFIN. "DID you make these?"

"Not entirely," I admitted. "I bought the mix and followed the instructions." It was the best I could do with my terrible cooking skills. I had vowed to learn how to cook, but so far, it wasn't going well.

Kevin grabbed a muffin from the platter in the center of the kitchen island. "I like it too."

Carol, who'd had two already, nodded. "I say keep practicing. You got these right. Soon, you'll be making them from scratch."

"If I don't burn down the house ..." I muttered.

They all laughed.

I rolled my eyes but ended up smiling too. What could I do? It seemed cooking wasn't for me. Thankfully, I had Lia, who would be home soon to make us dinner.

Like me, she had practically adopted Sabrina and Kevin, and if they weren't here, she asked me to find them. She was like that about Carol too, but it was harder to not find Carol in our house nowadays.

"Enough about cooking, what about homework?" I asked, glancing at the books and notebooks spread over the kitchen island. "Are you all done?"

"Almost, Mom," Carol teased.

"Good job, daughter," I played along.

She chuckled at me.

While they finished their homework, I pulled out one of the books I was studying for the GED. I wasn't in the mood to read it, but I couldn't bother them while they all did their homework. It was that, or watch TV, which would distract them, or read some fiction novel, but I had already finished the one Devon had given me. I needed to buy another one. Or ask Lia to bring a couple from the library.

I picked up my phone, hoping she was late and still there so I could ask, when the front door opened and Lia barged in.

"Hi, guys," she said, entering the kitchen. She deposited her purse on the counter and took a white envelope from inside. "Look. We've got an invitation to a fundraiser ball."

"Oh." Carol straightened. "The library fundraiser ball? That's cool."

"Library fundraiser ball?" I asked, lost.

"It's an annual thing," Carol said. "They raise money to buy books for the local schools. I heard it's pretty cool, though I have never been to one."

"You're going with me," Lia announced, with a big smile.

I frowned. She wanted us to go to a ball? Clearly, she wasn't thinking; otherwise she wouldn't suggest something like that. It was practically like pointing arrows and neon lights at us, yelling, "We're here!"

Guilt nagged at me, because I had gone to the festival and attracted demons. I didn't want to have that happen again so close to home.

Home.

I argued with Lia all the time because we should leave and never look back, but I couldn't deny it. This place felt like home now, the only home I'd had in many years, the only one I remembered. I also didn't want to leave.

"Can I go too?" Carol asked in a high-pitched voice.

"Sorry, I only have a plus one," Lia said. "I'm sure your parents will be invited, though. You should go with them."

Carol crossed her arms. "They're always invited, but they never go, and I can't go alone."

"I wish we could go too," Sabrina mumbled.

"I think you're too young for that, little lady." I flicked her nose and she wrinkled her face at me. "When you're older, I'll let you take my place and go with Lia."

Her eyes sparkled. "Deal."

Kevin chuckled. "Lia. You're always calling your mother by her name."

Shit. "It's my way of teasing her," I said quickly.

Lia laughed, a nervous thing that grated at my ears. "Yes, she's always being silly." She grabbed an apron from a drawer. "Anyway, you have your credit card." The one she had given me for emergencies, yes. "Go out tomorrow and buy a dress."

Carol almost jumped up from the stool. "I'll go with you! I'll help you pick a dress."

I ignored Carol and stared at Lia. "Are you sure?" Not about buying the dress, though she had barely received any salary yet and we were already short on money again, but about the ball. I would rather stay home, watching a movie and eating ice cream, hiding away from demons and strangers.

"I'm sure." Her tone was resolute.

I wouldn't argue about it now. I was going to wait until the siblings and Carol went home to remind her why we shouldn't go to this ball.

Meanwhile, Lia prepared a nice dinner for us, and I enjoyed being home.

PAST

Devon

DEVON HAD COME UP WITH FIVE HUNDRED EXCUSES WHY KIANNA and her mother shouldn't go to the ball at Lord Sandler's house, but none had satisfied Ophelia. In the end, the only thing he was able to do was to convince her that he should go with them.

Somehow, Lord Sandler had learned Ophelia and Kianna didn't have a carriage anymore, so he sent one to pick them up. He had also offered a nanny to stay with Selina and Calvin, but Ophelia had let him know the kids would stay with Giles and his family.

Standing beside the carriage parked in front of the manor, Devon sized up the driver, but the old man seemed harmless enough. He smoothed down the outfit he had bought—fancy trousers, a white shirt, and a fitted black jacket. Ophelia had asked where he got it, and he lied and said he had borrowed it from a wealthy merchant in the village. Thankfully, she didn't ask for details.

For the occasion, he had even combed his hair neatly and tied it in a tight ponytail at his nape. For some reason, he wanted to look his best for the occasion.

A couple of days ago, Devon had taken Kianna and Cat to the village to buy a new dress. Though he had accompanied them there, he hadn't gone in the shop.

The anticipation was killing him. Kianna was always beautiful. With an elegant dress and proper makeup, she would probably rival the goddesses.

Devon thought he was prepared, but when Kianna stepped out of the house with Ophelia, his heart stopped beating for a full four seconds.

Divine. Stunning. Dazzling.

A word to describe how beautiful Kianna looked hadn't been invented yet.

She wore a red dress with a tight bodice, covered in tiny red crystals, and a full skirt. The cleavage was modest, but the sleeves of her dress began below her shoulder line and extended to her elbows, showing the smooth skin of her neck and collarbone. Half of her long blond hair had been pulled up in an intricate bun, with red crystals weaved between the strands, and the other half fell down her back in perfectly pressed curls. Her makeup was simple but effective. Her bright blue eyes had been lined with kohl, and her lips were as red as her dress.

Lovely. Kianna was beautiful.

Devon couldn't strip his eyes from her as she paused on the steps. Waking up from his daze, Devon rushed forward and offered his arm to her.

She smiled at him and hooked her hand in his arm. "Thank you."

"My pleasure," he whispered.

After helping Kianna into the carriage, Devon helped Ophelia. The older woman had donned a dark blue gown, less opulent and fancy than Kianna's, but equally graceful. They made a beautiful pair, Devon realized.

On the way to the ball, the anxiety was palpable inside the carriage. Devon knew Ophelia was eager to find a good suitor for Kianna, and Kianna was nervous about being paraded like an animal for sale.

And Devon wanted to hide Kianna from the rest of the world.

The ball was being hosted at Lord Sandler's new home—a mansion in the village's wealthy section. Sprawling green lawn, a long stone road inside the property cutting through a carefully manicured garden, three stone fountains in front of the three-story brown stone building.

Carriages lined the road.

When it was their turn, a young page extended his hand to help Kianna out of the carriage, but Devon pushed him away. Instead, he gave her his arm once more. Without hesitation, she placed her hand in the crook of his arm and let him guide her out. Confused, the page helped Ophelia down from the carriage.

The page directed them around the mansion, down a wide stone path, which opened to a heavily decorated garden. White lights hung from strings zigzagging from pillars flanking the smooth stone pavement. Tables with flower ornaments and velvet-cushioned chairs lined the sides of the area, leaving the center open, probably for dancing later. At one end, long tables with pristine white tablecloths stood, piled high with food that probably looked much better than it tasted. On the other end, a small platform hosted a string group, who played a slow melody at the moment.

And all around them, the lords and ladies and their children mingling, greeting each other, talking, laughing, and drinking. The heavy scent of liquor and cigars filled Devon's nostrils.

Devon did his best to ignore the glances the others shot in their direction, most of them of disgust and disbelief. Were they that outraged that Kianna and Ophelia had been invited to the ball? Trying to keep them from noticing the stares, Devon steered the women toward the food. They grabbed a few hors d'oeuvres, then sat down at a table at the edge of the garden.

A moment later, Jocelyn, the nosy neighbor that once barged in to show off, sat at the table beside them with her husband, her son, and his wife. With a fake smile, she waved at Ophelia, then promptly leaned into her husband, her hand covering her mouth, hiding her certainly hurtful words.

Devon sighed. Could they go home already?

Ophelia started looking around. "Have you seen Lord Morris? If I'm not mistaken, he has a son your age. We should greet them."

Under the table, Devon's hands tightened into fists. He had to do something to stop Ophelia from securing a marriage contract for Kianna tonight. He couldn't bear it if she became betrothed.

Before he could think of anything, the crowd hushed. A man in his fifties, dressed in a tailored dark tuxedo, emerged from the side of the mansion, followed by a woman in a pearl-colored gown, and two teenagers—a boy and a girl.

"Welcome to my humble home," the man said. So, this

was Lord Sandler, and the others were probably his wife and kids. "Thank you for accepting my invitation. I'm eager to get to know all of you." He opened his arms wide. "Please, enjoy your night."

With that, he and his wife started making the rounds, stopping at table after table, getting to know everyone; the kids ran off, probably to hide from the party and cause mischief; and the music started.

Devon's senses were on high alert, but this time they weren't attuned to demons, but to evil people, like many of the rich men and women around them. He also noticed several young men ogling Kianna, which only made his gut twist in rage.

He tensed each time one of them walked by, thinking they would stop and ask Kianna to dance. If they did, he would draw out his sword and kill them on the spot.

What was he thinking?

Devon shook his head, ashamed of how his feelings were getting the best of him. If he didn't control them soon, he would be in big trouble.

Finally, Lord Sandler and his wife approached their table. Ophelia, Kianna, and Devon stood up to greet him.

"I'm so glad you were able to come," Lord Sandler said with a wide smile.

"We appreciate the invitation," Ophelia said, lowering her head slightly, as a thank-you gesture.

Lord Sandler tsked. "My pleasure." He turned his eyes to Kianna. "I had heard you were a beauty, but let me tell you, my dear, you're a lot more than that."

Kianna's cheeks gained a red tint. "Thank you."

"He's right," his wife said, with a warm smile. "I wish my son was older, so I could introduce you to him."

"Speaking of sons ..." Lord Sandler turned back and waved at someone. A tall young man with sand-blond hair and a thin mustache approached the table. "Noel is my business partner's son and my godson." He smiled at Kianna and winked. "He's only twenty-two, and unattached."

Kianna's cheeks reddened some more.

"It's a pleasure to meet you, Lady Kianna." Noel extended his hand at her. "Would you do me the honor of dancing with me?"

Kianna's eyes widened. She hesitated. Ophelia nudged her with her elbow, and Kianna moved, her hand unsure as she reached for Noel's. "Y-yes."

His hands clasped hers tightly.

Devon wanted to switch into his warrior uniform and burn down this party. This mansion. Maybe the entire village.

Noel guided Kianna to the dance floor. Red blinded Devon as Noel's other hand found the small of Kianna's back and pulled her close to him, before they started dancing.

Lord Sandler and his wife exchanged a few more words with Ophelia, but Devon heard nothing over his jealousy. He sat back down and crossed his arms, trying to think of anything but Kianna in some other man's arms.

Warrior. He was a divine warrior. He had important missions. He saved the world from evil. He fought demons all the time. He was immortal.

He wouldn't be bothered by this simple thing.

Yet, a painful pang cut through his heart when Noel said something and Kianna smiled at him.

That smile.

Devon didn't like anyone else seeing that smile.

"They look so beautiful together," Ophelia said. Devon whipped his head to her, but the older woman watched as her daughter danced with a stranger. There was a glint in her eyes, as if all her dreams were coming true. "I hope she likes him."

Devon bit his tongue before he said anything he would regret.

Thankfully, a couple approached them and sat down at the table. They greeted Ophelia warmly, and soon the three of them were engrossed in conversation—it seemed not all rich people were rude.

Seemingly forgotten, Devon slipped out of his chair and kept watch over Kianna and Noel. He found them on the other side of the dance floor. Once more Noel said something and Kianna smiled.

As he walked toward them, Devon realized something.

This wasn't Kianna's true, wide smile.

She was faking it.

With a new skip in his step, he walked right to their side and extended his hand to Kianna. "You don't mind if I cut in, do you?" Devon didn't wait for an answer. He took Kianna's hand in his and pulled her toward him. Noel stood frozen, his mouth wide open, as Devon spun Kianna away from him. "Tell me I'm saving you."

Kianna let out a long breath. "Yes, you're saving me. Thank you." She smiled at him—now her true, wide smile. Devon's heart sped up. He became too conscious of how her hand rested on his shoulder, of his hand on her back, of how close their bodies were, of how bright her blue eyes were, of how sweet her cherry perfume was. "He was really boring, talking about business nonstop."

"I'm glad I interfered, then."

"Me too." She relaxed in his arms and he tightened his hold on her, just slightly, enough to take the lead and spin around the dance floor with her effortlessly. "Do you know if my mother is bored? I hope she is. I'm ready to leave."

Devon shook his head. "I think your mother is having a good time."

Kianna pouted. Then, one corner of her lips tugged up. "Well, at least I'm dancing with you now. If anyone tries to cut in, please, don't let them."

Devon smiled, proud that she would rather spend her time with him than with anyone else from the party. "Will do." He let go of her, only to twist her under his arm, then pull her to him again.

Kianna's smile widened. "Look at you. You might not remember much, but you do remember how to dance."

"It seems like that, doesn't it?" As a divine warrior who was centuries old, Devon knew better than anyone that some things were impossible to forget, most of them reactions to certain situations.

Like fear and rage and jealousy when the woman he adored was dancing with some other man.

As if it was the most natural thing in the world, Devon and Kianna danced for a long time. Every time he saw a man watching Kianna, or approaching them, probably to cut in, he spun them away until they were out of range. If he could, Devon would dance away with Kianna until they were out of there.

That gave him an idea.

"Would you like to take a break?" he asked. Kianna's eyes widened. "Don't worry. I won't let anyone else take you dancing."

She nodded.

Devon took her hand and hooked it around this elbow. He guided her to the long table with food and drinks, and grabbed two flutes of wine. As they walked away, Devon noticed a man watching them from one of the back tables. Devon had seen him eyeing Ophelia and Kianna since they had arrived at the ball. He rummaged his mind until he remembered the man. Lord Cooper, a lord with whom Kianna's father did a lot of business. As far as Devon knew, they had never gotten along well. Lord Cooper watched Kianna with his eyes narrowed, like a predator. Devon didn't like that look.

He took a stone path that led deeper into the garden, where the tall hedges and trees hid them from the party. They slowed their steps and sipped their wine, admiring the neatly manicured flowers and bushes.

"It's beautiful here," Kianna whispered. She glanced from a flowerbed with yellow and orange flowers to the star-dotted night sky.

"It is," he said, looking at her.

They walked some more, until they were at the edge of a curved reflection pool that cut through the garden. Devon frowned when Kianna peeled her hand from his arm.

She sipped from her wine, before saying, "Thank you again for taking me out of there."

The knot between his brows deepened. "Your mother won't be happy to know you ran away from all your suitors."

Kianna rolled her eyes. "I'm not some animal she can sell. Most of those men have known me for a long while. They were watching me more closely tonight because of this fake gown and this fake hairdo."

"They aren't fake."

"Yes, they are." She paused. "I'm still poor, Devon, and they probably won't want to admit that." She glanced down at her outfit. "I should sell this gown. It might not be worth much anymore, but it's better than hanging it in my wardrobe and never wearing it again."

Why were things so complicated? Devon had lots of money. He could pay for the gown. He could buy them a carriage. He could even pay for more workers, so Kianna and her mother could lead a gentler life.

But he couldn't do that.

He was a damn warrior, and besides keeping her alive, he shouldn't interfere in her life. He had done it so many times, though.

What was he doing? He shouldn't allow himself to fall for her. He shouldn't allow himself to get this close to her. He shouldn't touch her, dance with her, smile at her.

That was it. He had to take her home, and patrol the manor in warrior mode. Nothing else, nothing more.

"Kianna—"

"Yes?" She turned her bright blue eyes at him and he felt lost again. How could he resist those eyes?

Like a fool, he surrendered.

Devon fished the ring from his pocket. "I have something for you."

Kianna's brows curled down. "For me?" He took her right hand and slipped the ring onto her finger. Kianna gasped as she admired the ring—a metal circle with a blue stone, as bright as her eyes. "The ring. From the festival."

"I thought you would like to have it."

"Devon." She stared at him, a new glint in her eyes— unshed tears. "I love it, but you shouldn't have. It was expensive and—"

"It's okay," he said, though he couldn't offer more explanation than that. "I want you to have it."

A tear escaped from her eye. "Thank you," she whispered.

Without thinking, Devon reached up, cupped her face, and wiped the tears with his thumb. Without thinking, Devon stared into her eyes, then at her mouth. Without thinking, Devon leaned into her.

Without thinking, Devon kissed her.

There had been moments in his immortal life when Devon had felt really powerful, proud of his strength, of his duty, satisfied with his performance. In these moments, he had slashed through his enemies as if they were smoke in the wind, raised hell on Earth, and sent demons back to the underworld. He felt strong, unstoppable, invincible.

Unlike this moment, when his lips moved against Kianna's and a gasp ripped through her throat. When her hands tightened on his jacket, keeping him close, as if she was afraid he would leave her. When her sweet scent and her even sweeter taste stormed all of his senses, and all he wanted was her. Just her. Always her.

This moment could bring him to his knees. It could break him in half. It could be his demise.

And right now, he didn't care, as long as he could still hold her. As long as he could still kiss her. As long as he could still have her.

Even though he had never kissed anyone in his immortal life—had he kissed someone when he was human? He would never know—having Kianna's soft lips against him, her tongue teasing his, felt as natural and perfect and simple as breathing. It felt right. It felt charged. It felt like fate.

Startled, Devon pulled away.

Kianna blinked, before looking down, red rising on her cheeks.

By the gods, how could he resist her?

Devon hooked his fingers under her chin and tilted her head up until her eyes met his. A small smile spread over his mouth before he leaned into her and brushed his lips on hers.

He was ready to deepen the kiss, to show her how much she meant to him with that simple, wonderful gesture, when thick, oily tendrils scratched at his senses.

Breathing hard, Devon looked around.

The darkness. The demons. They were close.

They were getting closer.

"Devon," Kianna whispered. "What is it?"

Trying to remain calm, Devon took her hands in his. "Kianna, listen to me. Find your mother, take the carriage, and go home. Don't leave the farm until I'm back."

"W-what?" She shook her head. He started retreating, but Kianna held on to his hands. "Devon, what's going on?"

Devon let out a long breath. He cupped Kianna's face. "Everything will be fine. Just do what I told you." He pressed his lips to hers once more. "Now go."

He knew she wouldn't leave even if he pushed her away, so hoping she would follow his order, Devon spun on his heels and took off first to meet the demons before they came. Before they got too close.

Kianna

THE CARRIAGE MOVED ROUGHLY OVER THE ROAD LEADING OUT of the village. Seated across from her, Kianna's mother seemed in a bad mood. After Devon left her, Kianna was too shocked to move.

First, she couldn't believe what had happened. She stared at the ring on her finger, thinking of the kiss. Of the fantastic way Devon's lips had closed over hers, of his hands securing her against him, of his powerful body pressed against hers.

Heat washed over her body.

But when she thought of the desperate way he looked at her afterward, the almost frantic tone of his voice when he told her to go, she pushed it all down and focused on his words.

She knew Devon. He wouldn't tell her to go and disappear like that without a reason. All she had to do was trust him.

So, she marched back into the party, ignored all the men trying to talk to her, found her mother engrossed in conversation with an old friend, and lied about not feeling well.

Moments later, they were inside the carriage, riding back to the farm.

Kianna leaned back in the seat, watching the dark exterior through the window, as if she could get a glimpse of Devon, wherever he was.

What had all that been about?

She brought her fingers to her lips and gently patted. Perhaps they looked different now? She had never been kissed before. Of course, like any girl her age—and younger —she had imagined it plenty of times, but nothing had prepared her for it, for how amazing it felt, for how perfect it could be. And it hadn't been just the kiss, but everything. The way he touched her, the way he looked at her, his spice and manly scent, his mint taste. It all had been perfect.

Could it always be like that, or was it because it had been Devon?

It wasn't the first time she realized she was falling for him, but it still scared the hell out of her. She glanced at her mother. Her mother liked Devon, but after seeing how eager her mother was to marry her off to a wealthy family, Kianna doubted she would approve of a relationship with their farm help.

Devon, who suddenly became agitated and left her there, after telling her to go home.

Worry overcame her delight. What was going on? Where was he? What was he doing?

"How are you feeling?" her mother asked, her voice tight.

Reminding herself that she was lying about being sick, Kianna relaxed against the seat, as if she had no strength left to stand upright. "Not too good." She pressed her hand on her stomach. "Perhaps it was something I ate."

Her mother's lips pressed tight. "Of all the days to get sick, it had to be tonight, when we could have finally—"

"Mother," Kianna said, more like begging than a reprimand. "I don't like it when you do that."

Her mother frowned. "Do what?"

"Put the fate of all of us in my hands, as if all I had to do is to get married to any rich man, and everything would be all right."

"Well ..." Her mother lowered her gaze. A moment later, she exhaled. "I understand what you mean. I'm sorry if you felt pressured. I didn't mean it that way. I guess I was anxious and excited to be invited to a ball again, and for the opportunities it would bring. I didn't think straight. I'm sorry."

Kianna knew her mother was sorry, not for forcing her to

go to the ball and trying to find a husband, but for being in this situation.

"It's okay," Kianna reassured her.

They were quiet the rest of the ride home. Since the kids were at Giles's house, it was unusually quiet, and Kianna felt cold and strange stepping inside.

She turned to the door as her mother closed it, hoping Devon would barge in at second now.

"Do you want me to make you some tea?" her mother asked. Kianna frowned. "For your upset stomach."

"Oh." For a moment, Kianna had forgotten about her lie. "No, I think I'll go straight to bed."

Another lie. As soon as her mother was out of sight, Kianna changed out of that huge dress into a simpler, brown one, and she went out to the front porch, where she sat on a wooden bench and waited for Devon.

She tried keeping her mind busy by reading a book under faint candlelight, but it proved to be harder than she wanted it to be. She read the same paragraph five times and still couldn't absorb one word. All her mind wanted to think about was Devon.

What was happening? Where was he? Why had he sent her off so fast, so urgently?

As time passed, her worry turned into despair.

Was he okay? What if he didn't come back?

Finally, after hours of waiting, Kianna heard his footsteps before seeing his silhouette walking up the hill toward the front porch. She stood from the bench and took two steps toward him.

Her heart dropped when the candlelight illuminated him, and she took him in.

He was still wearing the same outfit, but he was dragging

his feet with his shoulder hunched down, as if he was too tired to stand. His hair was loose and untidied, sweat covered his skin, and there was blood dripping from underneath his sleeve.

Kianna held her breath. "Are you okay?"

He halted before her. "I'll be fine."

A million questions sprouted to the tip of her tongue—where had he been? Who hurt him? And why?—but she held those in. She wouldn't bother him with her curiosity. It didn't matter now. All that mattered was that he was back, like he said he would be.

She slipped her hand in his. "Come on. I'll clean and dress your wound."

Brows pinched, Devon didn't resist her. He let her guide him through the house to the kitchen, where they sat down, and Kianna treated his wounds.

Once she saw the nasty cut on his forearm, more questions rose to her throat. The cut was clean, but shallow, like that of a sword. Why had Devon been fighting someone sporting a sword?

Kianna shook her head as she applied a mix of herbs to the cut. Devon hissed. A moment later, he let out a long breath. "Thank you."

She glanced up at him, at his dark eyes, at the worry and pain stamped on them. Whatever he had been doing, she was sure it had been the right thing. Because she knew Devon, she trusted him, and he would never, ever do something to harm her or her family.

She offered him a small smile. "I'm glad you're back."

Devon put his hand over hers. "Me too."

Kenna

Despite all my protests and hesitations, I ended up going to the library fundraiser ball with Lia. The previous day, I had gone out with Carol and bought a strapless red dress with a tight bodice and a flowing skirt. Dresses weren't really my thing, but I had to admit I liked this one. For the occasion, I let my hair down, only securing a few short strands to the side, and applied makeup for the first time in ... I didn't even know when—smoky eyes and red lipstick. Also not my thing, but according to Carol, who saw me before I left for the ball with Lia, I was elegant and hot, a combination hard to find.

I laughed at her description but chose to believe her words. At least for tonight. I would need them if I were to endure such a boring night.

The ball was hosted at a fancy hotel ballroom with thick carpet, big round tables all around, crystal chandeliers, and tall doors like windows that led to a balcony outside. There was a bar on one side of the room and a stage on the other, where a band was warmed up. Waiters weaved around the arriving guests, bringing them drinks and hors d'oeuvres.

A whiskey glass in hand, Devon stood beside one of the tables, talking to an older man. I wanted to deny it, but I couldn't, not to myself. With his hair combed back and in a black tuxedo, Devon looked dashing. Too handsome for his own good.

"I didn't know Devon had been invited to the ball," I said to Lia as we took our places at a table near the stage.

"Oh, I forgot to tell you," she said. "He's a patron at the library and one of the ball's organizers."

"Really?" That was surprising. And here I was thinking he was a playboy, who had too much money and didn't even know how to use it well since he lived in that small house. But it seemed he did. Investing in books was always a good thing.

A waiter came by and we ordered glasses of wine—thankfully, they weren't asking for IDs at the ball. Mine was fake, but it had my real age on it.

Amid the gathering crowd, I recognized many faces, even our neighbor, Roselyn, who loved to spread gossip. I was sure tomorrow the town would be on fire with some rumor she started.

A moment later, a handful of men came up to the stage.

"Good evening," one started. "Thank you for joining us tonight." He went on, explaining who he was—the director of the library—and more about the event. He introduced the other men standing with him—all patrons of the library. I glanced from the stage, to where Devon stood in the corner, as if he was hiding. Why wasn't he up there with the other patrons? The men took turns speaking about the library and the event, thanking us for our generosity and kindness.

"Let's get this party started!" the director announced. He and the others hopped off the stage and the band began playing.

Lia's coworker, Miles, stopped by our table with his wife to greet us, then a couple more people Lia had met while working at the library.

Then she stood. "I need to go greet some people. I'll be right back."

Before I could protest, she walked away, leaving me alone at our table.

Great. I had come to this damn ball because she had insisted, and then she just left me.

I took a long swallow of my wine.

When I lowered my glass, I found a man staring at me from the edge of the dance floor. He stood beside the library director and a patron and talked to them, but every few seconds, he looked at me. I frowned. He was ... handsome, in a way. Tall, with dirty blond hair, and what seemed an easy smile. He was probably in his early twenties, but his demeanor exuded pride and charm, as if he was the CEO of a big company, or a famous actor.

His eyes met mine again and a smile appeared on his lips.

Was he flirting with me now?

I didn't get to find out as Devon appeared across my table. "I expected to see Lia here, but not you."

I shrugged. "What can I do? She practically forced me to come."

"You don't seem too upset."

"I'm screaming internally."

One corner of his lips tugged up. "Well, maybe I can help

make this night a little less boring." He extended his hand to me. "Would you like to dance with me?"

I frowned at his hand. Behind him, couples started filling the open space between the tables, dancing together along the music. Why would I dance with him? "Hm, no, thanks." Devon frowned. I tipped my glass, finishing my wine in one big gulp. Glass in hand, I stood up. "I need to get another drink. Excuse me."

I walked to the bar, now almost empty as people directed themselves to the dance floor or tables to eat the little bites the waiters brought over, and sat down on one of the tall stools. "Another glass of wine, please," I told the bartender. He nodded at me.

Devon leaned on the bar counter right beside me. "Hey, Paul, can I get another whiskey, please?"

The bartender, Paul, paused and grinned. "Sure." He went to grab our drinks.

"Can I at least sit here, or should I just get my drink and go?"

I kept my gaze on the wall across filled with bottles across the counter. "It's a free country. You can sit wherever you like."

Devon took the seat, put his elbow on the bar counter, and turned to me. "Did I do something to upset you?"

I glanced at him. "No."

"Then why are you more hostile than usual?"

Why, indeed? Since putting on this dress and coming here, I had been in a bad mood. I let out a long breath and faced him. "I guess I'm rebelling since I didn't want to come. Sorry. I didn't mean to be rude."

The bartender placed the drinks on the counter in front of us, then moved on to the next guest.

Devon picked up his drink. "A peace treaty toast."

A soft laugh bubbled past my lips. "A peace treaty? Whoever hears us will think I was trying to kill you." He raised his glass. Rolling my eyes, I grabbed my wine goblet and clinked my glass on his. "Cheers."

"Cheers." He drank his whiskey.

I only took a sip of my wine. I wasn't used to drinking much. Ever since escaping with Lia, I had tasted alcohol a few times, but we had never gotten drunk—we couldn't afford it in case we needed to run at a moment's notice. Now, I felt like I was too young for this, but since I had come to this ball against my will, why not rebel some more?

I racked my brain, grasping for something to say. "I finished the book you gave me."

"You did?" He tilted his head slightly. "Did you like it?"

I nodded. "Yes. Very much."

"Want me to get you another one like that?"

My brows curled down. Why was he being so nice to me? He didn't know much about me, and everything he thought he knew was absolutely wrong. Was he trying to get invited to more dinners? He didn't need to be nice to me for that. I was sure Lia would still invite him over, no matter what. She wasn't my real mother, but she acted like one nonetheless. Not just to me, but to everyone around us.

At that moment, I realized he was too close to me. His stool was right next to mine, and if he turned one more inch to my side, his leg would brush against mine and his elbow would poke my arm. Heat crawled up my neck and cheeks when I inadvertently took in his handsome face, the clean-shaven skin stretched over the sharp angles of his chin and jaw, and his eyes. Those dark, intense eyes bored holes into me.

Holy shit, Devon was handsome.

And right at this moment, I felt like any girl would.

I felt attracted to him.

His gaze dipped to my mouth and he leaned into me.

My breath caught.

Something tugged inside my chest, then in my mind. Something familiar, something powerful.

"What the ...?" Narrowing my eyes, I reached for the collar of Devon's shirt. He stopped moving as I hooked my finger under the collar of his shirt and fished out the thin chain.

———

Devon

TWO SLITS, KENNA'S EYES TRAVELED DOWN FROM MY FACE TO my chest. "What the ...?" She reached forward, baffling me as she pulled down the neck of my shirt and fished the thin silver chain from underneath.

Her fingertips grazed my skin when she pulled the ring out and a quick vision appeared in my mind. The same blonde girl from before, standing in front of me with a big smile on her lips as I slid the ring, this same ring, on her finger.

I tried looking at her more, but her face was a blur.

The vision faded like smoke, and I stared at the fake brunette girl in front of me. The one cradling the ring attached to the silver chain in her hand.

"This ring," she whispered.

For once, I was at a loss for words. How ... how did she know about the ring? Had she seen me wearing it? I racked my brain, trying to remember. I had been shirtless in front of her before, when I had gone out running, but I always took the necklace off when I exercised.

There was no way she could have known about it.

Yet, here she was. Holding it in her hands as if she knew why I had it, why the gods had sent it to me.

"How did you know about the ring?" I asked, confused.

"I don't know," Kenna whispered, her gaze fixed on the ring. The blue of the stone and the blue of her eyes were exactly the same.

"Have you seen this ring before?"

"I don't think so," she said, but her voice trembled, as if she was unsure of her answer. "I just ..." She dropped the ring as if it had burned and pressed a hand on her heart. A second later, she let out a loud laugh. "That's crazy."

To a human, my entire existence and life were crazy. Divine warrior? Missions sent by gods? Demons? Magical powers? It was all crazy.

But not to me.

This—Kenna knowing about the ring—wasn't a coincidence, I was sure of it.

"Kenna, I—"

"Excuse me," a new voice cut through our conversation. I glanced at the newcomer and found Nigel standing beside us. "Hello, Devon, it's nice to see you again."

"Nigel," I said through gritted teeth. He was the son of a big real estate investor. I had seen him a couple of times in town when he had come to evaluate properties to buy. He had never stuck around before, though. What was he doing here now, during this ball?

He turned his grin to Kenna. "I'm sorry if this sounds bold, but I couldn't help coming over and introducing myself." He extended his hand to her. "I'm Nigel Monroe."

With a polite smile, Kenna shook his hand. "I'm Kenna Jones."

"It's so nice to meet you, Kenna." Holding firmly to her hand, Nigel stared at her as if he was totally enamored by her. What the hell? "Would you like to dance with me?"

"I'm ..." She pressed her lips tight, then stood. "Sure."

What the fuck?

I stared, my jaw on the floor, as Kenna walked away, holding Nigel's hand. She had told me no, but then said fucking yes to him. Why?

My insides burned almost as hot and painful as the fiery pits of the underworld while I watched Kenna dancing with Nigel, smiling and talking to him as if they were longtime friends.

I didn't know why I didn't expect to see her here. I knew Lia was coming, but I honestly thought Kenna would have stayed home with Carol, and maybe Sabrina and Kevin, and watched a movie while eating buckets of popcorn.

Instead, she waltzed into the ballroom and I felt my world turn upside down. Despite thinking she had a connection to my punishment, she was just too fucking beautiful to be ignored. In an elegant red dress that left her shoulders and her neck exposed, and some makeup, she was so stunning it hurt.

I tried reining in my curiosity—and my attraction to her —but I couldn't help myself. I marched to her and made a fool of myself. I invited her to dance and she flat turned me down.

My ego was wounded.

Until she started talking about the book I had given to her. At that moment, she seemed less guarded, a little vulnerable. At that moment, I felt an incredible urge to kiss her.

I was going to.

But then she found the ring.

How the hell did she know about the ring?

It didn't make sense.

Or it did. I just needed time to think this through and connect the dots.

Tonight wouldn't be the night, though.

Tonight, I was too anxious and … all right, I admitted it, jealous. Why deny it? I had been attracted to Kenna since I had first seen her. And the more she seemed connected to my dilemma, the more I liked her.

Kenna laughed with Nigel again, making my jealousy more painful.

All right, that was it. I had endured it for too long.

With determined steps, I marched to Kenna and Nigel. "My turn," I said, simply taking Kenna's hand from Nigel's shoulder and tugging her to me.

"Hey," Nigel protested.

I couldn't care less about him.

But Kenna frowned at me as I spun her away from him. "Devon, what the hell was that?"

"Nothing," I said, glancing at her hand on mine. I had expected to get another glimpse from the past, but I guess it didn't work every time I touched her.

She narrowed her pretty eyes at me. "Any more nightmares?"

I flinched. It had been a couple of days since Kenna had barged into my bedroom in the middle of the night and saved me from the worst nightmare I'd had in a while. At that moment, I had thought we had come to a truce, some sort of understanding, maybe even the faint traces of the beginning of a friendship. But today she was hostile again. I let it slide, only because she had said her sour mood was due to being dragged to the ball against her will.

To be honest, I wasn't in the best mood either.

"Every night," I confessed, surprising even myself. "But usually, they aren't as bad as that one."

"I'm sorry," she whispered.

I shrugged. "It's okay. I'm used to it."

We danced for a couple more songs, then I decided she could use a break from me. I was about to walk her back to the bar, to avoid the crowd, but the crowd found us.

The library director and the other patrons found us. They were accompanied by their wives and partners.

"Devon, you've been part of our family for a little over two years," the director said. "This is your third ball, and this is the first time I see you dancing." He glanced to Kenna, an amused glint in his eyes. He was curious about her. "I can see why." He winked at me. "She's a beauty."

A rush of rage and jealousy coursed through me.

"Oh, stop bothering him," his wife teased. Noticing my discomfort, she quickly changed the subject.

Kenna shifted her weight beside me, clearly as bored as I was. She glanced back over her shoulder. A knot appeared between her brows.

"Excuse me," she said, before walking back to her table. There, Lia sat alone, her hands on her temple. I followed Kenna. "Are you okay?"

"Just a nasty headache." Lia waved her hand, dismissing Kenna. "I can take it. Go have fun."

Kenna snorted. "As if I was having fun." I frowned. Did it

mean that she didn't enjoy dancing with me, or it was only the last part, when the library people crowded around us? She grabbed her mother's arm and tugged her up. "Come on. Let's go home."

"I can take you," I offered.

Kenna glanced at me. "No need."

"Thank you for offering," Lia said with a forced smile.

Without looking back, Kenna escorted her mother out of the ballroom.

Feeling aimless, I went to the bar and grabbed another whiskey. I drank half of the golden liquid in one swallow. Then, I glanced out to the crowd and regretted it instantly.

The director beckoned me to join them again.

Groaning, I dragged my feet back to the group. Why didn't I insist on taking Kenna and Lia home? Why didn't I just follow them out and go home too?

"Devon, you certainly remember Nigel, don't you?" the director asked the moment I stepped into the circle.

"Yes, we already talked briefly this evening," I said, my voice tight.

Nigel grinned at me, a smile full of disdain. "Yes, we did."

The director turned to him. "I heard your father is buying some property in town this time."

Nigel nodded. "Yes, he's negotiating the contract. It should be finalized in a couple of days."

The conversation went on, with Nigel explaining what his father wanted to use the property for. The director suggested they partner up for marketing and other events.

An old song started playing. The director's wife held his arm. "Oh, honey, remember this song? Come on." She tugged him to the dance floor behind our circle.

"Excuse me," he said, before taking her dancing.

This was my chance to leave. But as it was, Nigel stepped to my side. "So, you seem to be friends with Kenna," he said, a curious tone to his voice. I clenched my free hand. He showed me a sly smile. "I have to say, she's something else. Tell me, do you have her number?"

What the fuck?

I didn't answer him, because if I tried, I would end up punching his well-groomed face. Instead, I downed the rest of my whiskey, handed him the empty glass, and marched out of the ballroom.

I was done with this fucking event.

Ready for a fight, I undid the tie around my neck and opened up my senses, trying to find any demon or evil creature that was around, so I could ease my rage on them.

But as I drove around town, searching for them, I found none. The demons were all hiding tonight.

PAST

Kianna

Two days after the ball, Kianna felt as if it had never happened. Fancy gowns and carriages? Those belonged to a distant dream—especially when she was wearing her brown dress with several patched holes and her work boots with their half-gone soles, and was knee deep in the field, with her hands dirty and her forehead covered in sweat.

Another thing that seemed like a distant dream was the kiss she shared with Devon, and how he had come back late that night, covered in wounds. She hadn't asked him about it, she wouldn't, but at the same time, she hated that he didn't trust her enough to tell her. Was this a secret? Was it something about his past? Was he remembering things? He didn't tell her. Overall, things had been pretty cool between them. Besides a few longing glances, Devon had barely touched her these past few days. He only did when it wasn't on purpose, which filled Kianna with doubt. Did he regret kissing her? Or maybe he was too scared of her mother? No, that couldn't be it. Ophelia loved Devon ... but probably not enough to give him her daughter's hand.

There she went again. Her thoughts getting ahead of herself. No, she shouldn't think about it. No thoughts of Devon while she was working. None. None at all.

"Tell me I didn't come here for nothing!" Cat shouted from the edge of the field.

Kianna shook her head, glad Cat could steer her thoughts in another direction. Cat should have known she would be working hard today. Her mother and Devon had gone into the village to sell and buy supplies. It was only Giles and her until late afternoon.

"Why don't you join me?" Kianna teased. "It would go faster with four hands instead of two."

Cat wrinkled her nose. "Are you paying?"

Kianna laughed. "With a glass of water, maybe."

Kianna tried ignoring her friend for a few minutes more, but Cat was giving her a headache. If she took a break now and gave her unfiltered attention to Cat for fifteen minutes, she could then send her friend away without feeling bad about it.

"Fine," Kianna said, walking out of the field. She stopped by the pump beside the barn and washed her hands. "Only for a few minutes. Then, I need to get back to work."

Cat smiled wide. "Don't worry, I'll convince you to stay with me for the rest of the day no matter what."

Kianna rolled her eyes. "Don't make me regret this."

Cat hooked her arm around Kianna's. "When have I ever?"

Kianna snorted. She had lost count of how many times Cat had created trouble for them.

With a mischievous grin, Cat dragged Kianna toward the house, but they paused when Selina and Calvin ran up the hill, calling for their sister.

"What is it?" Kianna asked, realizing they never acted like that.

"A carriage," Calvin said, out of breath.

"A carriage is arriving," Selina explained.

Frowning, Kianna walked toward the hill, with Cat, Selina, and Calvin right behind them, as the carriage rounded the entrance and stopped in front of the manor. Four men mounted on big horses stopped behind the carriage.

Birch Cooper hopped out of the carriage and bowed his head. "Afternoon, Lady Kianna."

"Hello," she answered, a little wary. She remembered Lord Cooper. He had done business with her father. At one time, she could have said they had been friends. "What brings you here?"

"Where's your mother? I need to talk to her."

"She went to the village," Kianna said.

The man tsked. "Then I'm afraid I'll have to deal with you. I'm here to collect payment of your father's debt."

"Excuse me?" Kianna's brows deepened. "I didn't know my father had left any debts behind."

"Oh, he did," Lord Cooper said. "He has debts all over town. Most of us had decided to forget about it since your family didn't seem to be in a good financial situation. But you see, you just went to Lord Sandler's ball in a new dress, an expensive carriage, and even a servant. That tells me your family's situation isn't as bad as you made it look. So, I'm here to collect my debt."

He extended his hand, as if Kianna would simply fish a pouch of gold from her pocket and hand it to him.

"Lord Cooper, I'm so sorry, but you're mistaken," Kianna said. "The carriage was sent by Lord Sandler, the man you think of as a servant is actually a friend of the family, as for the gowns ... we repaired them ourselves." She lied about the dresses, but if she had told him she had bought it, he wouldn't stop pushing. "We really don't have any money."

"You don't have any money, hm." He glanced around. What was he doing? "Then, I'll take some of your farm tools. Heck, I'll take all of them."

He took a step forward, but Kianna jumped in his way. "Please, my lord, you can't. Those tools are the only things we have to work the field. If we can't work the field, we'll starve."

"Not my problem." He pushed her aside and marched on.

Kianna stumbled on her feet, but she raced after the man. She grabbed his hand and almost knelt in the grass. "Please, my lord, you have to believe me. We have nothing. We are nothing."

He halted and looked her up and down. "You're nothing, hm. Then I guess I'll take you as payment." He closed his hand around her wrist.

Panic laced her chest. Cat yelped, while Selina and Calvin protested.

"You can't do this."

"Leave her alone."

Letting her temper show, Selina stomped to the man and tried grabbing for her sister's hand. Lord Cooper slapped her hard on the face. Selina flew back, landing in the grass.

She didn't get up.

"No!" Kianna jerked against the man's grip to no avail.

"Selina!" Calvin yelled as Cat threw herself beside the little girl to check on her.

"Come with me." The man yanked on Kianna's arm, tugging her to his carriage.

Tears of fear and frustration and rage filled Kianna's eyes, blurring her vision. She tried jerking out of the man's grip, she tried calling for Selina, but nothing worked. Even her voice had run away.

The man shoved her toward the carriage's door.

Kianna's panic took life.

Her hands shook as she felt it again. That same sensation from before, that thick air around her, that pull and push inside her chest, a dark calling.

Whatever she was doing, it felt powerful. Invincible. She embraced it, willing it to take control of her, to find a solution for this impossible situation. A thick oily feeling filled her veins. The world around her darkened. Shadows grew from the trees and the manor.

Was this her? Was she doing this?

"Just go," Lord Cooper said, shoving her inside the carriage.

Kianna lost control over whatever that was when she tumbled onto the carriage's hard floor. The man stepped inside behind her, his eyes glinting with something Kianna didn't want to acknowledge.

Lord Cooper closed the carriage's door. "Let's go."

The carriage started rolling, taking Kianna away.

Devon

EARLIER, WHEN OPHELIA EXPRESSED INTEREST IN GOING TO THE village to get some supplies, Devon jumped at the opportunity. He didn't like leaving Kianna alone, but he was due to meet Ryder for a report.

The problem was, what would he tell Ryder? That everything was okay? That he still thought Kianna wasn't evil as the gods first thought? Though, he wasn't so sure anymore. He had sensed her at the festival, as she sensed the demons for the first time, as she grew scared by whatever was happening. But just because she could sense the darkness, it didn't mean she was evil, right?

Perhaps he was biased. Or rather, enamored.

Kissing her—by the gods, it had been the best feeling, the best sensation he had ever experienced. If he could, he would glue his lips to hers so he could kiss her for eternity.

But then he sensed them. The demons. Coming for her. He sent her away and went to meet the demons. He killed them all ruthlessly, but not before being injured.

That night, he almost didn't go back to the farm. He knew Kianna would be waiting for him, and he didn't want her to see him like that. But if he didn't go, she would wait for him all night. So he had gone, and he was glad when she just cleaned his wounds and provided him comfort, but didn't ask for details.

If she had asked, he didn't know what he would have told her. He didn't want to lie to her, but he couldn't tell her the truth either.

Feeling guilty, he tried to keep his distance the next day. What that meant was that he spent all of his time as near to her as he could, but he held back the desire flooding his senses and didn't kiss her again.

Confused and bothered, Devon stepped into the alley where he usually met with one of the warriors.

Ryder crossed his arms. "What's new?"

"Nothing," he lied. "Nothing happened. Everything is as quiet as it can be."

Ryder frowned. "That can't be."

"Why not?" Devon asked, ready to argue if necessary.

"It has been a while now," Ryder said, dropped his arms to his sides. "The gods wouldn't have sent you here for nothing."

If only he knew ...

"I'm afraid everything is calm. Too calm even."

It was like the heavens had heard him. The moment the words left his mouth, the air thickened and wavered. It wasn't darkness per se, but something familiar with it.

"You feel that?" Ryder asked, alarmed.

"I do." Devon closed my eyes and tried to sense it. He followed the disturbance. It went out of the village, down the road to the farm. His eyes shot open. "I've got to go."

He spun on his heels and ran.

"Devon, wait!" Ryder called, but Devon didn't stop. He didn't slow. In fact, once he ran out of the village, he used his warrior's powers to increase his speed.

In a flash, he found the source of the disturbance. A carriage and four riders behind it—he just knew Kianna was inside the carriage.

Red anger filled his veins.

Devon halted in the carriage's way.

The coach pulled on the reins, making the carriage stop. "Get out of the way," he yelled.

The carriage's door opened, and Lord Cooper stepped out of it. "What's going on?"

"This man won't move out of the way," the coach said, pointing to Devon.

Lord Cooper shrugged as if bored. "Run him over." He made to enter the carriage again.

Devon remembered him from the ball. He had glanced at Kianna and Ophelia one too many times, in ways that made Devon's stomach knot in disgust.

"You've got something that is mine," Devon said, his voice hard.

"Devon?" Kianna cried from inside the carriage. "Help!"

"Quiet, you wench." The man kicked inside the carriage and Kianna yelped.

Oh, the bastard.

Devon took a step forward, intent on squeezing the life out of this useless man, but he tried to control his urge. Killing them all in front of Kianna wouldn't gain him any points.

"Let her go," Devon warned.

The riders dismounted at once and drew their swords. He suppressed an amused chuckle. If only they knew who they would be fighting against.

"Why should I listen to you?" Lord Cooper asked.

"Because she's mine."

A loud laughter bubbled out of Lord Cooper's throat. "No, she's mine."

Devon was losing his patience. "How so?"

The man glanced Devon up and down, as if judging if he was worth his time. Finally, he sighed. "Her family owes me a lot of money. Since they don't have any money anymore, I'm taking her as payment."

This was barbaric. Slavery was ridiculous, and taking a lady from a family like that was even worse.

All Devon wanted was to run his sword through this man. He was sure that if he did that, his riders would be on top of him in five seconds flat—and Devon would be done with them all in two more.

But he couldn't kill them around Kianna. What would he tell her?

He was sure there was no way for him to reason with this man either. He would never let Kianna go out of the goodness of his heart.

There was only one thing he could do.

"How much is the debt?" Devon asked.

The man narrowed his eyes before rattling an absurdly high amount of gold. Devon reached behind his back and conjured a pouch full of gold—taken from his personal savings. This was a small dip in his fortune and he was more than glad to pay it and have this problem done with.

"Here." Devon offered the heavy leather pouch to the man. "There's an extra ten percent in here, so you'll keep your mouth shut and never bother this family again."

The man snatched the pouch from his hand and checked the contents. He turned a bit smile to Devon. "Done." Lord Cooper leaned over the carriage's door, but Devon put his arm out, on his way.

"I'll do it," he said, glaring at the man. Devon entered the carriage and sucked in a sharp breath. Kianna was on the floor, cowering against the bench, her hands shaking. Her lip was chapped and her cheek red. By the gods, the man had hit her.

Devon clenched his fist. He prayed for the gods to give him strength to endure this for only a bit longer. All he had to do was take Kianna out of there, and let the men go. Once they were out of range, he would focus on Kianna and forget about them.

That was the plan.

Devon knelt and gently reached for her. "Hey, it's me."

She startled when he wound his arms around her, but when she saw it was him, her bright blue eyes filled with tears. He picked her up, walked out of the carriage, and away from those men. When he was sure he was far enough that he wouldn't feel the need to go back and murder them all, Devon stopped and helped Kianna down to a low branch on the side of the road.

"Are you okay?" he asked, worried about her.

"What happened?" She stared at him and shook her head. "I heard you mentioning paying. How did you trick him like that?" Devon lowered his head, not sure what to tell her. "But ... I saw him with a pouch and some gold coins in his hands." Her eyes widened. "You really did pay him. How?"

Devon stilled. "Kianna ..."

"How?" Her voice rose.

"I ..." Devon sighed. He reached for her again, but Kianna scooted back on the branch, away from him. She was afraid of him. "Yes, I had some money, and I paid him."

"It wasn't just some money. It was a large sum."

"I know," Devon muttered.

Kianna frowned, her eyes staring at him as if he was a stranger. "Where did you get the money? Did you rob someone? Did you sell something of worth?" She sucked in a sharp breath. "You had money, which means you knew you weren't poor." She stood and took a few steps back. "Why are you with my family and me if you're not poor? Why are you submitting yourself to our conditions?" Her hands shook more. "That doesn't make sense."

"Kianna, please," he begged.

"Please what? Give me an explanation!"

But he couldn't. He couldn't tell her the truth.

Kianna, I'm an immortal warrior sent by the gods to protect you. By the way, I've been saving money for over a hundred years now. I'm rich.

Devon shook his head.

"You won't tell me because it's a secret, and it's probably bad, isn't it?" Kianna rounded him, keeping a safe distance from him, and stepped back into the road. "Stay away from me. Stay away from my family."

She spun around and ran in the farm's direction.

Defeated, Devon sat down on the branch and buried his face in his hands. By the gods, what had he done?

PRESENT

Kenna

LEANING AGAINST ITS TRUNK, I GLANCED UP AT THE BRANCHES of the cherry tree. The white flowers were now in full bloom and the scent of cherries filled the backyard. It was my favorite spot in the entire house. Hell, the whole world.

If only we could stay here forever ...

I shook my head, getting rid of those thoughts. No, I wouldn't think like that. I glanced down at the thick book in my lap and began reading again. I *hated* studying for the GED, but it was the only thing I could do now.

More interesting than the cherry tree or the GED test was my neighbor. I had barely seen him the last two days after the ball. I kept glancing over the fence, trying to get a peek at him.

That night ... two things bothered me about the ball. All right, three. One, the way I felt so guarded against him and how snippy I was. I had told him I didn't want to be there, and that was true, but still, I had been almost too bitchy for my liking. Two, at one point, I was sure he was going to kiss me. And I would have let him. But then three happened. I didn't know what had overcome me, how I had known Devon wore a ring on a necklace, and why that ring felt so familiar. But after that, I only felt snippier than before.

It was a relief when Lia and I went home.

Although, I admit that I stayed up half the night, watching out my window, waiting to see Devon arrive home.

Call me a stalker.

Carol poked her foot at my knee. "Are you done studying?"

Right, studying. I frowned at the words in my book. "No. Are you done with your homework?"

She chuckled. "Of course not."

"Then stop bothering me and finish it."

She poked me again. "Can't we take a break? Pretty please?"

I lifted my head and glanced at her. She was lying in the grass under the tree's shade, her books spread out on the ground around her. "And what do you want to do?" I asked.

She propped herself up on her elbows. "I don't know. Make some popcorn and watch something on Netflix."

I rolled my eyes. Typical. She loved popcorn and Netflix. I glanced down at my phone and checked the time. "Sabrina and Kevin should be arriving soon. After they're done with their homework, we can take a break."

She showed me a big pout. "Not fair."

I chuckled.

Taking a long breath, I glanced down at my book again, determined to focus and study this time.

"Kenna!" I shot up at the shout. Kevin ran up through the side of the house. "Kenna, help!"

His face was red and there were tears on his face.

I grabbed his arms. "What happened?"

"It's Sabrina," he said between sobs. "He's going to kill her!"

"What? What do you mean?"

"M-my foster father. He's going to kill her." He grabbed my wrist firmly and tugged. "Please, help her."

I didn't think, I just let him pull me. We ran to the front of the house, with Carol on our heels.

"Hey," Devon called as we ran past his house. "What happened?"

"No time to explain," Carol shouted back.

Kevin's legs were too short, and he ran fast for a little kid, but not faster than me. A little scared about what was happening, I let him go and ran ahead of him.

When I got to their foster home, the front door was ajar. I burst in just in time to see their foster father raising a thick belt and bringing it down on Sabrina, who was cowering in the corner of the couch. The girl let out a cry that broke my heart.

What the ...

The fury within me rose and exploded in a millisecond. I felt my power rising with it, so strong, it was hard to control. The lights in the house flickered and shadows grew in the corners.

"Let. Her. Go!" I said through gritted teeth.

The man turned around, tripping on his feet. From his clumsiness, his dazed eyes, and his ridiculous smile, not to mention his terrible odor, I knew he was drunk.

"What? You want a beating too?" he asked, his words slurred.

The shadows in the corners advanced. I would kill this man. I would beat him like he beat Sabrina and I would kill him. He would beg, but I wouldn't stop until he bled dry in my hands.

"What the fuck?" Devon's voice filtered through my head.

That startled me and I let go of my power. The shadows retreated and the lights stop flickering.

Had Devon seen it? Had he noticed what I had done? Even if he had seen the shadows, he wouldn't understand them. He would think it was a product of his imagination.

"Oh my," Carol gasped when she came in a few seconds after Devon.

The man lifted the belt toward me.

Devon tackled him before I could react—I would have. I was ready to grab his arm and take the belt from him—and threw the man on the floor.

I sidestepped them and reached for a crying, bleeding Sabrina. "Come on." I gently wrapped my arm around her shoulder and guided her toward the door. "Let's get out of here."

As we made for the door, Devon threatened the man. "Next time you touch the kids, you're done. I'll beat you to a pulp."

"Carol, go with Kevin and help him pack," I told my friend.

She snapped out of her shock and nodded at me. She took Kevin's hand and the both of them ran deep in the house, and I hoped they were fast. Meanwhile, I escorted Sabrina out of the house so she could get away from this horrible place as soon as possible.

From inside the house, I heard Devon say, "We'll report you to social services. You'll lose all the kids and all the money you get because of them."

Two minutes later, Devon, Carol, and Kevin joined us outside, and we headed to my house.

Devon

HALFWAY TO KENNA'S HOUSE, I PULLED SABRINA INTO MY ARMS and carried her. Her forearm had a thin cut, where she parried the belt when it came down on her.

My rage spiked again. That fucking man ... if Kenna, Carol, and the kids hadn't been there, I would have taught him a lesson. He had been so drunk, if I had worn my warrior's uniform and my sword, he would have dismissed that later as a hallucination, but he certainly wouldn't forget the beating he would have gotten.

I helped Sabrina down on a stool at the kitchen island and Kenna brought out the first aid kit. The air around the kitchen was tense while Kenna cleaned the cut and bandaged it. She gave Sabrina some medicine for pain, a lot of water, and told her and Kevin to go up to the guest bedroom.

"It's practically empty, but I'll find a bed and blankets for you two," she said, shooing them away.

"I've got an inflatable queen mattress!" Carol said, a little too eager to help. "I'll bring it over." She ran out of the house as the kids dragged their feet upstairs.

As soon as they were out of sight, Kenna let out a long

breath. She paced around the kitchen, her arms shaking. "Holy shit, that man. I could have—" Her hands clenched into tight fists. Then, she forced them open. "I swear, if you hadn't shown up, I think I would have killed him myself. That little piece of shit."

Once more, I was stunned by her attitude. She cared so deeply about these kids who, just a month ago, were strangers. She was even ready to fight for them, to help them even if it meant trouble for her. How could she have such a big heart?

I stepped in front of her, forcing her to stop pacing. My hands skimmed the bare flesh of her arms. "It's okay now," I told her. "Everything is fine now."

Kenna stared up at me with big, bright eyes. Her face was replaced by a blurred image of a blonde girl who rose from a low branch and took a large step back from me. She seemed scared of me. Inside, my heart was breaking because—

I loved her.

A heavy feeling of love suffocated me.

I inhaled deeply, and suddenly, Kenna appeared before me again. She was as still as a statue, her eyes on mine.

I wasn't sure what to think or what to do. Was the blonde girl Kenna? Was that why I felt so drawn to her? All I wanted to do was give in to the feeling in my vision, to that immense love that overwhelmed me. Why did I want to kiss her so desperately?

Slowly, my hand traveled up her arm and rounded her shoulder. Looking into her eyes, I inched closer, cutting the distance between us, and leaned into her. She didn't pull back. No, instead, she tilted her head up, holding my gaze steady, surely.

Her cherry scent hit me and I inhaled deeply, wanting more of it.

It was so fucking intoxicating.

My eyes flicked to her lips and I dipped into her.

"Kenna!" Kevin's voice rang through the house.

Kenna jumped back, her cheeks becoming red, and I inhaled deeply and took a large step back.

She turned to the hallway as Kevin stepped into the kitchen. "Yes?"

"Sabrina is saying she's hungry," he told her. "And me too."

"Of course," she muttered, reaching for the pantry. "What do you want?"

And just like that, Kenna went about the kitchen, preparing a snack for the kids as if we hadn't almost kissed— again. I hated that I felt cheated and ignored.

Shaking my head, I said, "I have some spare blankets at my house." Kenna stopped what she was doing and glanced at me. "I'll bring them over later."

"All right," she said. "Thanks." Once more, she focused on the snack.

Feeling like an idiot, I walked out of the house before I made a bigger fool of myself.

PAST

Kianna

During the last week, Kianna had felt lost.

Angry.

Scared.

Alone.

Betrayed.

When she went back to the farm without Devon, she cried. She lay down in her bed and pretended to be sick, lest the others bother her about what had happened. A couple of days later, when she was finally strong enough to get out of bed, she told the others Devon had left. No word, no explanation, no goodbyes. He had simply walked away.

Her mother was desolated. She couldn't understand why Devon would simply go. Had he recovered his memory? Had he found his family? Even so, he would have said goodbye before going.

And now that he was gone, work at the farm only accumulated. There was too much to do and not enough time in a single day. Kianna was working late into the night, until her body gave in, and she practically fainted in the field.

Her mother tried doing the same, but there was only so much her body could take. She usually ended up breaking down a couple of hours earlier.

Giles was working more than ever too, but the poor man was even older than Ophelia. And even Catherine, who liked to come visit to escape her own chores, now tried to help as much as she could.

But none of them had the strength and stamina Devon had.

Without him, Kianna was sure the crop would either wither, or rot before they could harvest all of it.

Almost a week after Devon was gone, Kianna forced herself to stop working before she fainted. She dragged her feet to the barn, where she washed her face and hands.

Then, she took in a long breath and looked up at the starry sky.

Her mind ran away from her and went back to the one topic that she shouldn't.

Devon.

If he knew he had money, he certainly remembered more about his life. Maybe he knew all of it. Maybe he lied to them and wanted to stay for a reason. But why? Why lie to them? Why stay behind when it seemed he had a pretty comfortable life somewhere else?

It didn't make sense.

Kianna had pushed him away and told him to stay back only out of anger. It was fear. She didn't know him. He could be playing with them all, only to hurt them at the end.

Her stomach revolved at the thought.

Pain shot through her core. She was hungry. She hadn't eaten since morning. After another long sigh, Kianna entered the dark manor. The kids were certainly in bed, and hopefully her mother was too.

She reached the kitchen and grabbed a piece of dried bread. With Kianna and her mother working all the time, the kids were left to fend for themselves. Selina was the one manning the kitchen—or the simple things she could cook by herself. Calvin tried helping, but he was too clumsy, and too agitated to help, which only made Selina more anxious. Calvin was supposed to stay away from the kitchen while Selina was cooking.

Kianna felt guilty. Calvin had lost his playing partner. The kids weren't studying because Kianna was always busy. Their mother was aging by the day and soon would collapse for real.

There had to be something Kianna could do to relieve their situation.

Munching on the bread, Kianna went to her bedroom and closed the door gently, so as not to wake up the others.

With a heavy heart, she opened the first drawer of her dresser and picked up the ring she had left inside a small box. When she found out Devon had been lying to her and her family, she took off the ring and threw it in the drawer. That ring had meant so much to her, but now she knew it had been lies. All the feelings and moments attached to that ring had been lies.

And because of that, she would sell it in the village tomorrow.

Devon

FOR DAYS, DEVON BEAT HIMSELF UP. HE RACKED HIS MIND, trying to think of another solution he should have used instead of paying the man, but other than showing his powers, he couldn't think of anything.

But now he had been expelled from the farm. Sent away. Cast out.

And it hurt like hell.

Though Kianna had told him to stay away from her and her family, Devon couldn't do that. It was his mission to protect her. To protect the world from her.

He stayed in the shadows. He watched as Kianna, Ophelia, Giles, and even Catherine worked themselves to death. It killed him to see them like that and not be able to help. He knew he had done more for the farm than all of them together. After all, when they weren't looking, he used his superior strength and agility to work the field.

Now it was all wasting away, because they couldn't care for the crops by themselves.

It took every ounce of his self-control not to interfere, not to sneak in there in the middle of the night and work the field for them. Several times, he had almost done it, but he stopped himself, because he knew Kianna would figure out what was happening and she wouldn't stay quiet. She would find him and tell him to leave again.

He couldn't take that heartbreak one more time.

Even though it killed him, Devon remained hidden, in the shadows of the trees and in the darkness of the night.

One morning, he saw as Kianna left the manor early, before everyone else had woken up, and walked toward the village with determination.

Devon frowned. What was she up to now? Shouldn't she be getting ready for a full workday ahead?

Like always, Devon followed her.

The sun was just rising, illuminating her golden hair, making her look like an angel. His angel.

His heart squeezed.

When Kianna was crossing the small wooden bridge, just a few yards from the entrance of the village, a group of men approached her. They halted right at the end of the bridge.

She stopped and lifted her chin. "What's the meaning of this?"

Lord Sandler appeared from behind his lackeys and stalked to Kianna. On instinct, she retreated a step. Meanwhile, Devon seethed, having a hard time staying put instead of just rushing in to protect her from this man and his lackeys, who were certainly up to no good.

He didn't do it because he knew Kianna wouldn't want him.

Not right now. Not this time.

"It's nice to see you again, Lady Kianna," Lord Sandler drawled, walking around her. Appraising her.

One of his lackeys approached him. "Are you sure it's her, my lord?"

Without taking his eyes from Kianna, Lord Sandler nodded. "I'm positive."

What were they talking about?

Kianna took a daring step forward. "Lord Sandler, I have somewhere to be. Excuse me, please."

"Somewhere to go?" he mused. One corner of his lips curled up. "The entire village is just waking up. Who could you possibly be meeting at this hour?"

The air changed. Devon felt the heaviness in the wind, the tendrils of evil advancing.

His heart stopped.

No, no, no.

Devon blinked and the demons appeared. The tall shadow monsters with their long limbs and sharp claws surrounded the bridge, trapping Kianna with Lord Sandler and his lackeys.

Dropping all his reservations, Devon rushed forward.

The demons saw him coming, but it didn't matter. Devon was ready for them. With the will of his thoughts, Devon's clothes changed. His full warrior uniform appeared, along with the sword strapped to his back.

He slashed through the first demon with a clean cut, but the second, Devon had to dodge. He was so close now. All he had to do was take a few more steps, kill a few more demons, and Kianna would be safe. A third demon came for him. Devon swung his sword in a diagonal, cutting the demon in half.

He slammed into an invisible wall and tripped back.

"What in the gods name?" Devon muttered. He raised his hands and pushed forward. A jolt cut through the air, toward him.

An invisible barrier.

He slammed into it again, not caring about the pain that coursed into his body each time he touched it. "Kianna!"

But she didn't move. She didn't even look at him. She couldn't.

Lord Sandler had his hand up, aimed at Kianna, who was kneeling on the ground, staring at her own arms with wide eyes.

Black tendrils enveloped her arms.

"See?" Lord Sandler asked. He twisted his hand and Kianna yelped. The black tendrils wrapped around her shoulders. "You have power. I knew it. I knew it was you."

What the ...?

Slander knew Kianna had darkness within her? And he was coaxing it out?

Devon's rage and desperation spiked. He used his feelings to ignite his power, his strength. Then, he held his sword high and brought it down on the barrier.

The invisible wall cracked and jerked, but faded away.

And Devon rushed in.

The demons turned to him, but Devon was ready. Pure rage and despair guided him, his movements. He twirled around, moving out of the way. He swept his sword out and wide, cutting across the demons. He stepped back, whirled his sword in his hand, changed holding hands, widened his stance, stabbed through, and moved forward. All the movements automatic, focused in one single thought: to kill the man hurting Kianna.

But Devon didn't have that chance.

The coward sent more demons to attack Devon, and fled, leaving Kianna gasping for air, the darkness pouring out of her unbidden.

Devon grunted. As fast as he could, he finished the demons. When they were all gone—either dead or running with their master—Devon sheathed his sword and slowly advanced toward Kianna.

He stepped into the darkness, and without seeing

anything, he knelt in front of her. Careful, he rested his hands over hers. The darkness disappeared at once.

But Kianna remained with her eyes closed, her hands trembling against his.

"Kianna," he called, his voice soft.

She only pressed her eyes harder and shook her head.

"All right." He had an idea. "Just ... hang on." He picked her up in his arms.

She gasped but didn't open her eyes. "What are you doing?"

"You'll see." Holding her in his arms, he took her somewhere safe. He put her down and after making sure she was steady on her feet, he said, "You can open your eyes now."

Slowly, Kianna's eyes fluttered open. She glanced around, but recognition shone in her eyes. She stared across the lake, to the manor sitting atop of the hill on the other side.

She took in a shaky breath. "I can't," she whispered, before her legs gave out.

Devon reached for her and held her by the elbows. He softened her fall, helping her sit in the tall grass. Then, he scooted back several feet, still afraid of what she thought of him.

This morning, she had seen too much. Her mind was probably reeling. He needed to give her space, but he wanted to be here to answer her questions. He didn't think he could answer them all yet, but he would do his best. For that, he didn't even shift out of his warrior armor. He wanted her to see it, to realize what happened was real, and not a nightmare.

Seated on the ground, Kianna stared at her shaking hands as if they were foreign to her.

"Are you okay?" Devon asked. She obviously wasn't, but he needed her to say something. Anything.

"D-did you see what happened?" she asked, her voice trembling as much as her hands. "Did you see what came out of my hands?"

"Yes," Devon told her, willing his voice to stay even and calm for her. "You can wield darkness, Kianna."

She lifted her eyes to him. "W-what?"

"You have darkness inside of you." He hated himself for saying those words. "But your heart is pure, the purest I've seen in a long time. You can control it. I'll help you."

Slowly, Kianna lowered her hands. "What about you?" Her pained eyes rummaged over Devon. "Your armor, your weapons. What are you?"

Devon took in a long breath. "The only thing I can tell you is that I'm here to protect you."

Kianna's delicate brows curled down. "Is that why you're here? Why you came to us?"

"Yes," he confessed. "But it's not why I want to stay."

Kianna's bright blue eyes filled with tears. "Don't say that."

Devon scooted a little closer to her. "But it's true."

"Aren't you afraid of me?" Kianna shook her hands. "Of the darkness in me?"

"Not even a little," he said, shaking his head. "Are you afraid of me?"

Kianna stared at his armor, at the weapons on his back, and finally into his eyes. He held her gaze, unyielding, unfaltering. He needed her to see that he wasn't lying. Perhaps he couldn't tell her everything just yet, but he wouldn't lie to her anymore if he could help it.

"No," she whispered, her shoulders relaxing. "Not anymore."

Those simple words clutched at his heart and warmed it.

There was still hope for them.

PRESENT

Kenna

THANKFULLY, LIA DIDN'T OBJECT WHEN I TOLD HER SABRINA and Kevin would be staying with us for a few days—I didn't tell her it was more like indefinitely. The only problem was that we had to pretend to be mother and daughter twenty-four-seven now.

The next day, I took Sabrina and Kevin to the bus stop and promised them to be there when they came back. And by the way the sky was darkening with heavy clouds, I would have to come with umbrellas.

"I won't let anyone take you from me, okay?" I whispered, hugging them both. Then, I ushered them inside the bus.

I dragged my feet back to the house, just as Lia was exiting the front door.

"Are they okay?" she asked, walking to her car in the

driveway. She had seen them briefly this morning when everyone was getting ready for the day.

"I think so." I halted by her side. "Sabrina didn't want to go because of the bruise on her face, but I covered it up with some makeup. I told them to call me if anything happens."

"Good." Lia nodded. "I'll try to get home on time this evening, so we can have a nice family dinner."

I smiled. Then, the smile was promptly gone. "Oh, but we need to buy groceries."

"Oh, shit." Lia glanced at her car. "I guess you can take me to work, then go grocery shopping."

I nodded. "I can drop the car off to you when I'm done." And then risk walking back in the rain. Well, it wouldn't be a problem if I got a little wet.

"I can take you." Devon's voice reached my ears and I froze. Lia and I turned to his house and saw him standing on the porch, wearing black jeans and a dark t-shirt. He had a mug of coffee in his hand. "I can take Kenna to the grocery store."

"That would be wonderful, Devon," Lia said with a huge smile.

"But—"

"Bye," she said, slipping into her car.

I stared as she backed away from the driveway with a go-get-them shine in her eyes. Goddamn it. I would have to have a freaking talk to her tonight.

Without any option, I smoothed my expression and turned to Devon. "Hm, I don't want to impose."

"It's fine. What time do you want to go?" He sipped from his coffee.

"Whenever you're free."

He lifted his mug one inch. "Let me finish my coffee. We leave in ten minutes."

Just like that, he turned around and entered his house. I stood in place, momentarily stunned. What had just happened here? Then, I snapped out of it. I went back into my house, grabbed my wallet and my phone, and stopped by the oval mirror Lia had hung in the foyer above a rickety end table she had found at a thrift store. I smoothed my hand over my brown hair, admired the pink streaks, and checked my face.

I froze, my eyes widening as I stared at myself in the mirror. What the hell was I doing?

Shaking my head, I stomped out of the house.

Devon was already beside his car, the driver's door open in front of him. "Ready?"

I nodded, crossed the small patch of lawn separating our driveways, and hopped in the passenger seat of his car. The air between us was tense, if not a little palpable, crackling a bit with all that had happened. We hadn't talked much since we almost kissed yesterday. Later last evening, he had brought the blankets he had promised, along with a couple of pillows. I had thanked him, and that had been it.

And now we were in his car, seated side by side, and his fresh, spice scent flooded my senses. Why was it taking so long to get to the grocery store?

Actually, it took us eight minutes to get there, but with him so close to me, mudding my thoughts, it seemed like an eternity.

Once at the grocery store, I ripped half of the list and handed to him. "Divide and conquer," I said, needing some space from him. I took a cart and scurried to the end of the store. I focused on the list, grabbing items as I went, and not on the handsome man who had given me a ride here.

Why had Devon done that? When Lia and I first moved here, he seemed so bothered about having neighbors and wanting to have his space and quiet. He even resisted many of Lia's invitations for dinner. Until he didn't anymore. He started coming on his own, for any number of reasons, and sometimes for no reason at all. Like now? What was his real intention by bringing me to the grocery store? Was he just super bored, or he had a secret agenda?

Suddenly, I stopped, a bag of chips in my hands.

If he worked for Slater, he would have tried something by now, right?

I shook my head, ashamed of my thoughts. *Stop it, Makenna,* I told myself and tried focusing on shopping again.

Soon enough, I was done with my side of the store. Devon found me in the middle, a basketful of things in his arms. "I didn't know what brand you wanted of each thing. Some I remembered from seeing them at your house, but others I just picked what I would choose."

I shrugged. "It's fine."

He placed the items in the cart and we moved on to one of the open cashiers. The lady behind the counter had just started scanning the items when my phone rang. I picked it up and frowned at an unknown number. There was no reason for me to answer a call like that, so I pressed the red button and continued paying attention to the lady as she placed the items in paper bags.

My phone rang again.

Devon shot me a curious look. "Won't you get that?"

"Nope." I turned the call off again.

And once more my phone rang.

Devon gently pushed me aside. "Just answer it. I'll take care of this."

"But—"

He pulled out his wallet. "For the many dinners your mother has made me." I frowned, not liking this. "Just go."

I wanted to argue, but a new thought came into mind: what if this call was from the school and Sabrina or Kevin were asking for me? I had to answer it.

I stepped away from the cashier and pressed the green button. But I was too late. The call had already stopped.

Now starting to feel a rising panic inside of me, I walked out of the grocery store and returned the missed call. Mindlessly, I walked to the side of the building, where there were fewer cars parked and fewer people walking by.

My phone rang and rang, but no one answered. I turned off the call and stared at my phone. Who the hell was it? I pressed on my phone's screen and tried calling again.

"Hello there," a voice reached me.

I looked around the corner of the store. A man walked toward me, a half grin on his lips.

I lowered my phone, forgetting about the call. "Hm, hi."

The broad-shouldered man stopped a good distance from me, but I tensed, not used to strangers being so nice. His brown hair was cropped short and tattoos covered his neck.

He glanced around us. "My boss is looking for you," he said with a snarl.

My stomach tightened as a single thought crowded my mind. This was no coincidence. This man was here for a reason. And that reason was me.

He had been sent by Slater to get me.

Pushing my insecurity aside, I focused on my strength, on my anger, on my willingness to *live*. I called my powers just as the sky darkened more. Shadows appeared from the side of the building.

Demons.

"You have nowhere to run," he snarled.

"Then I can fig—"

"Kenna!" Devon's shout came from behind me. I whipped my head and saw him rushing toward me, letting go of the shopping cart with the groceries. He stopped by my side, his face closed, his dark eyes impassive. "What's going on?"

I gaped at him for a moment. Holy shit, what now? Devon couldn't be here. He couldn't see this. More importantly, he was entirely human. If these demons attacked, he would be hurt.

He could be killed.

Shit. Knowing I would have to deal with the consequences later, I stepped in front of him. The demons ripped themselves from the shadows and lunged toward us. I threw my hands out and sent my darkness toward them.

Devon

FOR A MOMENT, I THOUGHT I WAS FUCKING DREAMING. I blinked. Nope. Shit was real. Kenna really was in front of me, harnessing darkness and pushing back the demons.

And her hair was turning blond again.

"Stay back!" she shouted at me.

That snapped out of my trance.

My black armor covered me, and my sword appeared on my back as I stepped right beside her.

"What ... ?" Her arms went slack with shock. A demon rushed at her, taking advantage of her distraction. I drew my sword and slashed the demon in half. It burst into smoke, disappearing above us. "Watch out!" she shouted, extending her hands toward two demons who were coming for me from the side.

With a whirl of her hands, Kenna invoked the darkness from the corners of the building, from our shadows, even from the dark sky above us, and spun the darkness around the demons. Even though they were creatures of hell, they couldn't fight this darkness. They were engulfed by it and disappeared within. The darkness cleared and it was as if they had never existed at all.

Side-by-side, Kenna and I fought the demons, taking them out in a few minutes. It was an odd thing, this sudden feeling inside my chest, which looked very much like pride.

When all the demons were gone, we faced the only human in the bunch. The man ran. I took two steps after him, then stopped. I didn't like killing humans, and if I could avoid it, I would.

"No!" Kenna said, catching up with me. "We can't let him leave."

I looked at her. "You want to kill a human?"

She groaned but didn't answer. Instead, she marched back to where I had left the cart with the groceries, and pushed it back to my car. I willed my armor and sword to disappear and followed her, glad this was a small town, and no one had been out and about while we fought demons in a public parking lot.

Shaking my head, I joined Kenna in my car, put the groceries in the trunk, and slipped behind the wheel.

We drove in silence, but it wasn't tense like before. It was a different silence, as if now we shared a secret, something unique no one else in the world shared.

Even though I wasn't saying a word, my mind whirled with so many fucking questions. How did she have powers? How did they work? Who was she? Who was that man? Did that happen often?

I parked my car in Kenna's driveway and helped her with the groceries. It was only when everything was atop the kitchen island that I finally asked her about it.

"Your hair is blond again," I said, starting with something light.

Kenna grabbed the boxes of pasta from the paper bag. "Yup."

"I'm assuming blond is your natural color."

She placed the pasta inside the cabinet behind her. "Yup." She let out a long sigh and faced me again, her bright blue eyes a little apprehensive. "I dye it brown, though every time I use my powers, the dye fades. I don't know why."

I frowned. "Why do you dye your hair?"

She averted her eyes and fussed with the bags over the island, but not really doing anything. "Because I don't like it blond."

It was a lie. And she knew I knew it was a lie, but she didn't care.

"What about your powers?"

She returned her eyes to me. "I was born with the ability to conjure and control the darkness. I don't know why or how. All I know is that my powers are evil, and there are people out there who would do anything to use them."

Was that the problem? Someone out there wanted her powers? That was why she dyed her hair, and was reluctant to let people get close to her? She and Olivia were running from someone?

I wanted to ask all of that out loud, but I was concerned about pushing it too far and having her kick me out. She was slowly opening up, answering something here and there. I had to go slow.

Though, I could tell her a bit about me.

I extended my hand to her. "Come with me."

Her brows curled down and her eyes fixed on my hand. "Where?"

"I want to show you something."

Kenna hesitated, then she slipped her hand in mine. At that moment, another vision hit me. The blonde girl sat on the ground, and I knelt in front of her, in desperate need to keep her safe.

That feeling was so intense, I sucked in a sharp breath. The vision was gone and I stared at Kenna's beautiful face.

She tilted her head at me. "What is it?"

I locked my eyes with hers, knowing that the same feeling from before applied now, for Kenna. The realization that I would do anything to protect her hit me hard and made it hard to breathe.

Holding tight to her hand, I pulled her with me, to my house, all the while conscious of her delicate hand in mine, of her closeness, of her sweet cherry scent so delectable whenever a breeze blew or she got too close.

I only let go of her hand when we arrived in the spare bedroom on the second floor of my house, where I kept the board with all the information I had gathered over the years.

Kenna froze in the doorway, her eyes bugged and her

mouth open. Slowly, she dragged her feet closer to the board and took a good look at it.

Here, I was entirely exposed to her. She might not understand a couple of things, but she could make sense that I was different. Not human. Her eyes scanned the piece of paper where I took notes of the visions I had each time I touched her, except for the one from a few minutes ago. Then, she saw a picture of the ring, the drawing of some demons who I found in town in the past few weeks, and lastly, a picture of Lia and her, and my random notes about them, followed by several question marks.

Kenna pointed to Lia's picture on the board. "She isn't my mother."

I gaped at her. To be honest, I had suspected that before, but chose to believe whatever they were selling. "Who is she, then?"

"Just someone I met," she said, her eyes rummaging the board. "Someone who helped me through the tough times. Someone who deserved a better life than the one forced on us."

So, she was running from someone. And Lia too. They were hiding here, and pretending to be mother and daughter. Kenna had gone as far as dying her hair to hide.

We were finally getting somewhere. She was opening up to me and I definitely didn't want to mess this up.

Suddenly, Kenna turned her eyes to me. To my surprise, she didn't look mad or suspicious, merely curious. "And who are *you*?"

I inhaled deeply. How much could I tell her? How much *should* I tell her? She was involved in all of this, I was sure, but what if I brought her in deeper, and the gods punished me? Punished her?

"I'm a warrior, sent here on a mission," I started, hoping I wouldn't overwhelm her with everything. "I don't have details of my mission, but I have a strong feeling that you're connected to it."

Her brows curled down. "You don't have the details of your mission? What does that mean?"

"That I have to figure out by myself what my mission is and what to do." Even to my ears, that explanation sounded insane, but it was the fucking truth.

"And why do you think I'm connected to it?"

I pointed to the list of visions. "Every time I touch you, I see what feels like memories. Old memories, from centuries ago." I reached under my shirt and pulled the necklace with the ring on it. "And you knew about this. I don't know how, but you knew I had it."

She stared at the ring. Slowly, she stepped closer to me and reached for it. The moment she touched it, a jolt of energy coursed through me, shaking my insides. Kenna slipped the ring on her finger and it fit perfectly.

"I don't know how I knew about it," she whispered, admiring the ring on her finger. "But it calls to me. Almost like ..."

She didn't finish her sentence, so I did. "Like it's ours."

Her eyes lifted and fixed on mine. Fuck, when did she get so close to me? If I raised my arm, I could wrap it around her waist. If I leaned down, I could easily kiss her. My gaze flickered to her pink lips. I really wanted to fucking kiss her.

Whatever was between us wasn't a simple connection. I knew it. I *felt* it. And I was dying to explore it.

Lowering my guard, I brought my hand up and cupped her cheek. Kenna leaned into my touch, as if this was something forbidden she couldn't have, but she wanted it anyway.

By the gods, she was so beautiful, and her scent was really making me mad.

"Kenna," I whispered, lowering my mouth to hers.

The doorbell rang.

Kenna jumped away from me, losing her balance as her finger snatched on the ring. The necklace pulled with the force, but then her finger slipped and she almost fell back. I reached for her, but she caught her footing and raised her hands, warding me off. "It's fine," she said, her voice hoarse. Her gaze turned downcast. "I'm okay. Go get the door."

Right. The door. "What about you?"

"I ..." She shook her head once, then met my gaze again. Whatever moment we had just shared was gone, and cold, guarded Kenna was back. "I should go home."

I didn't like it. There was too much for us to talk about, to figure out. Not to mention that I still really wanted to kiss her. But before I could protest, the doorbell rang again.

I nodded. "You know the way out."

Reluctantly, I backed away from the room and went downstairs. I heard as Kenna climbed down the stairs and made her way to the back of the house.

With a heavy sigh, I opened the front door.

A middle-aged woman smiled at me. "Hello there." She offered me a flyer of some new church in town. "Would you be interested in—?"

"No," I snapped, slamming the door in her face.

I scoffed. Of course it had to be something about God and church to interrupt Kenna and me. Because why not? The fucking gods had a dry sense of humor.

PAST

Devon

THINGS BETWEEN DEVON AND KIANNA DIDN'T GO BACK TO normal right away, though their connection deepened with their shared secret. Devon was careful around her, always making sure she was all right, and that she had no doubts of how much he cared about her, that he was there for her any minute, any second of the day.

On a beautiful spring day, Devon told Kianna he had to go to the village, to do something related to who he was. He didn't elaborate on it, and he was thankful that Kianna didn't ask more about it.

Because of the nice weather, Devon invited Kianna to go with him. He also invited Selina and Calvin, who didn't blink at the opportunity to escape schoolwork and their chores.

"What about the field," Kianna said, eyeing her mother and Giles already working.

"I'll make it up when we get back," he promised. "You know I can."

Finally, she agreed and they went into the village.

The first thing Devon did when they arrived was to take them to the sweets shop. Devon told them to get whatever they wanted.

Kianna tugged his arm. "You don't need to spend your money on us."

Devon offered her a small smile, his heart happy to see she was worried about that, but even happier knowing he could give her so much more. "I want to." He pressed a kiss to her cheek and her face warmed. "Stay here. I'll be right back."

He saw the question in the knot of her brow, but once again, he was glad she didn't ask.

Devon hurried out of the shop and went directly to the alley where he usually met the warriors. This time, Ryder waited for him.

"We found out who the man and his demons are," he said as soon as he saw the warrior approaching.

Devon halted before him, bracing himself. "Who?"

"They are members of the D'Ingur Order," Ryder said. "As we suspected."

Devon cursed under his breath. This wasn't good. If the D'Ingur Order was after Kianna, then it meant the gods were right. Maybe not about her being evil, but about the darkness inside of her. About evil people using her darkness for evil things.

Ryder promised to look more into it and to search for the D'Ingur Order, while Devon kept Kianna safe. Or kept the world safe from Kianna.

Frustration laced the warrior's muscles and even though

he saw Kianna, Selina, and Calvin laughing when he came back to them at the shop, he was still apprehensive. It was only a matter of time before the D'Ingur Order came after Kianna again. He couldn't let that happen. He wouldn't. He would protect her and her family, and kill every one of those evil men and demons.

If Kianna noticed how tense Devon was on their way home, she hid it well. Instead, she hooked her arm with his and batted her long lashes at him, making her blue eyes shine even brighter. An urge to stop right in the middle of the road and kiss her hit him hard, and he only didn't because the kids were running and playing as they walked.

Devon glanced at Kianna, then Selina and Calvin, and his chest filled with affection ... with love. Even though he was a warrior, even though he knew he shouldn't have human feelings, he couldn't help it.

He loved them, plain and simple.

Back at the farm, Devon handed a bag of candy to Selina and Calvin. The kids snatched it from his hands and raced into the manor.

Kianna blinked at Devon. "That's a lot of sugar. If they don't sleep tonight, you're the one taking care of them."

Devon slipped his hands on hers. "I wouldn't mind." He glanced past her shoulder, to the field in the back. He had to make up the time lost while out with Kianna and the kids, but he wanted a few more seconds with her. "Come on."

He tugged her to the cherry tree and the bench beside the lake. He sat down, but Kianna didn't. She pulled her shoes and socks off and lifted her dress to her knees, then she stepped into the lake.

"Ah," she said with a sigh. "This is refreshing."

The sun shone on the lake's surface. Kianna's hair looked

as if it was made of fire, and her smile was contagious. Devon's heart squeezed. And once more, he wondered how such a beautiful and kind person could have so much darkness inside of her. Why was it her? Why not someone else, with a rotten heart and soul?

Devon felt the tug around his middle, pulling him to her.

His eyes fixed on her, he followed it.

"Devon?" she asked, seeing as he was coming right for her.

He didn't stop. He wrapped his arms around her waist, brought his lips to hers, and took them into the lake.

Kianna let out a yelp against his lips, but that was her only protest. Half a second later, her arms were around his neck and she kissed him back. Her lips were soft and her cherry scent was like a drug. Devon would never tire of her. He would never get used to how amazing it felt to touch her, for her to touch him back.

They submerged under the water.

When they finally emerged, out of breath, Devon ran his hand over Kianna's wet hair, combing it away from her beautiful face.

"I love you," he confessed.

PRESENT

Devon

I KNEW IT WAS A FUCKING NIGHTMARE, BUT WHATEVER I DID, I couldn't wake up.

In my dreams, Kenna walked down a dirt road a few steps in front of me. Her jeans and t-shirt suddenly changed into a brown gown, and her hair had turned blond.

My ring on her left hand reflected the sunlight.

She turned around and smiled at me.

Then, darkness descended upon us and the demons swarmed her. She screamed, disappearing amid the swarm. I changed into my armor, but before I could draw my sword, the demons attacked me too.

"Kenna!" I cried, trying to get to her.

She screamed again, this time so shrill, so deafening, the piercing sound exploded in my head.

I woke up with a jolt and sat up in bed, a thin sheen of sweat over my bare chest.

By the gods, what the fuck was that nightmare? I usually dreamed I was back in hell, being tortured and punished for the mistakes I had made, the mistakes I couldn't remember.

But this time, I had dreamed about Kenna.

Something about this dream, about how Kenna was there, wearing my ring, smiling at me, and then being attacked by demons, tickled something in my mind. There was something in it. A clue, a puzzle piece ... something. I just couldn't put my finger on it.

Heavy footsteps came from the stairs. Two seconds later, Kenna burst into my bedroom, light from the hallway leaving her a dark silhouette.

"Are you okay?" she asked, breathing hard.

I stared at her.

She leaned against the doorjamb, her hair back to brown and falling like a cascade down her back and around her shoulders. The tank top she wore was glued to her body, but not more than the tiny shorts that hugged her thighs and ass.

I gulped and turned on the dim light of the bedside lamp. "Did I scream again? Did I wake you?"

"I was up, couldn't sleep." She brushed a strand of her hair aside. "It was even more terrifying this time." She took two steps into my bedroom. "Want to talk about it?"

I ran a hand through my messy hair, briefly lowering my eyes. When I looked back at her, she was standing a couple of feet from my bed, looking like a vision. "It was about you," I confessed.

Kenna's brows twisted down and she sat at the edge of the bed by my legs. "About me?"

"Yeah ..." A buzz ran through my body at her closeness. "Usually my nightmares are about my time in hell and—"

She went rigid. "Time in hell?"

Fuck. "A long time ago, I failed a mission, and my punishment was to spend time in hell."

"Shit," she muttered. "I swear, if I couldn't control darkness, I would say you're insane and spewing nonsense. Alas ..." She gestured to the sides. "Here we are. A magical warrior and a girl who isn't quite human either. What a pair."

A pair.

I couldn't help but wonder if she was the girl from my visions. She had to be. I had dreamed she had transformed from one to another, and for some reason, I believed this dream had been more than just that.

I felt attracted to her in a way I couldn't explain. She knew about the ring and she had magic of her own, dark magic, which attracted demons to her. Demons I was chosen to kill.

Her moving here, right beside me, and this push and pull between us wasn't a fucking coincidence.

Kenna tilted her head. "You don't look okay."

I realized I was staring and lowered my gaze. But only for a second, because I couldn't stop looking at her even if I wanted to. "The nightmare. It scared me."

Holding my gaze, Kenna asked in a whisper, "You were scared because of me?" I dipped my chin in affirmation. She scooted closer. "I'm fine. See, I'm right here."

Gods, she had no idea that I *felt* she was right here, and how much I was fighting to hold her, to fucking touch her, to make sure she was really fine.

"I ..." I reached over and caught her hand in mine.

A vision appeared before my eyes. Of me lunging toward

the blonde woman, of her yelping as I pushed her into the water and her brief hesitation as my lips met hers.

I blinked and stared at Kenna, my heart speeding up.

"Did you see something?" she asked, her voice low. I nodded. I brought her hand to my bare chest and laid her palm over my heart. "It's fast."

"It's because of you." My voice was rough, and my heart accelerated more with her skin pressed against mine.

Her blue eyes glinted in the dim lighting. Gods, I couldn't endure this anymore.

I tugged her arm and pulled her to me.

Kenna

I DIDN'T RESIST. HOW COULD I WHEN HE LOOKED AT ME WITH such intense dark eyes, when his heart beat so fast under my palm, when he looked so handsome and so vulnerable in his bed, his sculpted torso bare and calling for me.

I scooted into his lap and leaned into him at the same time he wrapped his arms around me and held me tight.

His breathing became shallow gasps as he tilted his chin up and our lips met. A jolt coursed through me, igniting my insides, fevering my desire.

His mouth moved against mine, so soft, so hard, so relentless. I parted my lips and he took over. He claimed my body and soul with his kiss, making me breathless, lightheaded. I never knew a kiss could taste this good, could make me feel so many things at the same time.

Devon tugged the hem of my tank top and I lifted my arms. We briefly broke the kiss so he could slip my shirt over my head. Then, his mouth was back on mine, my chest pressed to his. Holy shit, his skin was warm on mine, and I could feel his heart beating inside me.

A gasp escaped my throat when he suddenly broke the kiss again and flipped us over. He laid me on his bed, his powerful body hovering over mine. His dark eyes drank me in, exploring every inch of my face, of my bare breasts, of my midriff. Warmth spread on my cheeks.

"You're so beautiful," he whispered.

He lowered his body to mine and I gasped again, enjoying his weight pressed over me. He swallowed my gasp with his mouth before deepening the kiss and moving his hips against mine, drawing another gasp from me.

I felt like I was larger than life, like I would explode out of my own skin at any moment, like I couldn't get enough of him, of his lips, of his hard, hot body, of his hands on me. All of that only multiplied once all of our clothes were gone and we became one. Holy shit! I held on to him while he took me to heights I never knew possible, little moans escaping my throat every few seconds.

After, Devon lay beside me and pulled me to him. He wrapped his arms around me, holding me tight, his head nestled on my shoulder.

"You're my destiny," he whispered in my ear. "I'm sure of it."

That single thought clamped around my heart and squeezed hard. Because as much as I liked the idea of being his destiny and staying with him, I knew it wasn't possible. Cecilia and I would have to leave. That much was certain, especially since the demons had already found me in this town. Shit, I hadn't even told Lia about that yet. I wondered if she would just chalk it up to a coincidence and ignore it, since she was happy now.

I turned my head to Devon, wanting to see him, this new piece of my own happiness, but his eyes were closed. His breathing had slowed. He was deeply asleep.

I stayed there, letting him hold me, while I held him, wishing this was a viable future.

PAST

Devon

Devon knew he didn't deserve the happiness he felt. After all, he wasn't human. He shouldn't feel like a human.

He shouldn't love another human.

But he couldn't help it. He loved Kianna more than anything else in this world, and he had a feeling he had never loved anything, anyone like that in his previous human life.

Whenever he could, he spent time with Kianna. Touching her, making her smile, taking care of her, kissing her. He felt drunk, completely addicted to her. But there were moments when he forced himself to part from her, so he could work in the field. He worked relentlessly sometimes well into the middle of the night, all so he could take more breaks the next day, and be beside the woman who had stolen his heart.

One sunny afternoon, Devon worked the field with Ophelia and Giles, while Kianna was schooling the kids inside the manor. He was counting the minutes until supper time, when he could spend a few minutes with her. Hopefully, he would be able to take her to the cherry tree by the lake, where they could be alone.

A carriage appeared in the distance at the farm's entrance road. Devon stiffened, watching it.

"Who could that be?" Ophelia asked from behind him. She wiped her hands on her apron and quickly left the field.

After taking off the apron and washing her hands and face, Ophelia walked down the small hill to the front of the manor as the carriage stopped a few feet from her.

Devon eyed with curiosity as an older man and a younger one stepped out the carriage and bowed low to Ophelia. She smiled wide at them, then ushered them into the manor.

Something tugged in Devon's chest.

At first, he ignored it and went back to work.

But after a few minutes, the tug turned into a painful pull.

Dropping his tools, he walked out of the field too. He washed his face and hands, put on a shirt over his sweaty torso, and went to the back of the manor. He took off his dirty shoes and walked in.

He stopped short when he saw Ophelia had invited both men to sit down at their rarely used dining room and was now busy making tea.

"Just stop it," she hushed to Kianna, who held a silver tray in her hands. Ophelia placed the hot water from the kettle into a hand painted carafe, then over the tray. "Just listen to what they have to say."

Neither woman saw Devon there as they turned back to the dining room with their best china and the last slices of the cake Kianna had baked for the kids yesterday.

Ophelia directed Kianna to take a seat beside the young

man, while she took a seat across the table. The older man was seated at the head of the table.

Frowning, Devon approached the dining room, but remained hidden from view. Something told him he shouldn't be seen.

"You were saying," Ophelia urged, serving the tea to both men.

The older man smiled at her. Devon recognized them now. Lord Sandler and Noel from the ball. He was the one Kianna had danced with.

"It seems my godson here is enamored of your daughter," Lord Sandler said with a wide smile. "He has a question for you, Lady Ophelia."

Noel cleared his throat and straightened his back. "I would like to ask for Kianna's hand in marriage."

An invisible knife pierced Devon's heart and twisted.

Ophelia beamed. Kianna's eyes went wide, horrified.

"That would be wonder—"

"Mother!" Kianna snapped, cutting off whatever her mother would have said. But Devon knew what Ophelia would have said. She would have agreed. If it depended on her, Kianna would marry this young man tomorrow. Seeing as they were rich and had status, Ophelia would even give them Selina for free.

No. Devon shook his head. Ophelia wasn't this heartless. Yes, she wanted Kianna to marry someone rich, so she could have a better future, and also provide for them. But she wouldn't go against Kianna's wishes. Would she?

Ophelia turned an uneasy smile to both men. "Excuse us."

She grabbed Kianna's arm and pulled her to the kitchen.

Right into Devon's path.

Kianna's eyes widened even more, her mouth falling open. "Devon ..." she muttered.

A wave of rage and jealousy took over Devon's senses.

Before he said something he didn't mean, he walked out of the house and into the field. He commenced working, as fast and furious as he could.

What was he thinking? He was a divine warrior, not meant for human emotions. He was here to protect Kianna, to protect the world from her. Nothing more.

He shouldn't interfere in her life, not in this way. If she found a man who could give her a solid future, that was good. Wasn't it?

Still, he couldn't erase the feelings he had developed for her.

Kenna

THIS MORNING, I SLIPPED FROM DEVON'S BED BEFORE HE HAD awoken. It was harder than I expected, leaving his warm bed and his hot body. But I had to get back to my house before anyone woke up. I thought about leaving him a note, but decided it was too much. Later, I would send him a text.

At my house, I put on a long robe over my night clothes and washed my face, pretending I had just woken up in my own bed. I made breakfast for Lia, Selina, and Kevin, then I helped the kids get ready for the school and saw them all out.

Once they were gone, I made myself another cup of coffee and stepped out onto the back porch. I sipped my coffee and stared at the cherry tree.

Warmth wrapped around me as I remembered what had happened last night. After what had happened yesterday morning at the grocery store, and the board Devon had showed me at his house, I hadn't been able to sleep.

He had been right. We were connected in some way, and Slater and his demons were getting closer. This peace was temporary. My perfect world would shatter sooner rather than later.

Then, I had heard him screaming and dashed to his house.

The rest ... I sighed. My cheeks warmed at the thought of his mouth on mine, his body sliding against mine, his breath on my neck, on my ear, of him holding me tight while sleeping, hopefully dreamless.

I glanced at his house. There was no movement, no sound. He was probably still sleeping.

I went on about my day—I took a shower, cleaned my bedroom, put in a load of laundry, studied for the GED, all the while eyeing my phone. Several times, I started typing a text to Devon ...

What are you doing?
I left because of the kids.
Sorry I wasn't there when you woke up.
Want to come over?

But each time, I deleted it all. Everything I typed sounded lame, needy. I didn't want to become clingy before anything had even started.

Why didn't he text me either? Why hadn't he come over and talked to me? Did he regret having slept with me?

I didn't regret sleeping with him.

Shaking my head, I pushed thoughts of Devon from my mind and continued as if my life hadn't just changed in some way—I just didn't understand how yet.

I busied myself with other tasks to occupy my mind with something else until Carol returned from school. Sabrina and Kevin arrived soon after, and as usual, they all worked on their homework while eating snacks I prepared for them. I took that time to study too, even though I was sure Lia and I would have to move soon and I wouldn't be able to take the GED.

Carol had just gone home when Lia came back from the library.

"Kenna, where are you?" she called from the front door.

"Here," I shouted from the kitchen. I had been cutting onions and tomatoes with Sabrina for dinner later, while Kevin cleaned the counters. Lia entered the kitchen with a huge smile. "What's with the freaky grin?"

She cleared her throat and gestured to the hallway. A young man stepped into the kitchen. "Do you remember Nigel? From the library's fundraiser?"

I frowned, confused. "Yes, I do." I waved my hand at him. "Hello Nigel."

"Hello, Kenna," he said with a small smile of his own. "Sorry to barge in like this."

"Nonsense," Lia said. "I bumped into Nigel at the library. He asked about you, and I suggested he come for dinner." She quickly rounded the island and pushed me away from the counter. "You go keep him company while I cook dinner."

I stared at her, but she avoided my gaze, knowing all too well I would give her hell for this stunt. Was she crazy? Wasn't it enough to have Devon, Carol, Sabrina, and Kevin at our house all the time? Now she had to bring in another stray?

"Mom," I said through gritted teeth.

"I can take care of everything." She continued pushing me

until I was right beside Nigel. She waved us off. "Don't worry. Just ... have fun."

Nigel gestured to the living room and I awkwardly followed him there.

"Sorry about that." He stopped in front of the couch. All around us, cans of paint and brushes and other tools covered the floor, a reminder of the continuous home improvement we had been working on for some time now.

"It's okay." I halted a good way from him, still unsure what to do with him until dinnertime.

"I have to confess, I didn't bump into your mother by chance." His eyes fixed on mine. "I went there because I wanted to see you. I can't stop thinking about you. Not since the fundraiser."

I tucked in a strand of my hair around my ear, glad it was back to brown and not the blond. The last thing I needed was anyone else seeing past my disguise.

"I don't know what to say," I admitted. All right, it was nice to have the attention of a handsome guy, but I had already fallen for another, one who was even more handsome. My cheeks heated again just thinking about Devon. And of course, Nigel thought I was blushing because of him.

"Do you mind?" He pointed to the couch behind him.

"Of course not." I inched closer and ended up sitting on a small folding ladder, since I didn't feel like giving him mixed signals by sitting beside him.

Nigel started a conversation, telling me about his job and asking a little about me. I answered politely, but didn't ask much, all the while stealing glances to the front door and my phone, wishing Devon would either burst in or text me.

But he did neither.

In fact, he didn't even come for dinner. Instead, we ended

up entertaining Nigel, who seemed intent on pleasing me. Lia pushed me toward him, as if we were a match made in heaven, totally ignoring my signs to stop this nonsense. Sabrina and Kevin were either oblivious to it all, or they simply didn't care.

After dinner and dessert, Lia suggested I walked Nigel out to his car.

My belly tensed the moment I stepped out onto the front porch, following Nigel. What if Devon saw me with Nigel? What if Nigel tried something while Devon was watching?

I halted at the top of the front steps. Nigel realized I hadn't followed him after a few seconds and turned around.

"Everything okay?" he asked, returning. He stopped at the bottom of the steps, just a couple of feet away.

I wanted to push him away, to step back and put more distance between us, but I was afraid of being disrespectful. Nigel had been nothing if not polite tonight. There was no reason for me to be rude to him.

"Yes," I said, standing my ground.

"Kenna ..." He paused. He took the first step, putting his head at my height, and so, so close. "I—"

"Hey."

I pivoted, my eyes wide at the incoming figure.

Like a predator, Devon stalked from his front porch to mine.

Devon

WAKING UP IN THE MORNING AND NOT FINDING KENNA IN BED with me had been a fucking hit to my ego. What the fuck happened and why had she left? Did she regret sleeping with me?

I got up from bed in a bad mood and went about my day as if I had a stick shoved into my ass. I kept glancing at my phone, expecting a text from her, explaining why she had left, or asking me to come over.

Nothing.

I went out for a long run twice since it was the only way to burn off my frustration and calm down. But even that didn't last long. All I wanted was to check on her, but I acted like a child and refused to cave first.

Until I saw the car parked beside Lia's. Who the fuck had come for a visit? I kept spying from the side window, but couldn't see much. Whoever was here stayed past dinner.

Then, Kenna walked the person out the front door.

Nigel.

My blood boiled with jealousy, and before I realized what I was doing, I left my house and marched to hers.

"Hey," I snapped, catching the attention of both of them. Nigel instantly took a large step back, and Kenna stared at me with huge eyes, as if caught red-handed.

Nigel straightened his back. "Good evening, Devon."

I wasn't in the mood for bullshit. I climbed the front steps and halted right beside Kenna, my body touching hers. If he didn't get the hint, then he was a bigger fool than I first thought.

"What brings you here?" I asked, a discernable bite in my voice.

"I came to visit Kenna and Lia." His gaze shifted between Kenna and me, a question in his eyes. Then, it fell on Kenna.

"Thank you for your hospitality, Kenna. I'll talk to you some other time."

"Good night, Nigel," she said, her voice tight.

The moment Nigel backed out of the driveway and started down the road, I turned on Kenna. "So that's what you were doing all day? You sneaked out this morning so you could spend the day with him?"

She pressed her hand over my mouth. "Shhh. Someone will hear you."

I pushed her hand away, but held on to it, afraid she would get away again. Since when had I become obsessed with a girl? I wasn't human, for fuck's sake.

And yet, I couldn't ignore them. I couldn't ignore her.

I tugged her closer to me. "What? You don't want anyone finding out about us?"

She tilted her head up, closer to me. "Is there an us?"

I reached up and ran my fingertips along her jaw, down her neck. "I thought there was. But you left this morning without an explanation."

She shivered at my touch. "I didn't want Lia or the kids waking up and not finding me at home." Kenna balled her fists on the edge of my shirt, pulling me even closer. "I thought about leaving a note, but I thought you would just text me when you woke up."

"And why didn't you text me?"

She shrugged. "I guess I was waiting for you."

I let out a heavy sigh. "I guess we're both a little stubborn."

She chuckled. "A little?"

I felt the corners of my lips tugging up. I leaned into her, resting my forehead on hers, and wrapped my arms around her, holding her tight. "Come over again tonight. I promise I won't be mad if you disappear before I wake up." I brushed my lips on hers.

Kenna shivered again. "I will," she whispered.

Losing the battle against my self-control, I cupped her nape and closed my mouth over hers, kissing her.

PAST

Kianna

WHEN DEVON HAD ASKED TO TALK TO OPHELIA AND KIANNA after the kids went to bed, Kianna's heart started racing and her mind spun. What did he want to talk about? Would he ask for her hand in marriage? The idea was absurd. Devon wasn't entirely human, Kianna was sure of that. He wouldn't settle down and marry a human, even if he had told her he loved her.

But besides that one idea, Kianna couldn't think of anything else.

Finally, Selina and Calvin went to bed. Kianna made some tea and met her mother and Devon in the kitchen. They sat around the table, each of them holding mugs of steaming chamomile tea.

Devon let out a long breath and fixed his dark eyes on Kianna. "You have to leave. All of you. It's not safe here.

Tomorrow morning, when the kids wake up, just pack a few things and leave."

Whatever Kianna was waiting for him to say, that wasn't it. Leave? What was he talking about?

"Devon, you're not making any sense," her mother said, her brows knitting together.

"Go as far away as you can," he continued. "Even then, you might not be safe." He slapped the table, startling both women. "We should wake up the kids and leave right now."

"Wait, Devon." Kianna shook her head. "What are you talking about?"

"Remember that man? Those demons?" he asked. Kianna stilled. She didn't think he would bring that up in front of her mother. How would she explain that if even she didn't understand? Whatever she saw that day, she preferred pretending it didn't exist. "They are members of the D'Ingur Order, and they are after you. After your powers. They won't rest until they have you."

Kianna shot up and took a few steps back. "Stop," she muttered.

"You know I'm not lying." Devon rose to his feet, but didn't move from his spot at the table. "I promised I would never lie to you again. This is me, telling you the truth."

Her chest tight, Kianna shook her head. "That makes no sense." She faced him with big eyes. "I'm no one. I'm nothing."

"That's not true," he said in a low voice. "You can control darkness. For these people, you are the most precious thing they could have."

"But—"

"That's enough." Her mother stood from her chair and stared at Devon, her eyes hard. "I don't know what has gotten into you, Devon, but I have to ask you to stop. What you're saying makes no sense, and I won't allow you to stay if you continue."

"Ophelia, please," he started. "I haven't lost my mind, and I'm not lying." He dared rounding the table and walking closer to her. "You and your family have become special to me. I don't want any harm to come to you. I need you to be safe, and for that, we need to leave. Now."

"Devon!" Ophelia snapped, losing her patience.

Kianna gasped. She could count on one hand how many times her mother had lost her composure in her life, and now was one of them. Whatever she thought of Devon before was crumbling in the face of this side of him.

"Please," Devon said again.

A loud bang came from outside.

Devon went rigid. Kianna sucked in a sharp breath. Ophelia's face paled.

"What was that?" Ophelia asked in a whisper.

After blowing out the nearest candle, Devon went to the window and looked out.

He cursed under his breath. His grave eyes met Kianna's. "They are here."

PRESENT

Devon

For the last three nights, Kenna had come to my house after everyone in hers was sleeping. And she left again early in the morning, before they woke up. My bed felt empty once she slipped from it. To be honest, my entire fucking house felt empty and cold without her in it, which didn't make any sense since I had lived here for almost two years before Kenna had shown up, and I had always felt comfortable here.

Not anymore.

Now I only felt comfortable and relieved and relaxed when Kenna was close to me, at least within arms' reach, if not with my arm around her.

How the fuck could I feel like this for a woman I had just met? But I hadn't just met her, had I? Though I still caught glimpses of memories whenever I touched her, the visions hadn't cleared. Nevertheless, I was sure Kenna was the blonde girl from my memories. I had met her many years ago. I had fallen in love with her.

And whatever mission I had failed before, it was connected to her. Which meant my new mission was about her too. Not knowing what it was exactly brought an uneasy feeling to my chest I couldn't shake off.

Kenna and I didn't just spend the nights together. After the kids left for school and Lia left for work, I had been going to her house, and we had spent most of the day together. Sometimes just talking, sometimes in a familiar silence, and sometimes in her bed.

I wondered how had I lived before I met her? The answer was fucking simple: I hadn't lived. I had just survived.

After Kenna left that morning, I tried sleeping more. I had been spoiled by Kenna's presence. Since she started sleeping here, I hadn't dreamed. I just held on to her and slept. But now, the moment I closed my eyes, the images of my last nightmare came back rushing to me.

Kenna being swallowed by demons.

I sat up in bed with a loud inhale.

That wasn't a dream. It felt like a warning.

My muscles tightened with anxiety as I pushed from the bed, put on some pants, a shirt, and boots, and went downstairs. I paced my living room, watching from the windows, waiting for the others to leave. Once the kids and Lia were gone, I crossed the yard and knocked on Kenna's front door.

She opened the door and narrowed her eyes at me. "I wasn't expecting you so soon."

I pushed in and closed the door behind her. "I ..." I rubbed the heel of my hand over my chest as a dull pain started there. I faced her, still in her pajamas with a robe tied around her waist, and took her hands in mine. "I have a feeling. A feeling that things aren't going so well."

Her brows knitted. "You mean you and me?"

I shook my head. "No, I mean my mission. I feel like I'm missing a big piece of the puzzle, or pieces, and something is about to blow up in our faces." I pressed a hand over my heart again. "I don't like this feeling."

Kenna took a step closer to me and pressed her hand over mine. "I know what you mean. Since that day at the grocery store, I feel like my life is a ticking bomb. It'll be only a matter of time before he finds me."

"Who? Who are you running from?"

With a heavy sigh, Kenna dropped my hands and took a few steps back. "Slater. He's the leader of the D'Ingur Order." That name. It struck a chord, but I couldn't remember why exactly. "He kidnapped me when I was twelve. Whatever he did to me, I don't remember my life before that." She shrugged.

A ball of rage bloomed in my chest. This Slater guy kidnapped a child? "He kidnapped you because of your powers?"

She nodded. "Yes. He taught me how to use my powers. And before you think I was willing, I wasn't. He tortured me, and I met Cecilia there. I became like a daughter to her, so he used her against me."

I hadn't asked why Slater had kidnapped Lia, and I wouldn't now. It was clear she was just the side dish while Kenna was the main course. "What did he want with you?"

Kenna's hands started shaking. "It doesn't matter. All that matters is that he can't find me again." Her blue eyes grew wide. "He can't take me again, Devon. He can't. If he does, the entire world is doomed." She walked to me and looked deeply into my eyes. "Devon, you have to promise me. If he comes for me, don't let me go, even if that means you have to kill me yourself."

My heart squeezed painfully. I wrapped my arms around her and held her tight, inhaling her sweet cherry scent. "I won't let him take you. I won't let him hurt you."

She pulled back a little and searched my eyes. "Promise me."

I shook my head. "I can't."

"You have to. Promise me."

I brought a hand to her face and cupped her cheek. "Kenna, I can't do that, because I love you too much."

Kenna's breath caught.

I hadn't thought before saying those words; I hadn't even realized my feelings ran that deep until the words were out of my mouth. But now that I had said it, I knew it was true. I loved her. I fucking loved her so much.

She held on to my shoulders. "I love you too," she whispered.

Those words ...

I groaned and fell into her, claiming her mouth with mine. She parted her lips and let me in, her tongue entwining with mine. Holy fuck, she was divine. I didn't care about her powers. Even if she had pure darkness inside her, it had to be divine. There was no other explanation.

I backed her to the nearest wall, pressing my body against hers. It hadn't been a handful of hours since the last time we had sex, but I couldn't help myself. I needed her. I was addicted to her.

I ran my hands up her thigh, and pulled her up, intent on carrying her up to her bedroom, but I quickly dropped her and jumped back when footsteps came from outside.

The door opened and Sabrina and Kevin walking in with big grins.

"What are the two doing here?" Kenna asked, smoothing her hand over her hair. "Did you miss the bus?"

"No," Sabrina said, opening the door wider. A man appeared behind her. "He was waiting for you outside. He asked us to bring him here. He says he's your friend."

Nigel stepped inside the house, but he was different than before. There was an energy around him that wasn't there before. A heavy darkness. And from the way Kenna went completely rigid beside me, I knew she felt it too.

PAST

Devon

"W-what?" Kianna asked. Her hands started shaking.

"What are you talking about?" Ophelia stomped to the window. "Who's here?" She peered out.

Devon glanced out again, past Ophelia's form. The hill was illuminated by a hundred torches, maybe more, each of them being held by a man or a demon.

He blew out a long breath. "Kianna, take your mother, take the kids, and hide in the cellar under the manor. I'll create a diversion so we can escape." Kianna stared at him, but her eyes were unfocused. He grabbed her shoulders and shook hard. "Kianna!"

She blinked, as if waking up from a daze. "Yes, yes. I'll do that."

With stiff movements, Kianna grabbed her mother's arms.

She pulled her mother, who was now in shock after seeing the silhouette of the monsters outside her house.

But, as the women made their way up the stairs, a boom echoed throughout the house. The glass windows shattered as the demons burst in and advanced on them. Kianna pushed her mother to her back, Ophelia screamed, and Selina and Calvin clambered out of their beds, yelling for their mother.

Devon's outfit changed in the blink of an eye and he drew his sword, walking backward until he was standing before Kianna and her family. It was too hard to curb his rage, his frustration, as the demons surrounded them.

"W-what's happening?" Selina asked, holding on to Kianna's and Ophelia's skirts.

"Just do what I say," Devon told them in a low voice. "And right now, try not to move too much."

He closed his eyes for a second and sent a prayer to the gods. *I need help. Please, send the warriors.*

The demons, with their slick skin and red eyes and sharp teeth, snarled at them. Devon knew that they wanted carnage. If it depended on them, they would have already killed everyone. Devon wasn't sure he could contain that many demons, but he would sure try.

Something else was at play here. Someone else.

As if he had heard Devon's thoughts, a human stepped forward and the demons parted, letting him pass.

Noel, the young lord who had asked for Kianna's hand in marriage, stared at them with an amused grin. "So you're the warrior assigned to protect the girl. Interesting."

Behind Devon, Kianna gasped. "*Who* are you?"

"I'm Noel," he said simply, as if that answered the question.

Kianna groaned. From the corner of his eyes, Devon saw as she lifted her hands. He felt the trembling in the air as she summoned her powers. But she had no control over it, not yet. She hadn't practiced; she didn't know what she was doing. As soon as she got a hold of the darkness, it vanished from her control.

Kianna's face paled.

"Nice try." Noel snickered. "It's a shame we were told to keep one prisoner." He raised his hand above his head. "Take the girl. Kill the rest."

Fear gripped Devon. The demons lunged over them.

Devon swung his sword wide, cutting through three demons at once. Behind him, he felt the power coming from Kianna as she summoned it, trying to use it. A shadow ball appeared in her hands. It flickered, as if unstable. She threw it, but it disappeared before it hit any demon. Instead, the demons bared their razor-sharp teeth at her.

Then, they sank their teeth into her mother and her siblings.

Kianna's scream filled the manor. The lamps in the room flickered, then went out, immersing them in darkness.

Devon's eyes adjusted to the dark at once, but Kianna fell to her knees, shaking and sobbing. She reached for the bodies of her family, but the demons pulled them away—or what was left of them.

His chest tightened for Kianna.

He killed demon after demon, trying to keep them back, but they were too many. Creatures separated him from Kianna, and soon, she had been overrun by demons. They held her and she didn't even try to fight back.

"Kianna!" he screamed, swinging his blade harder, faster,

trying to cut a path back to her. But for every monster he killed, three more poured into the manor, keeping him busy.

It felt like a second and an eternity at the same time, but finally, the demons dragged Kianna out of the manor.

"No!" he shouted, his chest hurting, his muscles protesting, his head swimming. What was happening?

Defeated, Devon lowered his sword and sank to his knees.

He couldn't win this battle, not alone.

Kenna

FEAR GRIPPED ME AS NIGEL WALKED INTO THE HOUSE, AN EASY grin on his lips, his dark eyes fixed on me.

He wasn't the same Nigel as before, the one who had come to dinner with me and wanted to spend more time with me. No, that Nigel was gone. The walking body in front of me had been possessed by darkness, by a demon's power, and I only knew of one order that could have done something like that.

I grabbed Sabrina and Kevin and pulled them behind me. Understanding something was wrong, Devon stood beside me, a wall of power.

"My dear Makenna," Nigel said, his tone thick as honey. And completely fake. "Slater has missed you."

My eyes narrowed as I watched him. I could ask him to leave, but I knew he wouldn't. I could ask him why he was here, but I knew why. Besides telling the kids to run, I didn't see any other way around this situation.

Nigel took a step closer and I pointed my hand at him.

"Stay back!" I warned, summoning my power.

"Or what?" he asked, amused.

It was the middle of the morning, but suddenly, the skies outside darkened, and shadows appeared outside the house.

Demons.

We were completely surrounded.

"Or I'll kill you," I hissed. I didn't think of myself as a murderer, when all I ever did was kill evil demons and monsters, but for him, I would make an exception. Truth be told, he was already gone. The moment the demon withdrew his hold on him, Nigel would be a lifeless body.

A boisterous laughter exploded from his throat, and he pressed his hand over his stomach, as if I had told the funniest joke on the planet. The next second, the laughter was gone. His eyes fixed on mine again, a dark glint flashing in their depths.

"Get her," he snarled.

The demons burst into the house.

"The kids!" I yelled to Devon, pushing a screaming Sabrina and a crying Kevin to him. "Take them. Take them out of here!"

He hesitated for half a second.

Then, he grabbed the kids' shoulders and pushed them through the house.

And I faced Nigel and the demons, my magic at my fingertips.

Devon

ON INSTINCT, I SHOVED THE KIDS TO THE NEAREST DOOR, THE magic around me working and my outfit changing to my warrior's leather uniform, the swords at my back.

Demons that had broken the windows to enter the house now appeared in our path to the front door, making the kids scream more.

"Just ... stay close," I told them as I guided them both behind me.

Watching the demons, I drew my sword from its scabbard and lunged at the first demon before it could attack us. I cut through the demon's middle, its dark blood staining my sword and the floor at my feet. I moved on to the next demon, and the next, and the next, until the path was clear again.

"Come on." I turned to the kids, but both of them stood a few feet back, their eyes huge, their faces white, and their limbs shaking like bamboo in the wind. Fuck, this was too much for them. "I don't have time to explain." I grabbed their shoulders and steered them toward the door. More demons crawled into the house through the broken windows. I opened the door and pushed the kids out. "Go! Run to Lia at the library! She'll know what to do. Don't stop for anything." They both stared at me, too stunned to move. "GO!" I roared.

Tripping on their own feet, Sabrina and Kevin took off toward the street. I sent a silent prayer to the gods and hoped the kids would be fine, that they would find Lia and escape this town.

I twirled my sword in my hands and turned to the incoming demons crowding the hallway. I ran toward them, through them, slashing and cutting and pushing back wherever was needed. Although the hallway was only a few feet long, it seemed to take me an eternity to cross it.

The lights in the house, which had been off, flickered, and darkness filled the kitchen.

"Get out!" Kenna shouted, releasing her power into Nigel. Slowly, her hair began changing, the brown color fading away, showing the blond of her strands.

The man raised his arms and the darkness reflected off him, as if he was holding a shield. Kenna staggered, surprised by this.

"Like my new trick?" Nigel said, holding his sick smile. "Then try this one."

He threw his arm out, a dagger appearing in his hand and flying toward Kenna.

She yelped as the blade buried into her shoulder.

"Kenna!" I cried, slashing my sword through a demon's throat.

"Kill him," Nigel said, never taking his eyes from Kenna. More demons swarmed the hallway from the kitchen, putting themselves between Kenna and me.

Red rage filled my vision, and I swung my sword.

But it was not enough.

Hurt, Kenna couldn't fight against Nigel and the demons. Nigel leaned over her, pressed a white cloth over her nose and mouth, and when she fainted, a demon picked her up in its arms.

"No!" I screamed, moving quicker, killing faster.

But by the time I had killed all the demons in my way, it was too late.

Kenna had been taken.

A band tightened around my chest, making it hard to breathe. The world darkened and I fell on my knees, dizzy.

This pain ... this pain that assaulted my heart, this desperation to save her, I had felt this before.

A dull headache started behind my temples as my memories returned.

PAST

Kianna

INSIDE A CAGE AT THE BACK OF A CARRIAGE, KIANNA WAS KEPT drugged. From the few moments she gained clarity, she could tell she had been on the road for days now. But she didn't know how many, and whenever she looked around, she didn't recognize the countryside. Even the scenery had changed, not once, but multiple times. First, there were thick woods, then a long lake, and now a beaten path, and lots of rocks and cliffs.

But more than being locked up and not knowing where she was, what filled her with pure, unbidden fear, was the people around her.

No, not people.

Demons.

That was what Devon had called them, that was what Noel had called them when he had shoved her inside the cage. Her arms shook and her stomach twisted each time her eyes landed on the demons. Some looked alike, with slick, grayish skin, long limbs, and misshapen faces with yellow eyes and sharp teeth. But there were others too. Some short and stocky, some that seemed made up of shadows, and even ones that looked like ghosts with translucent bodies that hovered over the ground.

In her brief moments of clarity, Kianna lowered her head, closed her eyes, and told herself this couldn't be real. It wasn't happening. There were no demons, no people who were after her. She wasn't in a cage.

And her family hadn't been murdered right in front of her face.

Tears burned her eyes and she sobbed, remembering their terrified faces, their screams. Their blood splashing everywhere.

"You're awake," Noel said. Kianna scooted to a corner of the cage, but it was to no avail. Demons closed their claws around her arms through the wooden bars. The man rounded the cage and pressed the white cloth over her nose.

She tried not to breathe it in, but it was impossible.

Her eyelids grew heavy, her vision darkened, her limbs softened, and she fell into a deep sleep again.

***

WHEN KIANNA WOKE UP AGAIN, SHE WASN'T IN THE CAGE. No, she was on a cold stone floor in a cavernous room, with her hands bound by ropes that dug into her raw skin. The rope was tied to a hook in the floor.

She bit back a sob. She hadn't been dreaming. There were

demons everywhere, watching her with hungry eyes. If she moved the wrong way, they would eat her alive.

Did she even care anymore? Her mother, Selina, and Calvin were gone. And Devon? Was he still alive? God, she hoped he was, and that he was smart enough to stay away. Even with his powers, he wouldn't be strong enough to rescue her from so many demons.

The demons parted and a man walked to her. Not the same man from before—Noel was a few steps back. Another man, taller, with a rougher face, more imposing.

Lord Sandler, the one who had invited her to the ball weeks ago.

"Kianna, it's so nice to meet you again," he said, his voice grave. "It's a great honor to have you here with us."

She puffed out her chest, trying to be brave. "Who are you? Where is here? And what the hell do you want with me?"

Sandler showed her a brilliant grin. "I'm the leader of the D'Ingur Order, and you, my dear, are the key."

Kianna frowned. "Key?"

"You're the only person in the world who can conjure and wield darkness, which means you're the only one who can open this chamber." He stepped aside, his arm wide, gesturing to the darkness beyond him.

At first, Kianna didn't see anything other than the stone that made up the cavern, but then her sight adjusted and she saw it. Two tall doors carved into the stone, dark-light illuminated symbols engraved on its surface.

Invisible fingers ran down her spine, chilling her bones. "W-what is in that chamber?"

"Ingur, the greatest demon of all time," Sandler said, as if that was common knowledge. "Long ago, warriors fought against Ingur and were able to imprison and hide him here. It took time, but the order never gave up. And here we are." He smiled triumphantly at her. "We found him and we found you, the only one who can free him."

If he thought she would open the damn doors for him, he was sorely mistaken. "I' not opening that."

His smile faded. "Who says you have any choice in the matter?" He stalked to her, his steps measured to give her goose bumps. "I mean, it would be easier if you willingly opened it, but I doubted you would, so I have everything prepared." He poked the floor with his boots. The same symbols on the door were carved into the stone ground, forming a circle around her. "Once I activate the spell, there's no going back."

Desperation bloomed in Kianna's chest. She couldn't allow this madman to release a powerful demon. She jerked against the ropes tying her to the floor, but it only dug into her raw skin more.

"I won't let you!" she screamed, her frustration and panic rising to her throat.

Sandler laughed. "Poor little girl." He extended his hand and Noel stepped forward. He placed a silver dagger in Sandler's hand. "Thank you for your help." He leaned over her, the dagger aimed at her chest.

A whimper rocked her body, but Kianna closed her eyes and tried staying as still as she could. If she was going to die, then she would do it with dignity.

A zooming sound echoed through the cavern and the clang of metal. Kianna's eyes shot open and she stared at Sandler, the dagger on the stone floor several feet from her.

She looked around but didn't have to search long.

Devon.

He stood at the cavern's entrance, stoic and strong.

And he wasn't alone.

Devon

DEVON WOULD NEVER FORGIVE HIMSELF FOR NOT BEING ABLE TO save Ophelia, Selina, and Calvin. But he could still save Kianna.

Not long after Kianna was taken, the cavalry arrived. Ryder, Owen, and a dozen other warriors burst into the manor, killing all the demons in their way.

From there, they were called before the gods. Devon didn't want to go, since he had to go after Kianna, but he couldn't defy a direct order.

The gods explained to him what was happening. The famed D'Ingur Order was back. Truth be told, it was never gone, just quiet in the background, gathering members and researching. Until now. They had found the hidden place where the warriors had imprisoned Ingur centuries ago, and they had found the one human who could free him.

Kianna and her powers.

That was why he had been sent to protect her. To protect the world from her. Because if Sandler, the leader of the D'Ingur Order, got his hands on her, the world would be in grave danger.

The gods allowed Devon and the other warriors to go, to try to stop the D'Ingur Order before it was too late.

"Even if you have to kill her yourself," one of the

goddesses said right before he left. "If that's what it takes to stop this demon from rising, then you *have* to do it."

Devon wanted to argue, but he didn't have time to waste. Instead, he set out with the warriors, following the faint tracks left behind by the demons. All the while his mind spun fast, trying to come up with a solution.

By the time they arrived at the hidden cave in the middle of nowhere, Devon still hadn't found a solution. If it came down to it, he wouldn't be able to kill Kianna. If it came to it, he knew he would even fight the other warriors, his brothers, in order to save her.

Feeling agitated, Devon charged inside. Sandler held a dagger, poised to strike Kianna in her chest.

As fast as he could, Devon drew a smaller dagger and threw it, his aim true. The sword's tip hit Sandler's hand, sending the dagger flying away.

Sandler whipped to him, his teeth gritted. "Kill them all!" he roared, the words echoing in the cave.

The demons lunged at them, but the warriors were ready. They met the demons halfway. Devon slashed through the demons as if they were paper, trying to get to Kianna.

Sandler leaned over Kianna and grabbed her throat, making her gag.

"No!" Devon shouted. "Kianna!"

His rage turned red. He brandished his sword even faster, harder. He killed without thinking. If another warrior had stepped in his way, he wouldn't have even noticed. He would kill anyone to get to her.

His world froze.

Sandler plunged a dagger deep into Kianna's stomach.

"No!" Devon screamed.

The world froze. Devon halted, his sword fell from his hand.

Sandler released Kianna and she fell to the hard, cold ground, like a rag doll.

Shadows slipped from her, unbidden, strong, floating to the enormous doors across the cave.

Black light shone from the symbols carved in the door and through the cracks. A shudder rumbled through the cavern, and slowly, the doors opened.

Everyone in the cave stopped, watching the doors.

Another rumble echoed from the stone doors, like a sigh or a moan.

Then, big, black legs appeared from the door.

Ingur.

"Kill the demon!" Ryder yelled from somewhere behind Devon.

That snapped him out of his daze, but he didn't go for the demon. He went to Kianna.

Devon rushed to her, slipping on the deep red blood pooling underneath her. He suppressed a sob as he knelt beside her and scooped her up in his arms. "No, no, no."

Her head lolled back into the groove of his elbow and her eyes blinked, as if she was searching for his face.

"D-Devon?"

Her voice was so weak. Another sobbed racked his body. "I'm here." He held her tight. "Please, hang on. I'll fix this."

She lifted a trembling hand to his face, ran her fingers across his cheek. "Just ... stay with me."

He sobbed again. "Forever," he whispered.

Kianna let out a shallow sigh, blinked her eyes once more. Her hand slid down from Devon's face.

Her chest stopped moving.

Her heart stopped beating.

Devon yelled, a shrill sound that shook the walls, the entire world.

And yet, the fight went on, as if the love of his life hadn't died in his arms.

Because of him.

Because he couldn't protect her.

Because he couldn't keep her safe.

Devon gathered her onto his lap and tucked her hands on her chest. Then, he saw it. The ring he had given her. The ring she had not taken off, except during their brief misunderstanding.

Inhaling deeply and wiping away his tears, Devon slipped the ring from her finger and put it onto his pinky, the ring too tight, but he didn't care.

Gently, he deposited her on the ground, promising to come back, to give her and her family a proper burial.

Then, he picked up his sword and turned toward Ingur.

Even if it killed him, Devon would put this demon back in his place and make everything right.

Devon

I PRESSED A HAND TO MY HEAD AS THE REST OF THE MEMORIES came back to me.

I hadn't killed Ingur. Not then, not later.

The battle against him raged for years. It destroyed villages and towns, and killed many people.

But the war hadn't been mine to fight. I had been called by the gods and they rendered my punishment for not stopping Sandler from opening the chamber again: They sent me to hell for a few centuries.

And I knew now why they had brought me back. Because Kianna had been reborn into Kenna, and I had to do this all over again.

I punched the kitchen island beside me. I had already failed this fucking thing again. Noel, now Nigel, had taken her from me.

But this time ... this time, I wouldn't fail.

This time, I would save her.

PRESENT

Devon

ALL MY GRIEF, ALL MY DESPERATION TOOK A BACKSEAT TO THE
rage and determination I felt. Hanging on to those feelings, I
moved. I went to my house and called to the gods. For the
warriors. For whoever the fuck wanted to hear me.

Not five minutes later, Ryder appeared in my backyard. I
walked out and met him.

"You failed?" He glanced to the house beside mine, to the
broken windows and ruined porch. "Again?"

I crossed my arms and faced him. "I haven't failed yet.
And let me just say, this setback only exists because the
fucking gods didn't tell me shit about this mission!" My voice
rose. By now, the neighbors were probably watching us. The
destroyed house. The two guys in odd clothing, carrying
weapons. And now shouts. I didn't fucking care. "Now, where
the fuck is the tomb?"

Ryder let out a long sigh. "It's under an abandoned fort forty miles south of here." I nodded and started marching across the yard. He followed me inside. "I'm coming with you."

I gritted my teeth. "I don't need your help."

He grabbed my arm and tugged me back. "I'm your friend. I want to help."

I jerked my arm free of him. "Suit yourself."

The truth was, I was glad he was coming with me. I wasn't sure I could take Nigel and dozens of demons by myself. I wasn't sure if the two of us could do it. But I had to try.

Ryder and I jumped into my car. A moment later, we were on the road, headed toward the fort. I stepped on the pedal and went as fast as the car could go. As I expected, we caught up with Nigel in less than thirty minutes.

A line of black vans followed the curve of the road like a writhing snake. Speeding up a little more, I zoomed past them and threw my car in their way. The first van tried to swerve and pass me, but I put my car in reverse and hit its front, stopping it completely. The next van didn't have much time to brake. The driver turned the van off the road and slammed into the ditch, smoke steaming from its radiator. I hoped Kenna wasn't in that one. The next couple of vans all hit each other as they braked to avoid the stopped vehicles.

Ryder and I moved, going from van to van, searching for Kenna and taking down the demons. We cleared the first two vans. By then, demons had emerged from others the vans and lumbered into position around Ryder and me. And right behind them were Nigel and Kenna. Her eyes locked with mine and her name rose to my throat, but I held my tongue. Her wrists and arms were bound with thick ropes and a piece of cloth gagged her mouth, her blond hair blowing behind her. Nigel held a dagger above her chest.

"One more step and I'll kill her," he declared, his voice loud enough to be carried above the demons' hissing and growls.

"He's bluffing," Ryder whispered to me.

"I know," I whispered back. "He needs her alive until she's close to the chamber."

"Attack?"

"Oh, yeah."

Ryder and I rushed the demons. We slashed through them as if they were made of air. Out of the corner of my eye, I watched Nigel. As I thought, he simply held on to Kenna and retreated to the van in the back. He shoved her inside and hopped behind the wheel.

He turned the key. The van's engine sputtered but didn't come back to life.

When there were fewer than ten demons to deal with, I went after Kenna, knowing Ryder could take care of them.

Nigel saw me coming and threw open the driver door, the dagger poised in his hand. "Stop!"

"Or what?" I asked, through gritted teeth.

I didn't give him time to answer that. I swung my sword hard, knocking the dagger from the man's hand. Then, I plunged my sword into his chest, right through his heart.

I pulled my sword away and let his body fall at my feet. Disgusted, I stepped over the body and opened the van's doors.

Kenna cowered in the back of the van, her eyes slightly dazed. Whatever they had given her still muddled her mind. But when she saw me, her shoulders relaxed and a sob shook her body. I scooted to her, and tore the gag from her mouth and the ropes from her arms and torso. She leaned into me and I pulled her into my lap.

"Shh, you're safe now."

Her limbs were heavy, but she held my shoulders, her face in my chest. She lifted her chin and looked at me. "You came."

I nodded, as finally the dam broke inside of me. Relief poured through every inch of my body. I had done it. I had saved her.

And I wouldn't let her go.

I would protect her until the end of our days.

Nothing else, no one else, would hurt her.

"Of course I came." I cupped her face and ran my thumb across her cheek, glad she was okay. "I'll always come."

She leaned her hand into my hand. Her brows curled down and her gaze shifted to my neck. No, to my collarbone. She reached up and tugged the collar of my vest down, revealing the silver chain. She pulled the necklace out from underneath and stared at the ring—*her* ring—liked she had done before.

"This ring," she whispered. She rested the ring in the palm of her hand. A gasp came from her lips and her eyes widened. She blinked fast a handful of times, then she looked at me, her eyes on mine, still huge. "I remember," she whispered. "I remember everything."

Kenna

ON THE WAY BACK TO MISTY HILL, I REPLACED THE HALF-ASSED bandage Nigel had placed on the wound on my shoulder, the one he had inflicted. At least it wasn't deep and should heal nicely. I told Devon about my past in this lifetime. Or at least, what I knew about it. My guess was that Slater had erased my memories of my childhood to make it easier for him, so I wouldn't fight him. But I always fought. From the moment he abducted me and locked me inside his hidden mansion, I fought him. There had been other girls there, human girls he sold like cattle—Cecilia had been among them. Slater hadn't sold her, though. He kept her there to take care of the girls before they were sold to the highest bidder.

That and selling drugs was how he had money to own such a huge mansion and to have so many lackeys to run his main operation—find the tomb of Ingur.

This, of course, was broken into two steps: find the one who could open the tomb and find the tomb. I remembered how excited he had been when he first brought me to his mansion. He treated little me like a queen, giving me anything I asked for, but freedom. But as time passed and he couldn't find the tomb, he grew aggravated. He started lashing out at Cecilia and me. He started using me and my powers to his advantage—robbing people and undermining powerful demons. I always refused, but he threatened to hurt Cecilia, the only person I cared about, the mother I didn't have, the one who took care of me. So, I did all he asked, and after, I cried for days, unable to sleep because of the nightmares that assaulted me.

I tried escaping a few times, but gave up because each time I was caught. Slater had beaten me within an inch of my life, and then he hurt Cecilia too.

When I was older and stronger, a plan started forming in mind. My powers grew with me, but I didn't reveal that to Slater. I didn't show him all I could do, because if he knew, he would have tightened security around the mansion, around me. He would have had more demons watch every movement I made.

Instead, he thought I was weaker than I really was, and served only to open the chamber. Which he never stopped looking for. In fact, the clues started aligning, and it seemed he was getting closer to finding the damn tomb, which meant I had to get out. Cecilia and I waited for the right moment. It took a few months, but in one of the few outings he took us both on—when I was supposed to use my powers to his advantage, and he took Cecilia as leverage so I would cooperate—we fought back and escaped.

At first, it was a deadly wild chase, and Cecilia and I didn't stop running for months, afraid that if we paused for a second, they would catch us.

Until now.

"I should have known," I muttered, watching out the window to the passing landscape. "We shouldn't have stopped here for so long. Deep down I knew he would find us, and yet, I allowed us to stay."

Devon reached over from across the seat and took my hand in his. "I'm glad you stopped here. Otherwise, I wouldn't have found you again." He pulled my hand up and placed a quick kiss on my skin, his eyes always on the road.

A shiver traveled down my arm, filling me with love.

Despite our little time together in this life—and in my previous one—my feelings for him were exactly the same. I loved him with all my heart, and having him here, holding my hand, taking care of me, was more than my poor heart could bear.

Tears filled my eyes, but I glanced away before he could see them.

His car sputtered, the engine making a weird noise, making us both tense. But it turned smoother again. The side of the car had been badly banged up when he stopped the vans, but thankfully, it still turned on and was driving us home.

Then, it was his turn. When I was done telling him about me, Devon told me about himself. After I was killed in my previous life, Devon and the warriors fought Ingur, but he was too strong. And, before they could stop the demon, the gods punished him by sending him to hell.

To hell. Damn, these gods weren't fooling around.

When I was reborn, the gods sensed me and pulled him

out of hell. They gave him my ring and told him to figure out what his mission was and make it right this time.

I snorted. "That's nuts."

"I know!" He slapped the wheel. "I've told Ryder that thousands of times, but the gods never gave me another clue. Until you showed up and I started having visions, or rather memory flashes, of past you, I was lost." He gripped the wheel tight, his knuckles turning white. "Well, I wasn't good enough this time either, was I? After all, they took you and—"

"They *almost* got me," I corrected him. "You saved me this time." I squeezed his hand, reassuring him that I was here and well.

We drove into town and parked his car in his driveaway.

Lia and the kids burst from the front door of his house, with a tall guy following behind them.

"What are you doing?" I asked, exiting the car and pointing to Devon's house. Then, I frowned at the strange man. "And who's that?"

"It's Owen," Devon said, joining me on the other side of his car. "He's a warrior like me." This was the third warrior I had met. The first was Devon, the second was Ryder, who had helped Devon rescue me. He had stayed behind to clean up the mess we left behind on the road.

"I'm glad to you see you alive and well in this lifetime, Kianna," the warrior said, his voice deep and stoic.

"Thank you," I replied, not sure what else to say.

"I asked him to stay here with Lia and the kids to make sure they were safe," Devon explained.

I started walking to the porch, but Sabrina and Kevin rushed at me and bear-hugged me. I smiled as I hugged them back. These were Selina and Calvin. My sister and my brother. My heart filled with love for them, for meeting them again. Tears sprang to my eyes as I glanced up, looking at Cecilia. She was a friend and a mentor now, but long ago, she had been my mother. My real mother. I gestured for her to come to us, and she did. She wrapped her arms around the three of us.

"I was so worried," she said, a sob breaking her words.

"We're fine now," I told her. I kissed Sabrina's and Kevin's heads and Lia's cheek. "We'll be fine." Still embracing them, I glanced at Devon. "What's the plan?"

"I'll help you pack, all of you, and you hit the road," he said, his tone firm. "The sooner, the better. If we all work together, we should have you on the road in about an hour. Don't you think?"

Lia startled. "Run away again?"

I frowned, my thoughts matching hers. "I'm tired of running."

"But if you don't run, Slater and his demons will come back for you," Devon reminded me.

I glanced around, a little worried about the nosey neighbors listening to us talking about demons and powers.

"Can we talk about this inside your house?" I asked.

Devon nodded and gestured to the front door.

Once we were all inside his living room, Devon turned to me. "Why don't you want to run?"

"Because if we run, they will come after us anyway," I explained. "There's no safe place for us. We'll be on the run forever. Because of me." I glanced at Lia and the kids, who were standing close beside me. "I can't do this to them." I lifted my chin, trying to be stronger than I felt. "I want to face Slater and his demons once and for all."

"What?" Devon shrieked.

"I'm strong, but I can't do it alone," I told him. I glanced at

Owen, who seemed like a statue in the foyer. "I know it's in the warriors' interest to stop the D'Ingur Order. We need to find a way to kill Ingur."

"We can't kill it," Owen said.

"What do you mean?" I asked.

"Ingur is too strong even for all of us combined," Devon said. "We can't defeat him, only lock him away in that chamber."

Understanding fell over me. "So, when I die, hopefully of old age this time, I'll eventually be reborn and they will come after me again." Devon nodded. Shit. "The more reason to defeat the order now. We kill them all, and put an end to this. There will be no more order to try and free Ingur. In time, he'll be forgotten."

"She's right," Owen said.

Devon glared at him. With a heavy sigh, he returned his gaze to me. "Even if I agree to this, we need to send Lia, Sabrina, and Kevin away."

The three of them protested, but I nodded.

"I'll call the other warriors," Owen announced before disappearing into thin air.

I stared at the spot he had been. "You can do that?" I asked Devon. Despite knowing him from centuries ago, I had never understood the scope of his powers.

"Some of us," he said. "But not me."

Kevin walked closer to Devon and blinked. "So, you're an angel?"

He and Sabrina were taking all of this way too well. I had expected Lia, who knew about demons, not to be too surprised by warriors, but the kids were another matter.

Instead, Kevin batted his eyes at Devon as if he was a superhero.

Devon's lips curled up. "Not exactly."

I squeezed Lia's shoulder. "How about we all have a snack while we talk about where the three of you will go?"

Lia nodded at me, then steered the kids to the kitchen.

Devon crossed his arms and faced me, his eyes hard again. "I don't like this."

I walked to him, until I was a foot from him. I ran my hands over his tight arms. "We can do this."

"We can, but I would rather you left with Cecilia and the kids."

I rose on tiptoes and leaned closer, aiming my mouth to his. "Don't you trust me?"

His gaze flickered to my lips. "You know I do. That doesn't change the fact that I want to keep you safe, no matter what."

"For now, just hold me," I whispered. "And believe we'll be fine."

His arms wrapped around me. His hands splayed on my back, pressing me against him very tight. "We'll be fine," he repeated, as if he needed to say it out loud to convince himself.

I too had to believe we would be fine this time.

PRESENT

Kenna

I DIDN'T WANT TO RUN, BUT THAT DIDN'T MEAN I WANTED Lia, Sabrina, and Kevin here while we fought Slater. At first, Lia argued with me, saying she wouldn't leave me. But after telling her about the past, who she was to me, who the kids were, she started crumbling. Many years ago, Sabrina and Kevin had been her kids too. It had been her duty to make them safe, and I was hoping she felt the same way now. Thankfully, she did. But she felt that way about me too. Though, she understood. I had my magic and would fight alongside powerful and divine warriors.

After promising to see them again, I watched as they drove away. Sabrina and Kevin looked back and waved, while I stood at the curb, waving back at them, tears springing to my eyes.

Devon put an arm around my waist and pulled me to his side. "They will be fine."

"I know," I said, my voice low. "I'm just scared that I might not see them again."

When the car turned a corner and disappeared from my sight, Devon turned to me, his hands gently on my hips. "You will see them again. I promise you that."

I wrapped my arms around his waist and laid my head on his chest. "At least you're here with me."

He planted a kiss on the top of my head. "Always."

"What's going on?" That was Carol, arriving back from school.

"Oh." I disentangled myself from Devon but didn't move away. She already knew about us, of course. But now I was worried about her too. In the past, she had been Cat, my best friend, and she hadn't died with my family, but that didn't mean she wasn't in danger in this lifetime.

Her gaze went to the top of my head. "What's up with your hair?"

I ran a hand over my strands, blond once again. "Hm, nothing. Just changed a bit." I rocked on the balls of my foot. "So, you're already back from school."

"It's been thirty minutes since the last bell." Narrowing her eyes, Carol hiked her backpack higher on her shoulder. "I just saw Lia driving away with Sabrina and Kevin. Where are they going?" She glanced past our shoulders, to our houses. Mine half destroyed and Devon's full of warriors. I followed her gaze and saw many of them through the windows. "Hm, what's going on? Who are they?"

Shit. I exchanged a glance with Devon. "Carol, why don't you go to your house for now? I promise to come by and explain everything later."

She tilted her head, her eyes narrowed at me. "Oh-kay." She didn't sound too pleased, but I was grateful she didn't argue. She started turning toward her house, but something tugged inside me, and before I knew it, I grabbed her arm and pulled her into a tight hug. She stood frozen. "Hm, what's that for?" Then, her arms enveloped me too. "You're scaring me. Are you okay?"

I nodded, my chin grazing her shoulder. "I am. Everything will be okay." I forced myself to step back from her. "Now go. I'll stop by later."

"You promise," she reminded me.

"I promise." I just hoped I could keep it.

Watching Carol walk to her house brought back the same desperate feeling of watching Lia and the kids walk away.

Devon slipped his hands in mine and squeezed it tight. "She'll be fine too."

I let out a long sigh. "I know." Then, I turned to him again, in need to tell him something, at least once in this lifetime. "I love you," I whispered, my eyes on his.

His eyes rounded for a brief second, then they crinkled when the ghost of a smile took over his lips. "I love you more."

His hand found my nape and his lips found mine.

I just hoped that I would have the chance to tell him that again.

Devon

I reached over my car's middle console and slipped my hand into Kenna's. If I could, I would touch her, hold her, stare at her, every second of every day for all eternity.

I inhaled deeply, apprehension growing inside me as we drove out to meet the warriors. The plan was to lure the order to a place of our choosing. Kenna would be there as bait, waiting for them. As would the warriors and I. There had been at least twenty warriors in my house, but Ryder had guaranteed me that over a hundred warriors would be there, ready to kill Slater and his fucking demons, and keep Kenna safe.

Kenna placed her other hand over mine. "Relax, Devon. It'll be okay."

I spared her a quick glance before returning my eyes to the road. She was trying to be strong and brave, mostly for me, but I knew on the inside she was trembling, her heart going a thousand miles per minute. She had trained herself to run from Slater her entire life, and now she was willingly walking toward him.

If there was any chance this plan could fail, I didn't want to think about it. I wanted to believe nothing bad would happen. Kenna would stand in the middle of the clearing, the warriors and I lying in wait the moment Slater showed his face.

Kenna would be free forever.

Somehow, I would make that happen for her. I would give her all she ever wanted.

"I'm relaxed," I lied.

Kenna chuckled. "Right."

I glanced at her again.

A loud screech filled my ears, and my head was lolling back, my eyes seeing more than my brain could register, and not seeing anything at all. Pain started in the back of my head, but it was nothing compared to the panic I felt.

The car rolled down the side of the road a few times before stopping, the back smashed by a tree.

I blinked, my head spinning.

"K-Kenna," I tried calling her, but my voice wouldn't come out.

Before I could lift my arm, open my eyes fully, or scream, a band of demons surrounded the car. They had done this. Somehow, they had pushed the car off the road and sent us down the ravine.

One of them punched the remaining glass that hadn't shattered when we rolled and reached for Kenna. I yelled at my brain to wake up, to stop being so fuzzy, for my arms to grab her, for my sword to appear in my hands so I could send these demons to hell, but I couldn't do anything.

I could only watch as they closed their hands around Kenna's arms and pulled her from the wreckage.

Once more, they took her away from me.

———

It was like bad deja vu. I tried doing things differently, going through a different strategy, but when I entered the chamber where Ingur had been locked away for hundreds of years by the warriors, intent on saving the woman I loved and stopping the order from releasing the demon, chills covered my arms.

This time, the demon had been locked underneath the rubble of a fort, but the chamber where its door was located resembled the same cavern from many years ago.

And to my horror, Kenna was tied to hooks on the rough stone ground, her hair messy, and a smear of blood on her eyebrow. Dozens of demons surrounded her, and Slater stood in front of her, with the same fucking dagger from before.

My gut twisted.

"We're too late again," Ryker muttered.

No, we were not. We couldn't lose again. I couldn't lose Kenna again. Slater pulled the dagger back, ready to kill Kenna. Like before, I took one of my hidden daggers, held it by the blade and threw it at him, but this time, I aimed for his wrist. The blade nicked his wrist, sending the dagger flying.

Chaos ensued as the battle began.

I carved my way through the mass of demons who attacked me, cutting them in half, determined to not fail this time.

I couldn't fail.

Hope blossomed in my chest when Kenna called her darkness. A small, brief smile took over my lips. In this lifetime, she wasn't learning how to handle her powers. In this lifetime, she knew exactly what to do with them, how to use them.

Slivers of darkness wrapped around the ropes and snapped them apart. Darkness rose from the ground, enveloping Slater. But he wasn't the leader of the order for nothing. He had tricks of his own. Slater stomped on the ground and the darkness retreated, as if he had blown a strong wind over shadows.

What the fuck was that?

I pressed on, counting how many demons I had to kill before getting to Kenna.

Four.

Kenna sent her darkness to the ropes around her wrists.

Three.

Slater picked up his dagger.

Two.

Kenna released her hands and threw darkness at Slater.

One.

Slater waved the darkness away.

I turned, ready to strike Slater with my sword, but he was already moving, his dagger poised. I didn't even have time to blink.

His dagger lodged in Kenna's chest.

The emotion inside of me was more than I could bear. Red cloaked my vision as I swiped my sword, cutting Slater's throat and splashing his blood on my armor.

On Kenna.

I turned to her and held to her arms as her knees buckled. She folded to the ground, and I crouched with her, taking her in my arms. A sob ripped from my throat as her wide eyes met mine.

"No, no, not again," I whispered. I hovered my hand over the dagger embedded in her chest, darkness spilling from the wound, going directly to the markings on the door. If I took the dagger out, she would bleed to death. If I didn't, she would die anyway. "No, please, stay with me."

Kenna lifted her hand and touched my face. "I'm sorry," she whispered. "I-I'm sorry we couldn't stop the demon this time."

I leaned forward and rested my forehead on hers. "I don't care about the demon. I care about you. I love you. I want you to stay with me."

"I'm s-sorry about that too." Her voice was faint, her breathing choked gasps. "I love you."

She blinked, then her eyes closed and she didn't open them again. I held my breath, waiting for her to look at me, to say it was all a bad joke, and she was fine.

But she wasn't fine. Her arms lowered, heavy, and her chest stopped moving.

Another sob rose to my throat.

No, no, no ...

The doors opened with a loud groan, shaking the walls of the chamber, and a chilly wind blew into the chamber.

The demon had woken up.

Right now, I really didn't care about any fucking demon.

The sound of metal and shouts and grunts echoed through the chamber as the fight went on around us.

I leaned into Kenna again, touching her beautiful face, running my fingers through her hair. In this position, the necklace slipped from underneath my armor, and the ring shone between us.

The ring which belonged to her.

The ring the gods had given me as the only clue to this entire mess.

It'll bring you light, they had said.

Light in darkness.

My heart sped up and I tugged the necklace from my neck, breaking the chain, and slipped the ring on Kenna's finger. I watched, my breath still, as a surge of power rushed through her.

Kenna inhaled. Her lashes fluttered and her eyes opened.

She stared at me. "What ... what's happening?"

"The gods gave us a second chance," I said, my voice breaking with emotion. "I'm so glad you're alive."

She pushed up and cupped my cheek. "Me too." Then she looked around. "But we have to help."

The demon stepped out of the doors.

Ingur was a giant made of gray stone and ash. His big head, topped off by long, thick horns, almost reached the ceiling of the chamber. He let out a roar, exposing his razor-sharp black teeth, and sending a chill down my spine. His eyes, totally black, took in the room, sizing up his victims. To him, we probably looked like ants who could easily be squashed.

Grabbing her hand in mine, I stood and pulled her with me. "He's a powerful demon. We can't kill it. We can just lock it inside the chamber again."

Kenna's brows curled down as she glanced at her hands, then at the demon. "I can take the darkness from him," she whispered, the realization stunning her. Her eyes widened. "I can make him weak."

I watched her for a moment. Everything in me screamed to take her away from here, to run away as far as we could and never look back. But I knew it wasn't the right thing to do.

I nodded. "I'll keep the other demons back."

She offered me a small smile, then focused on her magic. With half of my attention still on her, I turned and engaged in the fight, helping the warriors get rid of the lesser demons, while trying to keep Ingur back.

My movements were automatic, practiced over centuries, especially now when Kenna raised her arms and called the darkness in the room from the demon.

Shadows seeped from its limbs, and the demon roared. It looked at Kenna, zeroing on her.

"Keep Ingur back!" I shouted.

A handful of warriors and I turned to Ingur and joined the other warriors already fighting him. To give Kenna a chance to do what she could, the demon couldn't reach her.

She went on, pulling more of his darkness to her. At first, only a few black tendrils floated from Ingur to Kenna, but as she struggled with her powers, more and more darkness left the demon.

And he changed.

The once giant and powerful demon started shrinking, his skin became dull, and his sharp teeth shortened. Soon, he was the size of a tall human, with not so scary features.

I pierced my sword through its body along with the other warriors.

The demon let out another roar, but this time, it didn't shake the walls of the chamber. It didn't strike fear into us. This time, the demon's black blood oozed from the wounds.

We pulled back our swords and it fell back.

The demon was dead.

Not just contained, not just weaker.

Dead.

A groan filled the cavern and I turned around.

My heart sank.

The darkness Kenna had taken out of the demon had seeped into her. She absorbed it all and it changed her. Her eyes were black, her once blond hair was now black, her fair skin was translucent white. And she looked at us with pure hunger.

She had become the demon.

"No," I whispered, my heart breaking at the sight. "No, Kenna, please." I dropped my sword and took a step toward her. "Kenna, please, fight this."

"Devon, stay back," Ryder said from somewhere behind me. "She doesn't seem to be herself anymore."

I ignored him because I knew, deep down I knew Kenna wouldn't ever hurt me, even when transformed into a demon.

She threw her hand out, sending a wave of darkness at us. I crouched down, only feeling it brush over me, but the wave slammed right into the chests of the other warriors and sent them flying across the cavern.

Demon Kenna snarled at me, showing off her razor-sharp teeth.

My blood went cold. This didn't look like my Kenna, but she had to be. My Kenna couldn't be gone.

"Kenna, listen to me." I raised my hands to my sides, a sign of peace, though I wasn't sure a demon would recognize it. "You're in there, I know you are. Fight this. Push it away. You can do this."

She sent her magic out again, aimed at me. I tried to dodge it but wasn't fast enough. Her darkness hit me square in the chest, robbing me of my breath. It enveloped me, hard and fast, and before I knew I was on the ground, writhing in pain as the darkness traveled through my body, claiming every inch of me.

Until it stopped my heart.

Kenna

THERE WERE NO WALLS AROUND ME, NO GROUND, BUT everything was dark and cold. I moved to one side, then to the other. I swung my arms wide. I called out. "Hello!" But there was nothing.

Just me and the darkness.

Suddenly, a voice, a tiny whisper sounded in the back of my mind.

"Kenna, please, fight this."

Fight? Fight what?

I didn't know where I was, what I was doing. I wasn't even sure who I was.

And yet, that voice ... it tugged at my chest. It made me want to find out. Who I was? Who did that voice belong to? What was happening?

I clawed through the darkness, listening to that voice.

"Kenna, listen to me."

It grew slightly louder the more I clawed and moved, the more I fought to swim toward it.

"You're in there. I know you are."

In there? In what? A big abyss?

Still, I followed the voice. Louder and louder.

"Fight this. Push it away. You can do this."

I could do this.

This ...

Then, I recognized the voice. I knew who it belonged to, even when I didn't even know my name.

"Devon," I whispered in the darkness.

I blinked and the darkness faded, like a fog lifting. There he was. Devon.

My heart squeezed as thick darkness wrapped around him. His eyes wide, he fell back, quavering under the darkness's power.

"No, no, no," I whispered, rushing to his side. I skidded forward, almost tripping over him and falling to my knees. I hovered my now shaking hands over his body, calling on the darkness inside of him, consuming him. "No!" I cried, pulling it out.

But I was too late.

His heart stopped.

Devon was dead and I had killed him.

I buried my face in my hands, ashamed of what I had done. Heartbroken because he had trusted me. He had called for me. He had held on to me.

And I had killed him.

I dropped my head to his chest and cried.

"Kenna," someone called from behind me. I ignored the voice. I didn't care about anything or anyone. All I wanted was Devon. "Don't worry, Kenna."

A rush of anger sliced through my sorrow. Don't worry? What the hell? I lifted my head and glared at Ryder. I opened my mouth to yell at him, but Owen stepped forward, a small grin on his lips. "He'll be fine."

I froze. "What did you say?"

"He'll probably be disoriented when he returns, but he'll be fine," Ryder said. I gaped at him. "It's the way we're designed. There's only one way to kill us. Otherwise, we're immortal. When dealt a killing blow, we'll 'die'—" He made quotation marks with his fingers. "—for a couple of minutes, but then we come back."

I returned my huge eyes to Devon.

Just then, he inhaled deeply and his eyes fluttered open.

I half-gasped, half-laughed.

Rubbing at his chest, Devon sat up. "Hey, you." He offered me his half smile. "I knew you could do it."

My gaze was blurred with tears. I glanced down at myself. Just moments ago, I had been a demon, with black hair, milk white skin, and razor-sharp teeth. Although I hadn't been aware of what was happening, I remembered it. And now I was myself again. The darkness had faded from me the moment I sent the killing blow to Devon.

"But I killed you before that," I whispered.

He shrugged. "Nah, you didn't. I'm fine." He wrapped his arms around my shoulders and pulled me to him. "We did it. We killed the demon. We sent it away. We destroyed the order. You're free now."

Another half-laugh bubbled in my throat.

I was free.

For the first time in my life, I was free to do whatever I wanted. To be whoever I wanted.

The emotion that overcame me with that news was too much to bear. I melted into Devon's arms, glad he was here with me. That we had endured it. That we had done it.

Together.

SIX MONTHS LATER

Makenna

LIFE COULDN'T BE MORE DIFFERENT THAN I HAD EVER imagined, but it couldn't be better either.

I stepped back and took a good look at the tree. At the large living room around it. At the stone fireplace in the corner of the room. I thought that decorating the house and setting up the tree would be enough, but something was still missing.

I touched the ring on my index finger with my thumb. It had become a habit since I started wearing the ring Devon had gotten me centuries ago. At first, I didn't notice what I was doing, but Devon had. He showed me I always reached for it with the tip of my thumb, as if I had to feel it, to make sure it was still there.

That I hadn't lost it again.

Kevin came running into the room, startling me. He held

a pink notebook in his hand, waving it wildly over his head. He ran behind me and grabbed my arms. "Save me."

I frowned. "From what?"

A moment later, Sabrina stomped into the living room, her gaze mortal. "You prick!"

I gasped. "Sabrina, language!"

"Ugh." She pointed at her brother. "He took my diary and won't return it to me!"

"Kevin," I called out, looking at him over my shoulder. He knew the rules. No messing with his sister like that. "Give it back."

"But—"

"No buts." I shook my head. "You have three seconds to return it." I lifted one finger. "One. Two. Three." He didn't do it, but I couldn't be mad at him for that.

So I channeled my magic. The lights in the living room flickered and darkness swirled around Kevin's middle, tickling him on the sides and under his arm. He laughed out loud, contorting his body to escape my tyranny. He let go of the diary.

It fell like a rock, but before it could hit the wooden floor, a mini cloud of darkness appeared beneath it and floated toward Sabrina.

She grabbed the diary. "Thank you," she barked, still upset. With a huff, she flipped her hair and stomped back upstairs.

Instantly, Kevin ran after her.

These two ...

I stared back at the tall tree in the corner, with white lights, red and golden streamers, a few other decorations, and a small star that had come with the ornaments on top. It still didn't feel like it was done.

A door opened in the distance. I turned to the kitchen and saw Cecilia entering through the garage door, her arms loaded with grocery bags. "Hi," she said, putting the bags on the kitchen island.

"How was the store?" I asked.

"Not too bad," she said. "With the storm coming and Christmas in a few days, I thought it would be packed, but it was okay-ish." She headed back to the garage.

"Want help?" I asked, raising my voice.

"Sure!" she yelled back.

I took a step in her direction, but then the sliding doors to the back porch opened, letting in a chilly wind that sent a shiver down my spine. Devon stepped inside and instantly took off his jacket and shoes.

Beyond him and the now closed doors, I could see the faint silhouette of the cherry tree we had planted In the back-yard, covered in snow. What would have been our lives without that tree?

"I can help her," Devon said, walking to me. He leaned into me, entwined his index finger In my blond hair—which had become a habit—kissed my forehead, then continued to the kitchen.

I smiled at his back.

Sometimes it was still strange to be here, living this life, and sometimes it just felt plain right.

After the warriors, Devon, and I defeated Ingur and erased the D'Ingur Order from the map, the gods granted Devon one wish, and he had chosen to become human and live his life with me.

His wish couldn't have been more perfect.

We had moved to a bigger house in Misty Hill and started the adoption process for Sabrina and Kevin. Cecilia continued to work at the library, and I had passed my GED and been accepted to a university—I had chosen to major in social work and do the entire course online so we didn't have to move again.

Devon continued with his life of the hottest and richest orphan in Misty Hill, who sponsored library events. Though now he wasn't the most eligible bachelor anymore.

Now he was hitched to me.

Sometimes we talked about a real marriage, but I had turned nineteen only a couple of months ago. I was still too young. Besides, we didn't need a signed paper to confirm our relationship. Our feelings. We had been in love for centuries. Nothing would change that.

I stared at the Christmas tree again. At the little snowman and the nutcracker on top of the fireplace's mantel, and the stockings with our initials. It all looked beautiful, I knew that, but it still felt like something was missing.

This feeling had started a couple of weeks ago, as our new life settled, and it wouldn't let go of me.

Noises from the kitchen sparked in my ears, and I joined Devon and Cecilia in taking the groceries out of the bags and placing each item in the right place. It didn't take thirty seconds for Sabrina and Kevin to join us—to eat. These two were always eating.

"What are we having for dinner?" Kevin asked, his mouth already stuffed with popcorn he had taken out of the microwave a second ago.

Cecilia gaped at him. "Do you only think about food?"

Devon snickered. "I thought that was a fact."

"What?" Kevin asked, after swallowing. "I like eating!"

"Speaking of which, what are we having for dinner?" Sabrina asked as she placed bottles of juice in the fridge.

Cecilia rolled her eyes. "You guys only think about food!"

"We're growing." Kevin's words were muffled by all the popcorn in his mouth.

The faint beep on the keypad sounded from the foyer, and a moment later, we all heard the front door opening and closing.

A few seconds passed and Carol entered the kitchen. She held up two large brown bags. "Who ordered lattes and yummy scones?"

"Oh my gods," Cecilia muttered. "There goes our dinner."

Carol frowned. "What dinner? This is snack. We can have dinner later."

Cecilia groaned and busied herself with taking the brown bags from Carol and distributing the lattes and scones. Though Carol had moved two a bigger town with a nice college two hours from here, she often came on weekends and holidays and probably spent more time at our house than at hers—especially because her parents were always busy at the hospital.

In the end, we never told her about what had happened to us. Not the truth anyway. We told her as much as we thought was enough—the kidnapping, the man after Cecilia and me, about Devon helping us, and us adopting the kids because we wanted them. We never told her about powers, magic, divine warriors, gods, and demons.

That would have been too much for her.

The moment Carol had arrived for winter break from college a couple of days ago, she had come to our house, and she had spent at least eighty percent of her time here.

With a smile, she pointed to the tree. "I like what you're doing there."

I narrowed my eyes at the tree. "I like it, but I think it's still missing something."

"Nothing is missing." Cecilia gestured to the new kitchen towels hanging from the oven door handle and the red cookie jar on top of the counter, also Christmas themed. "Soon, it'll look like Santa Claus lives here."

"Can't I go a little overboard with our first real Christmas?" I joked, but it was true. This was the first Christmas we would spend free and together, with a real family. I wanted to go as overboard as I could.

"Of course you can," Devon said, nudging me with his elbow.

"You know what we can do?" Sabrina asked, her eyes wide. "Christmas cookies."

"We did those last week," Cecilia reminded her.

Kevin swallowed the handful of popcorn in his mouth and said, "And they didn't last two days."

Cecilia snorted. "Jeez, I wonder why."

"Here." Carol pulled out her phone from her pocket. "Let's find a different Christmas cookie recipe. Like, I don't know, snickerdoodles."

Sabrina scooted closer to her. "Cool. We can do it tomorrow."

Kevin's lips turned down. "Tomorrow?"

They continued bickering about the cookies and when to bake them, and I just rolled my eyes at them, used to this kind of scene by now. Devon slipped his hand in mine and tugged me closer. He took a step back and I went with him.

We stopped right in the middle of the living room.

I glanced up at him, a little suspicious. "What is it?"

"I know you said you feel like something is missing." He let go of my hand. "I might be able to help. Wait here." He held up a finger, then turned around and disappeared out of the house again, through the sliding doors to the back porch.

What the hell was he doing?

He came back a second later, a large panel in his hands. "I was going to wrap it nicely and give it to you, to all of you, on Christmas." He handed the panel to me. "But I can see you might want it now."

Curious, I grabbed the panel from him, surprised by its weight, and turned it around. It wasn't a panel at all. It was a picture frame. A beautiful, intricate brushed bronze frame around an even more beautiful picture. It was all of us—Carol, Sabrina, Kevin, Cecilia, Devon, and I posing in front of our new house, on the day we moved in. The realtor had insisted on taking the picture. She had sent it to me via email, and I had saved it with every intention of printing it, placing it in a picture frame, and putting it somewhere in the house, but in all the busy days of the move and every day since—because let's be frank, with Sabrina and Kevin, and some-times even Carol, our days were always super busy—I forgot. I forgot about the picture. I glanced around. We had no pictures of us in the house. None. Zero.

That was what was missing.

Holding the large frame with both my hands, I walked to the fireplace. I lifted the frame high and placed on the mantel, behind the snowman and the nutcracker, which I promptly pushed to the sides, so as not to cover the picture.

Then, I stepped back until I stood beside Devon, and admired it.

The six of us, all smiling in front of our home. Our little, happy family.

It was perfect.

Tears blurred my vision. "This is beautiful."

Devon leaned into me and pressed his lips to my forehead. "I knew you would like it."

"I love it." I turned to him, snaking my hands over his shoulders and pulling him closer. "I love you."

One corner of his lips curled up. "I love you more," he whispered, his eyes fixed on mine. I rose on tiptoes and he met me halfway, his mouth pressing against mine.

The kiss was slow, sweet, and soft. A reminder of an eternal love that had endured too much, and yet stood strong.

We all stood strong.

I broke the kiss and just hugged Devon, my cheek resting on his chest. He held me tight, as he always did. In his arms. It was exactly where I belonged.

I glanced from the tree to the picture on the fireplace, to my friends and family, and to the man I loved. My heart never felt so full, and I intended to make sure this feeling never went away.

Now, everything was perfect.

fantasy series about a young woman who finds herself at the center of a mysterious supernatural world.

Destiny Gift (The Everlast Series book 1): a post-apocalyptic urban fantasy series about a young woman with a special power that can save the world.

Don't forget to sign up for my Newsletter to find out about new releases, cover reveals, giveaways, and more!

If you want to see exclusive teasers, help me decide on covers, read excerpts, talk about books, etc, join my reader group on Facebook: Juliana's Club!

ABOUT THE AUTHOR

While USA Today Bestselling Author Juliana Haygert dreams of being Wonder Woman, Buffy, or a blood elf shadow priest, she settles for the less exciting—but equally gratifying—life as a wife, a mother, and an author. She resides in North Carolina and spends her days writing about kick-ass heroines and the heroes who drive them crazy.

Subscribe to her mailing list to receive emails of announcement, events, and other fun stuff related to her writing and her books: www.bit.ly/JuHNL

For more information:
www.julianahaygert.com

facebook.com/julianahaygert
twitter.com/juliana_haygert
instagram.com/juliana.haygert

The Blood Pact (Book 9)

The Fire Heart Chronicles

Heart Seeker (Book 1)

Flame Caster (Book 2)

Sorrow Bringer (Book 3)

Earth Shaker (Novella)

Soul Wanderer (Book 4)

Fate Summoner (Book 5)

War Maiden (Book 6)

The Everlast Series

Destiny Gift (Book 1)

Soul Oath (Book 2)

Cup of Life (Book 3)

Everlasting Circle (Book 4)

Willow Harbor Series

Hunter's Revenge (Book 3)

Siren's Song (Book 5)

Breaking Series

Breaking Free (Book 1)

Breaking Away (Book 2)

Breaking Through (Book 3)

Breaking Down (Book 4)

Standalones

Daughter of Darkness

www.ingramcontent.com/pod-product-compliance
Lightning Source LLC
Chambersburg PA
CBHW051205190726
48288CB00006B/1815